UP
THE
DOWN
STAIRCASE

by

BEL KAUFMAN

HarperPerennial
A Division of HarperCollins*Publishers*

A hardcover edition of this book was published in 1964 by
Prentice Hall Press. It is here reprinted by arrangement
with Prentice Hall Press.

UP THE DOWN STAIRCASE. Copyright © 1964, 1988, 1991 by
Bel Kaufman. All rights reserved. Printed in the United
States of America. No part of this book may be used or
reproduced in any manner whatsoever without written
permission except in the case of brief quotations embodied
in critical articles and reviews. For information address
HarperCollins Publishers, 10 East 53rd Street, New York,
NY 10022.

First HarperPerennial edition published 1991.

Library of Congress Cataloging-in-Publication Data

Kaufman, Bel.
    Up the down staircase / by Bel Kaufman. — 1st
HarperPerennial ed.
        p.   cm.
    ISBN 0-06-097361-7
    1. Education, Secondary—Humor. 2. High school
teachers—Humor. 3. High schools—Humor. I. Title.
PS3561.A83U6' 1991
813'.54—dc20   90-56104

12 13 14 15   RRD H   30 29 28

*For all the dedicated teachers
still struggling up that down staircase,
and all their students,
present and future*

Contents

vii

Contents

Introduction

This book has had many lives. More than a quarter of a century ago a young editor discovered in a three-and-a-half-page story the novel you are holding in your hand. Now after many printings, editions, translations, and a gala silver anniversary publication, it has been newly discovered by the same editor, reborn as a trade paperback available to a new generation. The staircase that never seems to rust has come full round.

I never intended to write *any* novel, certainly not a bestseller or a "classic on education." I didn't even think of myself as a professional writer. I was a high school English teacher who published occasional short stories in magazines—a teacher with no dreams of glory beyond, perhaps, fewer clerical chores, a raise in salary to make thin ends meet, and now and then a word of appreciation.

The success of this book astounded me. It created dramatic reversals in my life that were like a soap opera I would never allow in my fiction. Denied a license to teach, I became a noted teacher. Having flunked the oral exams at the Board of Education, I became a professional public speaker. Struggling with poverty and loneliness, I was catapulted to fame, fortune, and the affections of thousands. Even the short story on which this novel is based was initially rejected by several magazines.

My story was composed of scraps of paper presumably found in the wastebasket of a large metropolitan high school classroom. Ironically juxtaposed, these papers told a story of chaos, confusion, cries for help, bureaucratic gobbledygook, and one teacher's attempt to make a difference in the life of one youngster. Magazine editors rejected it because, they said, it was "weird looking typographically" and its style was "too different."

I tend to give up easily, but somehow I could not abandon this story. It was finally accepted by *The Saturday Review of Literature*, which published it on November 17, 1962, under the title "From a Teacher's Wastebasket," next to sober articles on teacher shortages and inadequate salaries. Actually, I had written this story in 1961, thirty years from the time of this edition of *Up the Down Staircase*, in which it appears as a chapter; yet it seems more timely than ever, and more urgent.

Though I was paid $200 minus a $20 agent's commission—a substantial sum in those days—I was dismayed by the funny stick-figure drawings the magazine provided as illustrations. Anyone stumbling upon this story, I thought, would consider it just a collection of boners and jokes. I was wrong.

The day the magazine hit the newsstands, an enterprising young editor at Prentice Hall, Gladys Justin Carr (now vice president and associate publisher at HarperCollins), got in touch with me and asked me to expand the story into a novel. No, I replied, absolutely not. I had said everything that needed to be said in those three-and-a-half pages. But I didn't protest long, for she offered me a much-needed advance, which I accepted. And spent. So I *had* to write the book.

I became a novelist by chance, only because an alert editor happened to notice my short story. It was by chance, too, that I became a teacher. As an undergraduate at Hunter College, I took a course in Education because my best friend was taking it. One of the course requirements was student teaching. The first time I stood in front of the class and saw all those eyes upon me, I knew: For me this was it!

But I found it difficult to get a license to teach English in New York City high schools. I had come to this country from Russia at twelve, long corkscrew curls down my back and not a word of English on my tongue. I was placed in first grade with seven-year-olds. Small, skinny, scared, I was monitor of nothing. The first time I dared to speak in class, propelled by sheer necessity, I mouthed a frantic "Mwooom?" which I subsequently learned was supposed to be, "May I leave the room?"

I soon learned English by osmosis. Yet years later, when I came up for my orals, the Board of Examiners took a dim view of my overcareful enunciation, afraid, I suppose, that it would corrupt the speech of my students. They sent me a "Dear Sir or Madam" letter informing me of my failure. Each year I took additional speech courses; each year I received additional "Dear Sir or Madam" letters. I spent my youth flunking the orals.

This was in the depth of the Depression, when public school teaching jobs were few and candidates for them many. I was offered college teaching positions, but I was eager to work with adolescents in whose lives, I felt, it was still possible to make a difference. Until I got my regular license, I was what's known in the trade as a "permanent substitute." I had the same number of classes as a regular teacher, a lower salary, no tenure, and I was stuck with all kinds of nonteaching chores. As a sub, I taught in some of the best and some of the worst high schools in New York City, schools that later became the background for this book. In schools where I used to patrol the toilets, I am today "Required Reading."

I even served briefly as a "per diem sub": one who comes for the day only, is expected to teach any subject, wields no mighty mark, and has the children for just forty-five minutes out of their lifetimes. Once I taught gym. "All you have to do," I was told, "is blow the whistle." I blew— loud and clear.

In one school, I found a man standing outside of the classroom assigned to me, holding on to the doorknob. From the room came shrieks and the sound of breaking glass. "You the sub?" asked the man. "I'm covering the class for you till you get here." He vanished. I took a deep breath and opened the door. I knew I had to mesmerize those youngsters within the first few seconds, or all would be lost. I entered saying: *"Ya ne ponimayu ochervo toot tak shoomno! Kak mozhno sebya tak vesti?"* This stunned them into a bewildered silence: Who is this maniac? What is she saying? I was speaking Russian, but at least I had their attention. Maybe I could even teach them something. At the end of the period a boy came up to me said, "You're okay, you can come back tomorrow. Yesterday we had a man sub— we made him cry!"

This was way back when I was a very young teacher. Yet some schools in those "good old days" were not much different from today's. In one high school, in a special annex for boys, two tall boys served as my bodyguards when I walked down the hall. One walked in front, one behind me. One morning a boy came to class three months late. I greeted him with a feeble joke: "Welcome back! What happened? Did you rob a bank?" "No," he said. "A grocery store." And in an English class, while I was reciting Lady Macbeth's speech, a cop walked in: "Lady, that kid I gotta have," he said, and handcuffed him right out of the room.

But I also taught in some fine schools. I remember eager students, earnest class discussions, the children's touching compositions, the sound of laughter in the room. My one hope was to become a regular teacher in such a school.

I finally passed the orals the year the Board concentrated on the "Sibilant S." The sentence that got me through was, "He sstill inssisstss he sscezz the ghosstss." I hissed it to their satisfaction, got my license, and spent many more years within high school walls.

I was happy to learn that as of January 1991 the dreaded New York City Board of Examiners, which had given me such a hard time, was terminated. In its place is ORPAL. It stands for OFFICE of RECRUITMENT, PERSONNEL, ASSESSMENT and LICENSING, and to me it sounds even more threatening. When I read newspaper stories of teachers complaining about the "overwhelming rudeness and bureaucratic foul-ups" at the Board's Department of Personnel, I have a sense of *déjà vu*. Not only have I experienced this, but so did the characters in my book.

The opportunity to write this book came during the lowest point in my life. I was living alone in a tiny apartment with very little money or hope for the future. My children were grown and far away. My mother was seriously ill. Some of the funniest pages I was writing had to be torn up and retyped because of the blisters on the paper from my tears.

With the advance from my publisher I was able to resign from the school system in order to have the time and energy to write.

I found a job teaching three times a week at a community college, and another writing lyrics for a musical that was never produced. This was less fatiguing than teaching high school everyday.

All I knew was that the novel would begin with "Hi, teach!" and end with "Hi, pupe!" and that the opening chapter had to be spoken aloud, not "written" on paper. First a cacophony of voices striking the note of confusion and frustration in the classroom, then, in the rest of the book, nothing but a blizzard of papers, flying, crying to be heard.

I chose for my fictional school—a composite of all the schools in which I had taught—the name of one of our least memorable presidents: Calvin Coolidge. In the original short story, the characters were mere initials. I had to develop these initials into people, to follow the few clues scattered in the story, and to plunge Sylvia Barrett, the young, inexperienced, idealistic teacher, into the maelstrom of an average city high school, where, inundated with trivia in triplicate, she had to cope with all that is frustrating and demeaning in the school system, while dealing with larger human issues. I wanted to show the lack of communication all the way down the line, and to reveal glimpses of the children's lives outside of school through their own inarticulate eloquence.

The children in my story began to come into focus: the class comedian, the sycophant-politician, the over-ripe girl bursting with sexuality, the black boy with a chip on his shoulder, the Puerto Rican boy who finds himself, the silent girl who doesn't. Each of them, apple-polisher or window-smasher, seemed to be crying out: "Here I am! Care about me!" Gradually I became aware that I was saying something important, poignant, even desperate, through such notes as HIS MOTHER CAN'T COME, BEING DEAD. PLEASE EXCUSE.

Memory is short. Because the book is funny, I later began to think it was fun to write it. I had blocked out pain and remembered only chuckling at my inventions of absurdities, such as LATENESS DUE TO ABSENCE and POLIO CONSENT SLIPS. I recall waking up one morning laughing, because I had thought of something a boy might say about *The Odyssey*: "I wouldn't give it to a dog to read."

I did not realize how much work had gone into it until I went to the New York Public Library, to which in 1965 I had donated two huge cartons of my work in progress. There, in the Rare Books and Manuscripts Divison, behind a locked door, under the watchful eye of the guard, I dug into the past. In those cartons I found masses of messy manuscripts, hundreds of pages of outlines, lists of characters, and diagrams of my fictional school, with exact locations of rooms and timing of erratic bell schedules. I found pages bedoodled, scratched out, scotch-taped, blotted with ink or tears. I saw how relentlessly I had kept polishing my material, shortening and sharpening it. A chapter on racial prejudice became a paragraph, which in turn became one sentence. A child writes: "Can you tell by my handwriting if I'm white or not?"

The most difficult chapter to write, I saw, was the confrontation between Sylvia and her problem student Joe Ferone. He was vivid in my mind: leather jacket, toothpick, insolence, but it took many drafts to write that scene. But Joe refused to do what my careful outline dictated.

To let the children speak in their own words, I invented a SUGGESTION BOX in which they signed their comments with funny little pictures or pseudonyms. I had made lists of each child's pseudonym and real name, along with their characteristic misspellings and idiosyncratic styles. When the book was in galleys, a zealous copy editor kept sending me corrections of their misspellings, which I kept sending back, misspelled as intended.

Some reviewers paid me the ultimate compliment: They thought I had merely collected and arranged the material in the book. But everything in the novel is invented, except a few directives from the Board of Education, which I had to tone down for credibility. I made up reports, memos, notes, records, forms, announcements, confidential files of the school nurse and the school psychologist, class minutes, lesson plans, administrative circulars, and comments from the kids themselves. All of it sounded so authentic that I was delighted to learn that when the assistant principal of my former school sent directives to his teachers, he would add in red pencil: "Do not show this to Bel Kaufman."

I made long lists of possible titles for this book. I said them aloud. I typed them in caps on blank paper and stared at them. I pictured them on book jackets. I tried them out on friends. One wag suggested: *Don't Shoot Till You See the Pupils*. The title I finally chose came from the book itself—a picayune note by the administrative assistant: "Detained by me for going up the down staircase and subsequent insolence." In those days there were UP and DOWN signs on narrow school stairs to facilitate traffic. *Up the Down Staircase* stood for the pettiness of administration; at the same time, it was a metaphor for going against traffic, bucking the system. I worried that it sounded too clumsy and unwieldy. How would anyone remember it?

One thing I did not worry about was the morality of my book, so I was astonished to learn that the completed manuscript was going to be the subject of an obscenity conference at my publisher's, which I was invited to attend. An obscenity conference? *Me?* There we sat, several editors and I, with photocopies of the manuscript in hand, speaking in low voices so as not to corrupt the typists outside the door.

"Miss Kaufman, let's look at the words *fuck teacher*. We are also an educational publisher and sell a large number of books to schools, colleges, and universities. Can you see your way to spelling it *fuk*?"

"These kids," I said, "are poor students, lousy spellers, but that's one word they know how to spell!"

We compromised: The word was spelled with a *c* in one place, without it in another.

Next we turned to a page on which the word *balls* is scratched on the back of a seat in the auditorium.

"Miss Kaufman, we are also an educational publisher and sell a large number of books to schools, colleges and universities. Can you perhaps change it to *rats*?"

I was adamant. *Rats* was not a word worthy of being etched on wood. I prevailed.

Next—the page on which a girl passes a note to her friend about the class politician: "Harry Kagan is a prick."

"Miss Kaufman, we are also an educational publisher and sell a large number of books to schools, colleges, and universities. Can the girl possibly say he is a *louse*?"

"No," I replied, "that's not a word she would use. Besides, had you read the book carefully, you would have seen that Harry Kagan happens to be a *prick*."

At least they laughed. Nevertheless, we changed *prick* to *ass* in the book. As I left, I said, "Next time I write a book, I'll give it to a dirty publisher!"

My editor and I discussed the format of the book and settled on a hardcover that would sell for $4.95. (This was in 1964!) Why would anyone pay that much for a book about school? I wondered. Perhaps a few teachers might smile in recognition, a few readers might see that the book was more than merely funny. But would the general public be interested?

As is customary before publication, we tried to sell the first serial rights to one of the commercial magazines. It was refused by three. Again, its style was the problem. "It would probably stop our readers cold," wrote one editor. "Is it too 'special'?" wrote another. "I am returning the manuscript and will see how the book does."

My immediate fear was that I would be fired from my new teaching position at the community college when the book was published. I confided to a colleague that I had written a novel in which I satirized some school administrators, and I was afraid I would lose my job. "Forget it" my friend reassured me. "Who will review it? Who will know you wrote it?"

As soon as the book was published, letters came pouring in from friends, strangers, and teachers. I thought I wrote about one school in one city; I didn't know I had written about many schools in many cities. Teachers told me it was a book they should have written had they not been so exhausted after a day at school. "How did you know?" they wrote. "You described my class, my kids, my problems."

A letter came from the Board of Education: "You would be pleased to learn that a number of changes have been made with our Board of Examiners, including the elimination of 'Dear Sir or Madam.'"

A principal wrote: "We'd let you use any staircase you wish."

And a soldier in Vietnam, a former student, wrote he found my book in a tent. He addressed me: "Dearest Teacher," and signed: "Your devoted pupil."

I brought a copy of the book to my mother in the hospital where she was dying of cancer. She put it under her pillow, and the next morning she died. She never knew of its success.

I awoke one morning to find myself famous. I became an

instant authority—on everything, like the comedian who billed himself *the world's greatest authority*. I said what I had always said, but now people listened. I discovered a new career as a speaker at education conventions. Teachers who came to hear me laughed in recognition and felt better about their profession. For the first time, after years of feeling isolated and abandoned, they found someone like them, who knew, who had been there and told it like it was. At the same time, the general public became aware of what teachers have always known.

I achieved identity as "*the author of*." "You the one wrote the book?" asked the makeup man on a talk show where I was sandwiched in between a juggler and a transvestite. I was presented with plaques and scrolls and citations. My favorite, which hangs framed in my study, says in multicolored crayon: HUMER AND CHUCKELS AWARD FROM MRS. VINOGRAD'S CLASS. My latest and most unlikely honor, presented in October 1990, makes me a Kentucky Colonel.

I was photographed on staircases all over the nation, holding my book so that the title showed. I became a crossword puzzle item. I read my book into a record at the American Foundation for the Blind and received a fan letter from a blind reader: "Best book I ever heard." My novel was chosen for the Presidential Library. And it was banned in Knoxville, Tennessee. Parents of twelve students had the book removed from a list of approved books in Knoxville city schools because it contained "vulgar language." Someone must have caught that *c* in *fuck*. After the book was quietly reinstated, I took special pleasure in delivering the keynote address to the Tennessee Education Association at its annual convention in Knoxville.

Instead of losing my job at the community college, I was promoted to assistant professor. The style of the book, which had previously stymied editors, became a topic of study in writing classes. The title I worried about became part of the language, showing up in cartoons and headlines throughout the years. During the stock market plunge in October 1987 it was a front page headline in the *New York Daily News*: "Up The Dow Staircase" It even appeared in a Soviet newspaper: "Up the Glasnost Staircase."

The book was bound to become "a major motion picture." It

was sold to Warner Brothers for one of the largest sums paid at that time for a first novel by an unknown author—only because another studio, Twentieth Century Fox, was bidding for it at the same time. The legendary Annie Laurie Williams, theater and film agent whose word was honored by everyone in the industry, telephoned me every few minutes, quoting constantly escalating sums. She finally decided on Warner: "Alan Pakula wants to produce it and Robert Mulligan to direct it. They love it and they're good. Shall we say yes?" We said yes.

A few minutes later Annie Laurie called back to say that Twentieth Century Fox had just offered considerably more money, but she would stick by her word to Warner. At that point I was so benumbed by numbers, such large sums weren't real. What was real was the price of party invitations I went to buy the following day. Some cost five cents each; the prettier ones were ten cents—too expensive.

The movie was filmed in New York City, in and around what was then Haaren High School, emptied for the summer. As "technical consultant," I was allowed to hang around. It was thrilling to realize that all those people—actors, electricians, cameramen, script girls, director, producer, assistants, makeup people, scenic designers, and kids selected from schools and settlement houses, some with switchblade knives that had to be confiscated—were all there because one day I had sat down and put a blank piece of paper into my typewriter.

Since the film was shot in a real high school with real kids, I found it uncanny to see the names of the teachers I had invented printed on the school mailboxes, as if they were truly alive. And it was strange to see artificial snow on one of the hottest days in August, actors bundled up in winter coats and earmuffs on the street, while makeup people wiped the sweat off their faces and wilted New Yorkers on a passing bus stared out of the windows in disbelief.

None of the youngsters, so touching in the film, went on to an acting career. They had their one brief moment on the screen. I often wonder what became of them.

Look magazine was doing a picture story about the movie, and we went to the home of the Puerto Rican boy, a school dropout, who played Jose Rodriguez—whose own name happened to be Jose Rodriguez. His mother hugged me and said, "Please, Miss Kaufman, write another book soon so my boy could be in it."

I, too, appeared in the film in a cameo bit. For a few seconds, I was one of the teachers punching in with Sandy Dennis, who played Sylvia Barrett. There we were, Bel and Syl, side by side.

At the end of the filming, at a party for the cast and crew, I found myself, along with the others, singing the school song, "The Purple and Gold," with tears in my eyes. "Idiot!" I said to myself. "Why are you crying? You made up the song, you made up the school...."

The film opened in New York at Radio City Music Hall, and in 1967 was chosen to represent the United States at the Moscow Film Festival. There it was shown in the huge Kremlin Palace of Congresses to an enthusiastic audience of some five thousand people.

The Russian translation of *Up the Down Staircase*, called *Verkh Po Lestnize Vedooshchei Vneez (Up the Staircase Leading Down)*, is so lively, it reads as if I had written it in that language. I couldn't tell much about the other translations I saw, although I was intrigued by some of the titles:

Swedish: *Hei, Fröken!*
Czech: *Nahoru Poschodisti Dolú* by Bel Kaufmanova
Spanish: *Subieno por la Escala de Bakada*
Italian: *Su Per la Discesa*
Estonian: *Allakäigutrepist Üles*
Hebrew: *Bamalá Hamadregót Hayordót*
Japanese: vertical and unrecognizable, except for the photo of Sandy Dennis on the cover.

I learned that "Hi, teach!" in Finnish is: *"Terev, ope!"*; in Czech:*"Cau, pancelko!"*; in Spanish: *"Hola, 'Profe'!"* The French, with a sexy Gallic touch, transformed the book into a movie, *L'Escalier Interdit—The Forbidden Staircase*. And I heard of a pirated edition I couldn't trace, which gave the book a whole new dimension. It was called *Upside Down on the Staircase*.

In 1968, invited to the Soviet Union to spend my royalty rubles, I discovered that my book was widely popular there, perhaps because bureaucracy is not unknown in that country, and because the Russians have a strong affection for children. Soviet teachers were especially enthusiastic. "Just like here!" one of them told me, but of course, it wasn't, except that good teachers, like Tolstoy's happy families, are alike everywhere. Soviet teenagers I met seemed to identify with the book, or wanted to. And I learned only recently that the American edition of *Up the Down Staircase* is used in some Soviet schools to teach Russians contemporary English.

I have been back in the Soviet Union many times since then, always welcomed with open arms as the author of *that book*. I saw Russian plays based on my novel, some with music and lyrics. I read a new Russian edition of the novel in one volume that included a half dozen of my articles on education. I attended round table discussions of the book by Soviet authors. I was invited to meet Gorbachev at receptions in Moscow and in Washington—all because of the popularity of *Up the Staircase Leading Down*. In October of 1990, on a plane from Moscow to New York, I met a sixteen-year-old Soviet girl who told me in Russian how much she enjoyed appearing in my play in her high school in Tashkent. "Who were you?" I asked. "Sexpot," she replied in English.

Back home, when *Up the Down Staircase* was dramatized for amateur performances in the United States, youngsters who appeared in it wrote to me:

"Now that I am a movie star, this is my favorite future career."

"If not for you, I never would of got a curtain call."

"On opening night the crowd laughed when I was supposed to commit suicide by jumping out of the window, but that's not your fault."

When my book was published in an inexpensive paperback edition that the kids could afford, I began to get "Dear Miss Barrett" letters from them:

"Dear Miss Barrett we going down the drains. Keep in touch."

"You helped me overcome school."

"This is the first book I ever bought. For money."

"I am seventeen years old and I just read your book and I put it in my underwear drawer so that when I get married my forthcoming offsprings can read it too."

"When I was young I had a lot of griefness, but tomorrow will be worse."

Today is that tomorrow, and it *is* worse. Much worse and more serious than an insolent boy going up the wrong staircase. Education in this country is in crisis. If Sylvia Barrett were to step out of the pages of this book, she would find dramatic changes in the world. Yet she would immediately recognize her school.

The more it changes, the more it remains the same. Schools today are *exactly* the same as they were over a quarter of a century ago, only now they are more so. Everything described in my fiction is today reality. Only computers and condoms are new.

Teachers still cope. They cope with demeaning nonteaching chores, deadening bureaucracy, paper miles of clerical work, inadequate facilities, and heavy teaching loads. The same problems that have been "shelved for lack of time" and ignored for lack of attention have remained, have proliferated, have become chronic. Minor infractions—whispering in assembly, chewing gum in class, smoking (cigarettes) in the lavatory— have swelled into major crimes: assault, vandalism, arson, robbery, and worse. The "mugings and rapings" children wrote about in *Up the Down Staircase* have become more frequent. Teachers today lock their doors from the inside, hide their window poles, hold on to their wallets. They are still trying to teach, but for many it has become a question of survival.

In some schools, in overcrowded classes, children sit on radiators, as they did in my book. Even the old controversy about the "moment of silence," the fear that it may, God forbid, turn into a moment of prayer rather than meditation, is still, in some states, unresolved. No longer "bowed and cowed," teachers now speak for themselves, but they are seldom heard.

The "staggering statistics on dropouts" mentioned in this book are still staggering: today huge numbers of dropouts, mostly minority children, functionally illiterate, spill out of our schools and self-destruct. Drug pushers are more brazen. Glue sniffing is now cocaine and crack. In rereading my book, I see how innocent the "epidemic of chalk stealing" sounds; today it's robbery at knife-point. The sassy boy in *Up the Down Staircase* who dared to say to the chairman "Aw, go jump in the lake!" would today call him "motherfucker." Pregnant girls walk casually in school corridors; others bring their babies to school daycare centers. The school nurse who, in this book, was not allowed to give aspirin or touch wounds is dispensing controversial condoms.

Now, as then, the school system is strangulated by its own red tape. Now, as then, it is mired in rigidity and befogged by empty rhetoric. Now, as then, teachers are overworked, underpaid, and unappreciated. Now, as then, children wage war against their schools. Many see no reason to attend classes; one boy told me, "My future is forget it!"

I recently asked a teacher in my former school what has changed since my time. He shrugged and said, "Truants are now non-attenders!"

Absurdities remain the same. Teachers from all over the country keep sending me directives from their principals, such as these:

DO NOT ISSUE LAVATORY PASSES TO ANY STUDENT UNLESS PRESENTED WITH A MEDICAL CERTIFICATE TO COVER THE CONDITION

and

PLEASE DISTRIBUTE THESE CARDS TODAY TO EVERY STUDENT IN ALL YOUR CLASSES, INCLUDING ABSENTEES.

Fact follows hot upon the footsteps of fiction. In *Up the Down Staircase*, my invented phrase: "Staircase which terminates in the basement" has become real. A teacher in the Midwest sent me this:

FROM NOW ON ALL STAIRCASES MARKED UP WILL BE MARKED DOWN; ALL STAIRCASES MARKED DOWN WILL BE MARKED UP, AND ALL STAIRCASES LEADING TO THE BASEMENT WILL BE DOWN ONLY.

Another phrase in my book, "Please disregard the following," was echoed in this directive a teacher has recently mailed me:

FORTUNATELY, THE MESSAGE WE ASKED YOU TO DISREGARD WAS NOT SENT . . .

In one school, above the time clock, I saw a notice that could have come straight out of *Up the Down Staircase*:

THE CLOCK IS BROKEN. PUNCH IN ANYHOW.

A broken window was a constant in my fictitious classroom. Many public schools today are in worse disrepair than Calvin Coolidge High School. Not only broken windows but broken toilets and holes in the ceiling are unattended.

Uniformed guards provided by the Board of Education are stationed at school entrances to stop "intruders" like the ones who disrupted the assembly in my book. Some schools have installed metal detectors to spot knives and guns. When I recently went back, as a *per diem* substitute, to one of the toughest schools in New York, I had to show my identification to the guard and explain my reason for being there. I'm not sure how effective this method is: the Deputy Chancellor of Education, investigating high schools, wrote as his reason for visiting one: "child molester." He went in, unchallenged by the guard. Inside the school, I saw cops in the lobby, pot on the stairs, chaos in the halls. The principal, barricaded behind the door of his office, popped out long enough to say to me: "If you see a kid with a knife, take it away. And give him a receipt!"

In *Up the Down Staircase* the children's problems sprang from the same sad soil of poverty, joblessness, racism, and hopelessness. A boy in my book writes: "They tried to integrate me, but it didn't take." It didn't.

As far back as 1961, Dr. James B. Conant warned about the "social dynamite" building up in our schools. Now, thirty years later, it is exploding all over the place. At their historic meeting on education in 1989 at the University of Virginia, President Bush and state governors wondered how to solve all of society's ills in the classrooms. So do teachers. A recent ad for Apple Computer summed it up: "We expect our teachers to handle teenage pregnancy, substance abuse and the failings of the family. Then we expect them to educate our children."

In the last few years there has been a spate of books, articles, news stories, radio programs, and television documentaries with frantic titles: "A Nation at Risk!".... "High Schools on the Brink!".... "Save Our Schools!..." National reports have lamented the quality of public education, trying to "stem the tide of mediocrity." And what do these reports tell us? Everything that can be found in a book written almost thirty years ago. They inform us that:

"Teachers are troubled by loss of status, bureaucratic pressures, negative public image and lack of recognition."

"Teachers should be relieved of the burden of record keeping, paperwork, security duty and other chores."

"Teachers scrounge for chalk and paper clips while being bombarded with procedural directives."

A recent article in the *New York Times* speaks of teachers' "monumental frustrations over lack of authority and working conditions." My book could have been written today; perhaps that is why it has endured.

At least the problems are being recognized. The governor of New York recently called our schools "a disaster." And a member of the Board of Education said, "There's a lot of talk but no action." I think a youngster who wrote to me said it better: "DEAR WHO—NOBODY DOES NOTHING. YOUR TRUE READER."

My sources, as always, are the kids. I approached a boy loitering outside his classroom. He looked at me suspiciously: "You puttin' my name down?" No—I only wanted to ask him what we should do about our schools. His answer was direct and to the point. "Burn them," he said.

As in *Up the Down Staircase*, children today are still *writting* their *opions*. Even their spelling mistakes are the same. I have faithfully kept all the letters they have been writing to me through the years:

"If my mother didn't have a abortion of me, why should I complaint?"

"I am Vivian in your book, but I'd rather be a geneticist."

"Hi, Bel, I guess you don't know me but I love your book and will never stop reading it. Please don't forget me if possible."

"I wish you could be my teacher and not enough pressure in the water fountain."

"Sometimes I feel like throwing myself out."

Whether in 1964 or in 1991, good education means good teachers. All over the country, in spite of all difficulties, teachers have been working their daily miracles in the classrooms. I see them at their statewide conventions; I meet them in their schools—teachers devoted to their students, teachers committed to education, teachers to whom this book is dedicated.

They are there because of the rewards. No outsider can see what these rewards are. They are not on any plaque or medal. They are certainly not on any paycheck. But they are immeasurable. A child's face lights up: "I get it! I see!" A child, grown to adulthood, says, "I had a teacher once…" A teacher who had made a difference. Perhaps at this very moment, someone someplace is saying this about a Sylvia Barrett. It's a kind of immortality.

The potential power of good teachers is awesome. Today our children need them more than ever.

A new generation will be reading this book. The "forthcoming offsprings" of youngsters who used to write me fan letters may find it's about them.

A young reader wrote me: "I know your book is made up, but what happened to Joe Ferone?" I wish I knew. I wish I knew what happened to all the people in Calvin Coolidge High. Mr. McHabe, the disciplinarian, is still around, though he goes by another name. So are the teachers and the students, all with different names but the same old problems.

Sylvia Barrett still exists—not only between the covers of this book, but someplace, everyplace, in rural schools and city classrooms, wherever there are children. She's hanging in there, calling the roll, as new students crowding in the doorway greet her: "Hi, teach!"

JANUARY 1991
NEW YORK CITY

PART I

Hi, teach!
  Looka *her!* She's a teacher?
  Who she?
  Is this 304? Are you Mr. Barringer?
No. I'm Miss Barrett.
  I'm supposed to have Mr. Barringer.
I'm Miss Barrett.
  You the teacher? You so young.
  Hey she's cute! Hey, teach, can I be in your class?
Please don't block the doorway. Please come in.
  Good afternoon, Miss Barnet.
Miss Barrett. My name is on the blackboard. Good morning.
  O, no! A *dame* for homeroom?
  You want I should slug him, teach?
  Is this homeroom period?
Yes. Sit down, please.
  I don't belong here.
  We gonna have you all term? Are you a regular or a sub?
  There's not enough chairs!
Take any seat at all.
  Hey, where do we sit?
  Is this 309?
  Someone swiped the pass. Can I have a pass?
  What's your name?

3

My name is on the board.
    I can't read your writing.
    I gotta go to the nurse. I'm dying.
    Don't believe him, teach. He ain't dying!
    Can I sharpen my pencil in the office?
    Why don't you leave the teacher alone, you bums?
    Can we sit on the radiator? That's what we did last term.
    Hi, teach! You the homeroom?
    Pipe down, you morons! Don't you see the teacher's try-
ing to say something?
Please sit down. I'd like to——
    Hey, the bell just rung!
    How come Mrs. Singer's not here? She was in this room
last term.
    When do we go home?
    The first day of school, he wants to go home already!
That bell is your signal to come to order. Will you please——
    Can I have a pass to a drink of water?
    You want me to alphabetize for you?
    What room is this?
*This is room 304. My name is on the board: Miss Barrett. I'll
have you for homeroom all term, and I hope to meet some
of you in my English classes. Now, someone once said that
first impressions——*
    English! No wonder!
    Who needs it?
    You give homework?
*First impressions, they say, are lasting. What do we base
our first——Yes? Do you belong in this class?*
    No. Mr. McHabe wants Ferone right away.
Who?
    McHabe.
Whom does he want?
    Joe Ferone.
Is Joe Ferone here?
    Him? That's a laugh!
    He'll show up when he feels like it.

Put down that window-pole, please. We all know that first impressions——Yes?

Is this 304?

Yes. You're late.

I'm not late. I'm absent.

You are?

I was absent all last term.

Well—sit down.

I can't. I'm dropping out. You're supposed to sign my Book Clearance from last term.

Do you owe any books?

I'm not on the Blacklist! That's a yellow slip. This here is a green!

Hey, isn't the pass back yet?

Quit your shoving!

He started it, teach!

I'd like you to come to order, please. I'm afraid we won't have time for the discussion on first impressions I had planned. I'm passing out——

Hey, she's passing out!

Give her air!

——Delaney cards. You are to fill them out at once while I take attendance from the Roll Book. Standees—line up in back of the room; you may lean on the wall to write. Print, in ink, your last name first, your parent's name, your date of birth, your address, my name—it's on the board—and the same upside down. I'll make out a seating plan in the Delaney Book. Any questions?

In ink or pencil?

I got no ink—can I use pencil? Who's got a pencil to loan me?

I don't remember when I was born.

Don't mind him—he's a comic.

Print or write?

When do we go to lunch?

I can't write upside down!

Ha-ha. He kills me laughing!

What do you need my address for? My father can't come.
Someone robbed my ball-point!
I can't do it—I lost my glasses.
Are these going to be our regular seats—the *radiator?*
I don't know my address—we're moving.
Where are you moving?
I don't know where.
Where do you live?
I don't live no place.
<u>*Any*</u> *place. You, young man, why are you late?*
I'm not even here. I'm in Mr. Loomis. My uncle's in this
class. He forgot his lunch. Hi, Tony—catch!
Please don't throw——Yes, what is it?
This Mrs. Singer's room?
Yes. No. Not anymore.
Anyone find a sneaker from last term?
Hey, teach, can we use a pencil?
You want these filled out *now?*
There's chewing gum on my seat!
First name last or last name first?
I *gotta* have a pass to the Men's Room. I know my rights;
this is a democracy, ain't it?
<u>*Isn't.*</u> *What's the trouble now?*
There's glass all over my desk from the window.
*Please don't do that. Don't touch that broken window. It
should be reported to the custodian. Does anyone——*
I'll go!
Me! Let *me* go! That's Mr. Grayson—I know where he is
in the basement!
All right. Tell him it's urgent. And who are <u>*you?*</u>
I'm sorry I'm late. I was in Detention.
The what?
The Late Room. Where they make you sit to make up your
lateness when you come late.
*All right, sit down. I mean, stand up—over there, against
the wall.*
For parent's name, can I use my aunt?
Put down your mother's name.

I got no mother.
Well—do the best you can. Yes, young lady?
The office sent me. Read this to your class and sign here.
May I have your attention, please. Please, class! There's been a change in today's assembly schedule. Listen carefully:

> PLEASE IGNORE PREVIOUS INSTRUCTIONS IN CIRCULAR #3, PARAGRAPHS 5 AND 6, AND FOLLOW THE FOLLOWING:
>
> THIS MORNING THERE WILL BE A LONG HOMEROOM PERIOD EXTENDING INTO THE FIRST HALF OF THE SECOND PERIOD. ALL X2 SECTIONS ARE TO REPORT TO ASSEMBLY THE SECOND HALF OF THE SECOND PERIOD. FIRST PERIOD CLASSES WILL BEGIN THE FOURTH PERIOD, SECOND PERIOD CLASSES WILL BEGIN THE FIFTH PERIOD, THIRD PERIOD CLASSES WILL BEGIN THE SIXTH PERIOD, AND SO ON, SUBJECT CLASSES BEING SHORTENED TO 23 MINUTES IN LENGTH, EXCEPT LUNCH, WHICH WILL BE NORMAL.

I can't hear you—what did you say?
They're drilling on the street!
Close the window.
I can't—I'll suffocate!
This a long homeroom?
What's today's date?
It's September, stupid!
Your attention, please. I'm not finished:

> SINCE IT IS DIFFICULT TO PROVIDE ADEQUATE SEATING SPACE FOR ALL STUDENTS UNDER EXISTING FACILITIES, THE OVERFLOW IS TO STAND IN THE AISLES UNTIL THE SALUTE TO THE FLAG AND THE STAR-SPANGLED BANNER ARE COMPLETED, AFTER WHICH THE OVERFLOW MAY NOT REMAIN STANDING IN THE AISLES UNLESS SO DIRECTED FROM THE PLATFORM. THIS IS A FIRE LAW. DR. CLARKE WILL EXTEND A WARM WELCOME TO ALL NEW STUDENTS; HIS TOPIC WILL BE "OUR CULTURAL HERITAGE." ANY STUDENT FOUND TALKING OR EATING LUNCH IN ASSEMBLY IS TO BE REPORTED AT ONCE TO MR. McHABE.

Water! I gotta have water! My throat is parching!
He thinks he's funny!
May I have your attention?
No!

TOMORROW ALL Y2 SECTIONS WILL FOLLOW TODAY'S
PROGRAM FOR X2 SECTIONS WHILE ALL X2 SECTIONS
WILL FOLLOW TODAY'S PROGRAM FOR Y2 SECTIONS.

Where do we go?
What period is this?
The two boys in the back—stop throwing that board eraser.
Please come to order; there's more:
Is this assembly day?

BE SURE TO USE THE ROWS ASSIGNED TO YOU: THERE
IS TO BE NO SUBSTITUTION.

Excuse me, I'm from Guidance. Miss Friedenberg wants
Joe Ferone right away.
He isn't here. Will you pass your Delaney cards down,
please, while I——
I didn't start yet! I'm waiting for the pen.
How do you spell your name?
Hey, he threw the board eraser out the window!
Will you please——
Here's my admit. He says I was loitering.
Who?
McHabe.
Mr. McHabe.
Either way.
Now class, please finish your Delaney cards while I call the
roll.
I didn't finish!
I never got no Delaney!
Any. Yes?
Mr. Manheim next door wants to borrow your board eraser.
I'm afraid it's gone. Please, class——
You give extra credit for alphabetizing?
We go to assembly today?

You want me to go down for the stuff from your letter-box, Miss Barnet?
All right. Now we'll just have to——
I can't write—I got a bum hand.
You gonna be our teacher?
Please come to order while I take attendance. And correct me if I mispronounce your name; I know how annoying that can be. I hope to get to know all of you soon. Abrams, Harry?
Here.
Quiet, please, so I can hear you. Allen, Frank?
Absent.
Absent?
He ain't here.
Isn't. Amdur, Janet?
Here.
Mr. Grayson says there's no one down there.
How can he say that when <u>he's</u> there?
That's what he says. Any answer?
No. Amdur, Janet?
I was here already.
Arbuzzi, Vincent? Yes, what do I have to sign now?
Nothing. I came back from the bathroom.
Can I have the pass?
Me, I'm next!
I said it first!
Blake, Alice?
I'm present, Miss Barrett.
Blanca, Carmelita?
Carole. I changed my name.
Blanca, Carole?
Here.
Borden——Yes?
Miss Finch wants you to make this out right away.
I'm in the middle of taking attendance. Borden——
She needs it right away.
Excuse me, class.

IN THE TWO COLUMNS LABELED MALE AND FEMALE,

INDICATE THE NUMBER OF STUDENTS IN YOUR HOME-
ROOM SECTION BORN BETWEEN THE FOLLOWING DATES—

*Please don't tilt that chair——Boy in the back—I'm talking
to you——Oh!*

So I fell. Big deal. Stop laughing, you bums, or I'll knock
your brains out!

Are you hurt?

Naw, just my head.

You've got to make out an accident report, Miss Barrett,
three copies, and send him to the nurse.

Aw, she ain't even allowed to give out aspirins. Only tea.
Get your feet offa me!

You call this a *chair?*

He can sue the whole Board of Education!

*Perhaps you'd better go to the nurse. And ask her for the
accident report blanks. Yes, what can I do for you?*

Miss Friedenberg wants last term's Service Credit cards.

I wasn't here last term. And what do you want?

Miss Finch is waiting for the attendance reports and absentee cards.

I'm in the middle of——Yes?

The office wants to know are the transportation cards
ready?

The what cards?

Bus and subway.

No. Yes?

You're supposed to read this to the class. It's from the
liberry.

Library. May I have your attention, please?

THE SCHOOL LIBRARY IS YOUR LIBRARY. ALL STUDENTS
ARE ENCOURAGED TO USE IT AT ALL TIMES.

STUDENTS ON THE LIBRARY BLACKLIST ARE NOT TO RE-
CEIVE THEIR PROGRAM CARDS UNTIL THEY HAVE PAID
FOR LOST OR MUTILATED BOOKS.

THE LIBRARY WILL BE CLOSED TO STUDENTS UNTIL
FURTHER NOTICE TO ENABLE TEACHERS TO USE IT AS A
WORKROOM FOR THEIR PRC ENTRIES.

Yes, who sent you here?
>You did. Here's the stuff from your letter-box. Where do I dump it?

Is that all for me?
>Excuse me, the nurse says she's all out of accident reports, but she wants the missing dentals.

The missing what?
>Dental notes.

I see. And what is it you want?
>New change in assembly program. Your class goes to different rows. X2 schedule rows.

I see. And you?
>Mr. McHabe says do you need any posters for your room decoration?

Tell Mr. McHabe what I really need is——Yes?
>The office wants the list of locker numbers for each student.

I haven't even——Yes?
>This is urgent. You're supposed to read and sign.

TO ALL TEACHERS: A BLUE PONTIAC PARKED IN FRONT OF SCHOOL HAS BEEN OVERTURNED BY SOME STUDENTS. IF THE FOLLOWING LICENSE IS YOURS—

Tell Mr. McHabe I don't drive. Now, class——
>Hurray! Saved by the bell!

Just a minute—the bell seems to be fifteen minutes early. It may be a mistake. We have so much to—— Please remain in your——
>That's the *bell!* You heard it!
>All the other teachers are letting them out!

But we must finish the——
>When the bell rings, we're supposed to *go!*
>Where do we go, assembly?

Please sit down. I'd like to——We haven't——Well. It looks as if you and I are the only ones left. Your name is——?
>Alice Blake, Miss Barrett. I just wanted you to know how much I enjoyed your lesson.

Thank you, but it wasn't really a——Yes, young lady?

I'm from the office. She says to announce this to your class
right away.

PLEASE DISREGARD THE BELLS. STUDENTS ARE TO RE-
MAIN IN THEIR HOMEROOMS UNTIL THE WARNING BELL
RINGS.

I'm afraid they've all gone.
    I've got to go too, Miss Barrett. I wish I had *you* for Eng-
lish, but my program says Mr. Barringer.
*I'm sure he's a fine teacher, Alice, and that you'll do well
with him.*
    You Barrett?
What's that, young man?
    Late pass.
*That's no way to hand it to me. Throwing it like that on my
desk——*
    My aim is bad.
*There's no need for insolence. Please take that toothpick out
of your mouth when you talk to me. And take your hands
out of your pockets.*
    Which first?
What's your name?
    You gonna report me?
What's your name?
    You gonna give me a zero?
I'm afraid I've had just about——What's your name?
    Joe.
Joe what?
    Ferone. You gonna send a letter home? Take away my
lollipop? Lecture me? Spank me?
All I asked——
    Yeah. All you asked.
I don't allow anyone to talk to me like that.
    So you're lucky—you're a teacher!

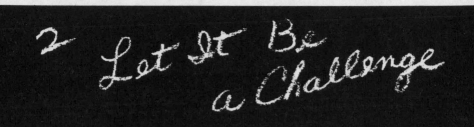

2 *Let It Be a Challenge*

INTRASCHOOL COMMUNICATION

FROM: Mrs. Beatrice Schachter, Room 508
TO: Miss Sylvia Barrett, Room 304

Dear Syl–

Welcome to the fold! I hope it goes well with you on this, your first day. If you need help, just holler; I'm in 508.

What's your program? Can we synchronize our lunch periods?

Fondly,
Bea

* * *

INTRASCHOOL COMMUNICATION

FROM: Miss Sylvia Barrett, Room 304
TO: Mrs. Beatrice Schachter, Room 508

Dear Bea–

Help!

I'm buried beneath an avalanche of papers, I don't understand the language of the country, and what do I do about a kid who calls me "Hi, teach!"?

Syl

13

INTRASCHOOL COMMUNICATION

FROM: Room 508
TO: Room 304

Nothing. Maybe he calls you *Hi, teach!* because he
likes you. Why not answer *Hi, pupe?*

The clerical work is par for the course. "Keep on file
in numerical order" means throw in wastebasket. You'll
soon learn the language. "Let it be a challenge to you"
means you're stuck with it; "interpersonal relationships"
is a fight between kids; "ancillary civic agencies for
supportive discipline" means call the cops; "Language
Arts Dept." is the English office; "literature based on
child's reading level and experiential background"
means that's all they've got in the Book Room; "non-
academic-minded" is a delinquent; and "It has come to
my attention" means you're in trouble.

Did you get anything done in homeroom today?

Bea

*   *   *

INTRASCHOOL COMMUNICATION

FROM: 304
TO: 508

Dear Bea–

I checked off 2½ items from some 20 on the list of
things to be done.

A boy fell off his chair.

Nothing in my courses on Anglo-Saxon literature, or
in Pedagogy, or in my Master's thesis on Chaucer had
prepared me for this. I had planned to establish rapport, a climate of warmth and mutual respect. I would
begin, I thought, with First Impressions: importance of
appearance, manners, speech, on which I'd build an
eloquent case for good diction, correct usage, fluent
self-expression. From there it would be just a step to
the limitless realms of creativity.

That's what I thought.

What happened was that I didn't get beyond the B's in taking attendance. And I forgot to have them salute the flag, and I have an uneasy feeling that it's illegal.

Syl

* * *

INTRASCHOOL COMMUNICATION

FROM: 508
TO: 304

You're in the clear. On assembly days they salute in the auditorium. What's illegal now is the Bible reading.

Bea

* * *

INTRASCHOOL COMMUNICATION

FROM: 304
TO: 508

Dear Bea—

What does the SS stand for in Eng. SS? Secret Service? Social Security? Sesame Seeds? Super-Slows?

Syl

* * *

INTRASCHOOL COMMUNICATION

FROM: 508
TO: 304

You're warm: special slow classes. The new teachers are stuck with the toughest assignments. Don't despair —by the time you get to be my age, you'll earn the choicest seniors.

I see by your program you're a "floater"—that means you travel from room to room. Insist on a desk drawer of your own in each room where you teach; if not, get a strong-armed boy to lug your things.

You have Hall Patrol—that's a cinch now that we have Aides to help with the non-teaching assignments. It means walking up and down the corridors and stopping kids without passes. It's a higher-class job than Cafeteria Duty, but carries less prestige than the Book Room or Staircase Patrol. All of us have one such "building assignment" a day, besides five teaching classes, a homeroom, and one "unassigned" (don't ever dare to call it "free") period. Those who play their cards right are relieved of homeroom, or even a teaching class, by becoming Lateness Coordinators or Program Integrators or Vocational Counselors or some such thing. We also have a lunch period. Yours, I see, is at the end of the third period, which means we can eat together on Wednesdays. Your gastric juices must start to flow at 10:17 A.M. It's a challenge.

Bea

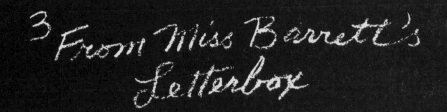

From Miss Barrett's Letterbox

PROGRAM FOR TODAY'S HOMEROOM PERIOD:
(CHECK OFF EACH ITEM BEFORE LEAVING BUILDING TODAY)

½ MAKE OUT DELANEY CARDS AND SEATING PLAN

TAKE ATTENDANCE

FILL OUT ATTENDANCE SHEETS

SEND OUT ABSENTEE CARDS

MAKE OUT TRANSCRIPTS FOR TRANSFERS

MAKE OUT 3 SETS OF STUDENTS' PROGRAM CARDS (YELLOW) FROM MASTER PROGRAM CARD (BLUE), ALPHABETIZE AND SEND TO 201

MAKE OUT 5 COPIES OF TEACHER'S PROGRAM CARD (WHITE) AND SEND TO 211

SIGN TRANSPORTATION CARDS

✓REQUISITION SUPPLIES

ASSIGN LOCKERS AND SEND NAMES AND NUMBERS TO 201

FILL OUT AGE-LEVEL REPORTS

✓ANNOUNCE AND POST ASSEMBLY SCHEDULE AND ASSIGN ROWS IN AUDITORIUM

ANNOUNCE AND POST FIRE, SHELTER AND DISPERSAL DRILLS REGULATIONS

CHECK LAST TERM'S BOOK AND DENTAL BLACKLISTS

CHECK LIBRARY BLACKLIST

FILL OUT CONDITION OF ROOM REPORT

ELECT CLASS OFFICERS

URGE JOINING G.O. AND BEGIN COLLECTING MONEY

17

APPOINT ROOM DECORATIONS MONITOR AND BEGIN DEC-
ORATING ROOM

SALUTE FLAG (ONLY FOR NON-ASSEMBLY OR Y2 SEC-
TIONS)

POINT OUT THE NATURE AND FUNCTION OF HOMEROOM:
LITERALLY, A ROOM THAT IS A HOME, WHERE STU-
DENTS WILL FIND A FRIENDLY ATMOSPHERE AND
GUIDANCE

TEACHERS WITH EXTRA TIME ARE TO REPORT TO THE
OFFICE TO ASSIST WITH ACTIVITIES WHICH DEMAND
ATTENTION.

* * *

CALVIN COOLIDGE HIGH SCHOOL
Maxwell E. Clarke, Principal
James J. McHabe, Administrative Assistant

CIRCULAR # 1A

TOPIC: ORGANIZATION

PLEASE KEEP ALL CIRCULARS ON FILE, IN THEIR ORDER

DILIGENCE, ACCURACY AND PROMPTNESS ARE ESSENTIAL
IN CARRYING OUT ALL INSTRUCTIONS AS TO PROCEDURES.

PROGRAM FOR MONDAY, SEPTEMBER 7

LONG HOMEROOM PERIOD (SEE CIRCULAR #H16)

SHORT SUBJECT CLASS PERIODS (SEE CIRCULAR # 7C,
SECTION 4)

ASSEMBLY BELL SCHEDULE (SEE ASSEMBLY CIRCULAR
3D, PAR. 5 & 6)

PUPILS ARE TO REPORT BACK TO THEIR HOMEROOMS TO
BE CHECKED OFF AT 2:56. DISMISSAL BELL WILL RING AT
3:05 SHARP. THIS, HOWEVER, IS UNCERTAIN.

* * *

TO: ALL ENGLISH TEACHERS

PLEASE SEND TO THE ENGLISH OFFICE BEFORE 3 TODAY
YOUR REGISTERS IN ALL SUBJECT CLASSES IN ORDER TO

ENABLE US TO EQUALIZE THE TEACHER-LOAD AND
ACHIEVE A GOAL OF 33 STUDENTS PER CLASS.

> SAMUEL BESTER
> CHAIRMAN, LANGUAGE ARTS DEPT.

❖ ❖ ❖

FROM: JAMES J. MCHABE, ADM. ASST.
TO: ALL TEACHERS
RE: REQUISITION OF SUPPLIES

PLEASE ANTICIPATE YOUR NEEDS AND REQUEST SUPPLIES
BEFORE THEY ARE NEEDED. PLEASE DO NOT MAKE EX-
CESSIVE DEMANDS.

TO PREVENT NON-AUTHENTICITY OF SIGNATURES, PLEASE
SIGN YOUR FULL NAME IN INK ON YOUR REQUISITION
SLIP.

IF YOU WISH TO DECORATE YOUR ROOM WITH POSTERS,
WE HAVE A FEW LEFT:

> BLOCK LETTERS, BLUE ON WHITE:
> "KNOWLEDGE IS POWER"
> YELLOW, ON GREEN BACKGROUND:
> "TRUTH IS BEAUTY"

ALSO SOME TRAVEL POSTERS IN BROWN AND TAN OF
SWISS ALPS, SLIGHTLY TORN BUT STILL USABLE.

> JJ McH

❖ ❖ ❖

TO: ALL TEACHERS

LATENT MALADJUSTMENTS MAY EXHIBIT THEMSELVES
IN SOCIALLY UNACCEPTABLE BEHAVIOR IN THE CLASS-
ROOM. THIS IS A CRUCIAL PERIOD IN THE DEVELOPMENT
OF THE ADOLESCENT IN THE SCHOOL ATMOSPHERE
WHICH CONSUMES A LARGE SEGMENT OF HIS TIME. IN
ORDER TO PROVIDE PROPER ORIENTATION TO ADULT
RESPONSIBILITIES IN A DEMOCRACY, PLEASE SEND ALL
NEW PUPILS TO ME ON ALTERNATE TUESDAYS FOR

DEPTH-COVERAGE ON PERSONAL INTERVIEW SHEETS.
THEY WILL BE EXCUSED FROM CLASSES ON THOSE DAYS.
IN THE MEANTIME, TEACHERS ARE TO ACQUAINT THEM-
SELVES WITH THE PPP OF EACH STUDENT AND SEND
THE DISRUPTIVE ELEMENTS TO MR. McHABE.

ELLA FRIEDENBERG
GUIDANCE COUNSELOR

*   *   *

TO: ALL TEACHERS

THERE HAS BEEN AN EPIDEMIC OF THEFTS FROM LOCK-
ERS AND WARDROBES. IMPRESS UPON YOUR STUDENTS
THE NECESSITY OF KEEPING THEM LOCKED UP AT ALL
TIMES, EXCEPT WHEN IN DIRECT USE.

JJ McHABE
ADM. ASST.

*   *   *

FROM: JAMES J. McHABE, ADM. ASST.
TO: ALL TEACHERS

THE FIRST FACULTY CONFERENCE OF THE TERM IS
SCHEDULED FOR MONDAY, SEPTEMBER 28, IN THE
SCHOOL LIBRARY, PROMPTLY AT 3:05.

ATTENDANCE IS MANDATORY. NO TEACHER IS TO BE EX-
CUSED FROM THE CONFERENCE EXCEPT ON WRITTEN
REQUEST SIGNED BY THE CHAIRMAN OF THE DEPART-
MENT AND COUNTERSIGNED BY THE PRINCIPAL OR AD-
MINISTRATIVE ASSISTANT AT LEAST TWO DAYS PRIOR TO
THE DATE SCHEDULED.

THE TOPIC FOR DISCUSSION WILL BE "EDUCATION AS
GROWTH IN A DEMOCRACY." BE PREPARED WITH SUG-
GESTIONS ON: SHOULD MARKS BE ENTERED ON THE
RIGHT OR LEFT OF THE BLUE LINE ON THE PRC?

JJ McH

TO: ALL TEACHERS

STUDENTS DELINQUENT IN OBTAINING GYM SUITS ARE TO BE ALPHABETIZED AND SENT TO ME.
GIRLS WHO WISH TO BE EXCUSED FROM GYM ON "CERTAIN DAYS" ARE TO BE SENT TO ME WITH ALL THE PERTINENT DATA.
PLEASE DISCOURAGE EXCESSIVE DIETING IN YOUR HOMEROOM.

> FRANCES EGAN
> SCHOOL NURSE

* * *

CIRCULAR # 5B

TOPIC: TEACHERS' WELFARE

PLEASE KEEP ALL CIRCULARS ON FILE, IN THEIR ORDER

TEACHERS SHALL BE REQUIRED TO REPORT TO PRINCIPALS AND PRINCIPALS SHALL BE REQUIRED TO REPORT TO THE ASSOCIATE SUPERINTENDENT FOR PERSONNEL AND TO THE LAW SECRETARY ALL CASES OF ASSAULT SUFFERED BY TEACHERS IN CONNECTION WITH THEIR EMPLOYMENT.

* * *

TO: ALL TEACHERS

CALVIN COOLIDGE IS WAGING AN ALL-OUT CAMPAIGN AGAINST LATENESS AND SMOKING IN LAVATORIES. SEND LEGITIMATE LATENESSES TO LATENESS COORDINATOR, ROOM 201. IF EXCUSE IS INVALID OR SUSPECT, SEND OFFENDERS TO ME, ROOM 211. PLEASE READ TO YOUR STUDENTS THE ENCLOSED LIST OF INFRACTIONS AND PENALTIES TO INSTILL IN THEM A SENSE OF CIVIC RESPONSIBILITY AND PUNCTUALITY.

POST IN PROMINENT PLACE IN HOMEROOM:

A STUDENT WHO IS LATE MAY FAIL TO GRAD-U-ATE

> JAMES J. MCHABE
> ADM. ASST.

TO: ALL TEACHERS

STUDENTS ARE NOT TO BE SENT TO THE SCHOOL LIBRARY FOR ANY REASON WHATSOEVER WHILE TEACHERS ARE USING IT FOR THEIR RECORDS.

NO BOOKS ARE TO BE REMOVED FROM LIBRARY SHELVES BY STUDENTS OR TEACHERS UNTIL CARD CATALOGUE IS BROUGHT UP TO DATE.

CHARLOTTE WOLF
LIBRARIAN

*   *   *

TO: ALL ENGLISH TEACHERS

PLEASE SEND TO THE BOOK ROOM FOR THE FOLLOWING BOOKS SELECTED FOR YOUR CLASSES BY THE COMMITTEE ON CURRICULUM INTEGRATION:

ENGLISH 3—ESSAYS OLD AND NEW
or
MYTHS AND THEIR MEANING

ENGLISH 5—THE MILL ON THE FLOSS
or
A TALE OF TWO CITIES

DO NOT ALLOW STUDENTS TO PURCHASE PAPERBACK EDITIONS OF SHAKESPEARE AND OTHER AUTHORS: BECAUSE OF OUTSIDE PRESSURES, WE SHOULD NOT EXPOSE THEM TO INSUFFICIENTLY EDITED OR UNEXPURGATED TEXTS.

SAMUEL BESTER
CHAIRMAN, LANGUAGE ARTS DEPT.

*   *   *

FROM: JAMES J. McHABE, ADM. ASST.
TO: ALL TEACHERS

RE: DISTRIBUTION OF BOOKS

BOOKS ARE THE MAGIC DOORS TO ADVENTURE AND KNOWLEDGE; THEY SHOULD BE TREASURED. KEEP ON

FILE A BOOK RECEIPT FOR EVERY BOOK DISTRIBUTED.
ALL BOOKS SHOULD BE COVERED AND STUDENTS SHOULD
BE WARNED NOT TO DEFACE OR MUTILATE BOOKS. SIGN
THE BOOK LABEL, INDICATING THAT YOU AGREE THAT
THE LABEL HAS BEEN PROPERLY FILLED OUT, AND MAKE
SURE THAT EACH BOOK HAS A NUMBER WHICH APPEARS
ON THE INSIDE FRONT COVER AND AGAIN ON PAGE 43,
IF THE BOOK HAS THAT MANY PAGES.
DISREGARD THE NUMBER ON THE FLY-LEAF.
LOVE OF READING LASTS A LIFETIME.

JJ McH

* * *

DEAR COLLEAGUE:
LOOKING FORWARD TO A NEW SCHOOL YEAR?
EEZYTERM CONFIDENTIAL LOAN COMPANY, WHICH I
REPRESENT, CAN SOLVE YOUR FINANCIAL PROBLEMS:
BROCHURE ENCLOSED.

* * *

Dear Miss Barette,
I need a dropout slip to work because I'm of age and
my income is needed at home. Most of school is a waste
anyhow, every period another subject Algebra French
Eco English one after the other what good is it, it's all
a Jumble and in each class the teacher tells you something different until you don't know who to believe.
I'm better off out.

Your pupil
Vince Arbuzzi

(I wasn't in Home Room due to the office unable to
find my records this morning)

FROM: JAMES J. McHABE, ADM. ASST.

TO: ALL TEACHERS

SINCE WE HAVE A LARGE PERCENTAGE OF DROPOUTS,
PLEASE MAKE EVERY EFFORT TO ENCOURAGE YOUR STU-
DENTS TO REMAIN IN SCHOOL BY POINTING OUT THE
VALUES OF EDUCATION.

JJ McH

* * *

CIRCULAR # 4

TOPIC: ETHICAL STANDARDS

PLEASE KEEP ALL CIRCULARS ON FILE, IN THEIR ORDER

TO PROTECT OUR STUDENTS FROM THE TEMPTATION OF
FRAUDULENT PRACTICES AND TO ASSURE TEACHERS OF
THE AUTHENTICITY OF ALL DATA, THE FOLLOWING PRE-
CAUTIONS MUST BE TAKEN:

1. SUBJECT TEACHERS ARE TO SIGN STUDENT PROGRAM
   CARDS IN INK, WITH THEIR FULL NAME, AS PROOF
   THAT STUDENT HAS APPEARED IN CLASS. NO INITIALS,
   PENCIL OR NAME-STAMPERS ARE ACCEPTABLE.

2. THE ABOVE IS ALSO TRUE OF ALL PASSES SIGNED BY
   THE TEACHER.

3. CHECK THE ROLL BOOK FOR NON-EXISTENT ADDRESSES
   AND NON-AUTHENTIC PARENT OR GUARDIAN, TO FA-
   CILITATE WORK OF TRUANT OFFICER.

4. IN MAKING ENTRIES ON RECORDS, DO NOT ERASE,
   SCRATCH OUT, OR USE INK ERADICATOR. CORRECTIONS
   ARE TO BE MADE ONLY WITH THE SIGNATURE OF THE
   PRINCIPAL OR ADMINISTRATIVE ASSISTANT WHO WILL
   APPROVE THE CORRECTION.

5. DURING FIRE, SHELTER AREA OR OTHER EMERGENCY
   DRILLS, INFORM STUDENTS TO BE PARTICULARLY
   CAREFUL ABOUT THEIR VALUABLES. BOOKS AND NOTE
   BOOKS ARE TO BE LEFT BEHIND, BUT POCKETBOOKS

AND WALLETS ARE TO BE HELD ON TO. WE HAVE HAD AN EPIDEMIC OF UNFORTUNATE INCIDENTS.

WITH THESE PRECAUTIONS IN MIND, WE CAN HELP OUR STUDENTS ACHIEVE THE HIGH ETHICAL STANDARDS WE EXPECT OF THEM.

JAMES J. McHABE
ADM. ASST.

* * *

I WISH TO TAKE THIS OPPORTUNITY TO EXTEND A WARM WELCOME TO ALL FACULTY AND STAFF, AND THE SINCERE HOPE THAT YOU HAVE RETURNED FROM A HEALTHFUL AND FRUITFUL SUMMER VACATION WITH RENEWED VIM AND VIGOR, READY TO GIRD YOUR LOINS AND TACKLE THE MANY IMPORTANT AND VITAL TASKS THAT LIE AHEAD UNDAUNTED. THANK YOU FOR YOUR HELP AND COOPERATION IN THE PAST AND FUTURE.

MAXWELL E. CLARKE
PRINCIPAL

4 Intraschool Communication

INTRASCHOOL COMMUNICATION

FROM: 508
TO: 304

Dear 304 – Just got your latest SOS. Don't let them lead you by the nose. They're testing you. Sit on them from the first moment to show you're boss; they can find out later how nice you really are. There *is* no such thing as an Early Dismissal Monitor or a Permanent Pass to the Water Fountain.

Bea

* * *

INTRASCHOOL COMMUNICATION

FROM: 508
TO: 304

Dear Syl – Serves you right! Never turn your back to the class when writing on the board—learn the overhead backhand. Never give a lesson on "lie and lay." Never raise your voice; let *them* stop talking to hear you. Never give up. And to thine own self be true.

(There is no such thing as a Social Intercourse Period!)

Bea

INTRASCHOOL COMMUNICATION

FROM: 304
TO: 508

Dear Bea—
  What's a PRC?

* * *   *Syl*

INTRASCHOOL COMMUNICATION

FROM: 508
TO: 304

Dear Syl—
  Sorry I couldn't answer sooner; was busy disentangling a kid from a wrong program.
  PRC is the Permanent Record Card; in it you will find the CC, or "Capsule Characterization"—a pregnant phrase composed about each student at the end of each term by his homeroom teacher. In the PRC is the PPP (It almost *sings*, doesn't it?). That's the "Pupil Personality Profile," invented by Ella Friedenberg, Guidance Counselor. She thinks she's Freud, but actually, she's Peeping Tom. She has based her PPP's on such interviews with kids as: "Why do you hate your parents?" "What is your sexual problem?" Avoid her. Also avoid McHabe—he's in charge of Discipline and Supplies. He can't bear to part with a paper clip; ask him for a red pencil and he blanches. Dr. Clarke will avoid *you*. He's really a Mr. but prefers, for reasons of prestige, to be called Dr. Do so. He exists mainly as a signature on the circulars; sometimes he materializes in assembly and makes a speech on "Education For Life"; occasionally he conducts important visitors through the school. Most of the kids think Grayson is principal: he's the distinguished gentleman with the white mane who is "The Custodial Staff." If your ceiling should fall down, send

a note to the basement. He'll probably say he isn't there, but at least you've tried.

Crumple this piece of paper into a small ball and swallow it!

Bea

* * *

INTRASCHOOL COMMUNICATION

FROM: 304
TO. 508

Dear Bea – Paper swallowed. Who is Paul Barringer?

Syl

* * *

INTRASCHOOL COMMUNICATION

FROM: 508
TO: 304

Glamor boy of Eng. Dept. Unpublished Writer. He drinks too much, such men are dangerous. He'll woo you with rhymes. Now you're on your own.

Bea

* * *

INTRASCHOOL COMMUNICATION

FROM: 304
TO: 508

Dear Bea – Can we meet for a smoke in the Teachers' Lounge between classes? I've got to talk to an adult!

Syl

* * *

INTRASCHOOL COMMUNICATION

FROM: 508
TO: 304

Dear Innocent – So-called Teachers' Lounge is Supply Room in basement. Has beat-up couch someone once donated; also sink and chair. But can't be used because of steam pipes in ceiling. Besides, smoking there is against fire regulations. Only place to smoke is Women's Toilet on third floor landing. Let's meet there right after 6th period. Get key to toilet from Sadie Finch. We'll have four whole minutes—if we're lucky and traffic in halls is with us. Sorry I can't come down now—trying to dissuade salvageable youngster from quitting school.

* * *
                                                    Bea

INTRASCHOOL COMMUNICATION

FROM: 304
TO: 508

Dear Bea—
   What am I supposed to do about the number of basketballs I need?

* * *
                                                    Syl

INTRASCHOOL COMMUNICATION

FROM: 508
TO: 304

   Nothing. Notice was put in your box by mistake. Health Ed teacher is right under you.

                                                    Bea

* * *

INTRASCHOOL COMMUNICATION

FROM: 304
TO: 508

   Dear Bea – I am about to send in my registers to Bester: I've got unexcused students, unauthorized students, non-authenticated students, illegitimate students, loitering students and absent students—and still they add up to 223 in my subject classes, besides the 46 in my homeroom. Will someone drop out tomorrow? Will it be I?

                                                    Syl

INTRASCHOOL COMMUNICATION

FROM: 508
TO: 304

Don't you dare! We need you! This is just the first
day; you'll get used to it. The rewards will come later,
from the kids themselves—and from the unlikeliest ones.

Bea

5

And Gladly Teche #1

Sept. 7

Dear Ellen,

It's a far cry from our dorm in Lyons Hall (Was it only four years ago?); a far cry from the sheltered Graduate School Library stacks; a far cry from Chaucer; and a far and desperate cry from *Education 114* and Prof. Winters' lectures on "The Psychology of the Adolescent." I have met the Adolescent face to face; obviously, Prof. Winters had not.

You seem to have done better with your education than I: while you are strolling through your suburban supermarket with your baby in the cart, or taking a shower in the middle of the third period, I am automatically erasing "Fuck Teacher" from the blackboard.

What I really had in mind was to do a little teaching. "And gladly wolde he lerne, and gladly teche"—like Chaucer's Clerke of Oxenford, I had come eager to share all I know and feel; to imbue the young with a love for their language and literature; to instruct and to inspire. What happened in real life (when I had asked why they were taking English, a boy said: "To help us in real life") was something else again, and even if I could describe it, you would think I am exaggerating.

But I'm not.

31

In homeroom (that's the official class, where the kids report in the morning and in the afternoon for attendance
and vital statistics) they went after me with all their ammu-
nition: whistling, shouting, drumming on desks, clacking
inkwell lids, playing catch with the board eraser, sprawling
in their seats to trip each other in the aisles—all this with
an air of vacant innocence, while I stood there, pleading for
attention, wary as a lion-tamer, my eyes on all 46 at once.

By the time I got to my subject classes, I began to stagger
under an inundation of papers—mimeos, directives, circulars,
letters, notices, forms, blanks, records. The staggering was
especially difficult because I am what's known as a "floater"
—I float from room to room.

There's a whole glossary to be learned. My 3rd termers
are "special-slows"; my 5th termers are "low-normal" and
"average-normal." So far, it's hard to tell which is which, or
who I am, for that matter.

I made one friend—Bea Schachter, and one enemy—Administrative Asst. who signs himself JJ McH. And I saw hate
and contempt on the face of a boy—because I am a teacher.

The building itself is hostile: cracked plaster, broken windows, splintered doors and carved up desks, gloomy corridors, metal stairways, dingy cafeteria (they can eat sitting
down only in 20 minute shifts) and an auditorium which
has no windows. It does have murals, however, depicting
mute, muscular harvesters, faded and immobilia under a
mustard sun.

That's where we had assembly this morning.

Picture it: the air heavy with hundreds of bodies, the principal's blurred face poised like a pale balloon over the lectern, his microphone-voice crackling with sudden static:

". . . a new leaf, for here at Calvin Coolidge we are all
free and equal, with the same golden opportunity . . ."

The students are silent in their seats. The silence has
nothing to do with attention; it's a glazed silence, ready to
be shattered at a moment. The girl next to me examines her
teeth in her pocket mirror. I sit straight on the wooden seat,

smoothed by the restless bottoms of how many children, grown now, or dead, or where? On the back of the seat directly in front of me, carefully chiseled with some sharp instrument, is the legend: *Balls.*

". . . knocks but once, and your attitude . . ." *Tude* booms, unexpectedly amplified by the erratic microphone, "towards your work and your teachers, who so selflessly . . ."

The teachers dot the aisles: a hen-like little woman with a worried profile; a tall young man with amused eyebrows; a round lady with a pepper-and-salt pompadour—my colleagues, as yet unknown.

". . . precious than rubies. Education means . . ."—he's obviously winding up for a finish—"not only preparation for citizenship and life *plus* a sound academic foundation. Don't forget to have your teachers sign your program cards, and if you have any problems, remember my door is always open." Eloquent pause. "And so, with this thought in mind, I hope you will show the proper school spirit, one and all."

Released at last, they burst, clang-banging the folding seats, as they spill out on a wave of forbidden voices, and I with them, into the hall.

"Wherezya pass?" says the elevator man gloomily. "Gotcher elevator pass?"

"I'm a teacher," I say sheepishly, as if caught in a lie.

For only teachers, and students with proof of a serious disability, may ride in the elevators. Looking young has certain disadvantages here; if I were a man, I'd grow a mustache.

This morning, the students swarming on the street in front of the entrance parted to let me pass—the girls, their faces either pale or masked with makeup; the boys eyeing me exaggeratedly: "Hey eeah—howzabadis! Gedaloadadis—whee-uh!" the two-note whistle of insolent admiration following me inside.

(Or better still—a beard.)

It seems to me kids were different when I was in high school. But the smell in the lobby was the same unmistakable school smell—chalk dust? paper filings? musty metal? rotting wood?

I joined the other teachers on line at the time clock, and gratefully found my card. I was expected: Someone had put my number on it—#91. I punched the time on my card and stuck it into the IN rack. I was *in*.

But when I had written my name on the blackboard in my room, for a moment I had the strange feeling that it wasn't spelled right. It looked unfamiliar—white and drowning in that hard black sea. . . .

I am writing this during my lunch period, because I need to reach towards the outside world of sanity, because I am overwhelmed by the sheer weight of the clerical work still to be done, and because at this hour of the morning normal ladies are still sleeping.

We have to punch——

6
No One Down Here

FROM: James J. McHabe, Adm. Asst.
TO: Miss Barrett, 304

Why do you need so many paper-clips? Supplies are running low. All out of desk blotters. All out of rubber bands. All out of board erasers. No red pencils—only blue. Can let you have half envelope of chalk—all out of boxes. Chalk is not to be wasted. *No unauthorized students are to use it.*

JJ McH

❋   ❋   ❋

TO: all teachers

Please ignore the bells.

Sadie Finch
Chief Clerk

❋   ❋   ❋

FROM: sylvia barrett
TO: dr. samuel bester

Dear Dr. Bester,
Enclosed are my registers in my five English classes. I find that my teaching-load is 223 students per day

and that my average is not 33 but 44⅗ students per class.

$$
\begin{array}{r}
39 \\
46 \\
46 \\
51 \\
41 \\
\hline
5\overline{)223} \\
\hline
44\tfrac{3}{5}
\end{array}
$$

Also, the Book Room has no *Mill on the Floss*—only *Julius Caesar*, and only enough for three-fourths of the class.

S. Barrett

* * *

FROM: DR. SAMUEL BESTER
           CHAIRMAN, LANGUAGE ARTS DEPT.
TO: MISS BARRETT

Dear Miss Barrett,
   Let it be a challenge to you.

S. Bester

* * *

ADDENDUM TO ETHICAL STANDARDS:

TRANSPORTATION CARDS ARE NOT TO BE SIGNED UNLESS STUDENTS ARE ENTITLED TO TRANSPORTATION. WE HAVE HAD AN EPIDEMIC OF MISREPRESENTATION ON TRANSPORTATION CARDS.

INSTILL IN YOUR STUDENTS PROPER BEHAVIOR ON PUBLIC VEHICLES TO AND FROM SCHOOL. INFRACTIONS OF COMMON COURTESY IN OR AROUND THE VICINITY OF THE SCHOOL REFLECT ON CALVIN COOLIDGE AND DISTORT OUR PUBLIC IMAGE.

NO WRITTEN PASSES ARE TO BE ISSUED TO LAVATORIES, SINCE THEY ARE EASILY DUPLICATED BY THE STUDENTS. ONLY WOODEN LAVATORY PASSES ARE TO BE HONORED.

JAMES J. McHABE, ADM. ASST.

* * *

Miss Barrett—
Joseph Ferone disrupted my 5th period math class through the door. He belonged in your English class that period but left your room without a pass.
Edward Williams of your homeroom talked in Assembly this morning.
Please take appropriate measures.

Frederick Loomis

* * *

Dear Mrs. Barnet, He said to apoligize in writing but I didn't even talk in assembly today, teachers have it in for me because I am color. Loomis flunked me in math last term, it's not fair because I was in class a lot. He flunked me in hist. too even though it's not his subject. Teachers give the subject a bad name. He said he'll report me because he's prejudice.

Edward Williams, Esq.

* * *

FROM: JAMES J. McHABE, ADM. ASST.
TO: ALL TEACHERS

AT THE END OF THE HOMEROOM PERIOD, PLEASE SEND TO ME THOSE STUDENTS WHO HAVE FAILED TO REPORT FOR CHECK-OUT BECAUSE THEY HAVE LEFT THE BUILD-ING.

JJ McH

Bea—As for above—I'd like to oblige him, but how do I send him kids who aren't there?

Puzzled

INTRASCHOOL COMMUNICATION

FROM: 508
TO: 304
Dear Puzzled—
    Let it be a challenge to you.

                                                    Bea

*   *   *

FROM: James J. McHabe, Adm. Asst.
TO: all teachers
DUE BEFORE THREE

Please fill out and send to 211 before 3 today the enclosed report on Physical Condition of Room. This is
done monthly to insure the safety of all students. Check
defects, if any, and name specifically any deviations or
hazards.

                                                    JJ McH

*   *   *

ROOM: 304
TEACHER: s. barrett   september 9

Door off hinge & banging—hazard!

Sliding wardrobe panel doesn't close; side blackboard
is on it and cannot be used. Deviation.

Book case in back of room missing ½ its door; can't
be closed. Also, shelf splintered. Deviation *and* hazard.

Teacher's desk missing two drawers. Deviation.

Window in back of room broken; scattered glass—
hazard.

                                                    S. Barrett

TO: ALL TEACHERS
Disregard Bells.

Sadie Finch
Chief Clerk

＊　＊　＊

FROM: JAMES J. McHABE, ADM. ASST.
TO: ALL TEACHERS

THE FOLLOWING MATERIAL AND NO OTHER IS TO BE PLACED IN THE <u>CENTER</u> DRAWER OF YOUR DESK IN THE ROOM WHERE YOUR OFFICIAL CLASS MEETS AND LOCKED UP WITH KEY PROVIDED FOR THE PURPOSE. THIS MATERIAL IS TO BE KEPT LOCKED UP AT ALL TIMES EXCEPT WHEN IN USE BY TEACHER OR OTHER AUTHORIZED AGENT: ROLL BOOK, ATTENDANCE PADS, ABSENTEE POSTAL CARDS, SEATING PLAN, EMERGENCY SLIPS, EXCUSE SLIPS, TRANSCRIPT SHEETS, PROGRAM CARDS (IN ALPHABETICAL ORDER), CONSENT SLIPS, TRUANT SLIPS (BLUE), PARENT LETTERS #1 (YELLOW), PARENT LETTERS #2 (PINK), EXTRACURRICULAR CREDIT CARDS, AND LUNCH PERMITS.

JJ McH

＊　＊　＊

Dear Mr. McHabe–

My problem is: I've got the material all right, and the key, but no center drawer. As a matter of fact, two whole drawers are missing from my desk. Please advise.

S. Barrett

＊　＊　＊

ADDENDUM TO CIRCULAR # 108 ON SHELTER AREA DRILLS:

AT SIGNAL (THREE BELLS REPEATED THREE TIMES) FOLLOW EXITS AND CONVERGE INTO CENTER AREA BETWEEN

PARALLEL BARS IN BASEMENT GYM. TO INSURE MAXIMUM
SAFETY, ABSOLUTE SILENCE IS TO BE MAINTAINED AT
ALL TIMES DURING THIS IMPORTANT DRILL. DO NOT
LEAN ON HORSES.

> JAMES J. MCHABE
> ADM. ASST.

*   *   *

FROM: S. Barrett, 304
TO: Mr. Grayson, Custodian, Basement

Dear Mr. Grayson,
    I need 11 additional chairs for 304, and someone to
repair broken window and clean up scattered glass—
health hazard!

> *S. Barrett*

No one down here.

*   *   *

INTRASCHOOL COMMUNICATION
FROM: 304
TO: 508

Dear Bea—
    What a curious place this is, where bells are rung to
be ignored, where children are safe from atomic anni-
hilation if they do not lean on gym horses, where a cry
in the wilderness remains unheard. Is there "no one
down there," ever?

> *Syl*

COPY TO: Dr. Clarke
Dr. Bester
Mrs. Egan

Dear Miss Barrett,

It has come to my attention that you have neglected to fill out a Form B221 Accident Report of a fall from a chair incurred by a student in your official class. Such negligence may result in serious consequences. The safety of the students in our charge is paramount at all times. Before leaving the building today, you will please make out this report in triplicate, signed by the witnesses who witnessed the above accident.

JAMES J. MCHABE
ADM. ASST.

(No purpose is served in blaming defective equipment for failure to comply with instructions on locking up confidential records.)

JJ McH

* * *

Miss Barrett,

The theft of a valuable wallet from a student's unlocked locker on or about the 5th period today has just been reported to me. One of your students was observed loitering in the vicinity without a pass and is a strong suspect.

See me at the end of the afternoon homeroom.

JJ McH
Adm. Asst.

TO: ALL TEACHERS

Please ascertain and send to me before three o'clock today the number of students in your homeroom who have not had a hot breakfast this morning. POOR NUTRITION IS FREQUENTLY THE CAUSE OF POOR MARKS.

Frances Egan
School Nurse

Sept. 7

Dear Ellen,

I had begun a letter to you this morning but was interrupted, and now I can't find it in the flood of papers in which I am drowning.

Perhaps it's just as well; I couldn't possibly succeed in describing this place to you: the homeroom, the Assembly, the chaos of clerical work, the kids—whom I had come to guide and "gladly teche."

I've been here less than a day, and already I'm in hot water. A boy had "incurred a fall" in class, and I failed to report it on the proper form. Another left the room without a pass and is suspected of stealing a wallet from a locker which wasn't locked because I had neglected to inspect it. This was Joe Ferone, *the* problem-boy of Calvin Coolidge, who earlier, in homeroom, had been flagrantly rude to me, and insolent, and contemptuous.

While I was writing you the other letter (Where can it be? Among the Circulars? Directives? Faculty Mimeos? Department Notices? In the right-hand desk drawer? Left-hand? In my wastebasket, perhaps?), during what was presumably my lunch period, Admiral Ass (a Mr. McHabe, who signs himself Adm. Asst.) appeared in my room with Joe Ferone.

43

"This boy is on probation," he said. "Did he show up in homeroom this morning?"

"Yes," I said.

"Any trouble?" the Admiral asked.

There we stood, the three of us, taking each other's measure. Ferone was watching me through narrowed eyes.

"No. No trouble," I said.

I am writing this during my free . . . oops! unassigned period, at the end of my first day of teaching. So far, I have taught nothing—but I have learned a great deal. To wit:

We have to punch a time clock and abide by the Rules.

We must make sure our students likewise abide, and that they sign the time sheet whenever they leave or reenter a room.

We have keys but no locks (except in lavatories), blackboards but no chalk, students but no seats, teachers but no time to teach.

The library is closed to the students.

Yet I'm told that Calvin Coolidge is not unique; it's as average as a large metropolitan high school can be. There are many schools worse than this (the official phrase is "problem-area schools on the lower socio-economic levels") and a few better ones. Kids with an aptitude in a trade can go to vocational high schools; kids with outstanding talents in math, science, drama, dance, music, or art can attend special high schools which require entrance tests or auditions; kids with emotional problems or difficulties in learning are sent to the "600 schools." But the great majority, the ordinary kids, find themselves in Calvin Coolidge or its reasonable facsimile. And so do the teachers.

Do you remember Rhoda, who left Lyons Hall before graduation? She is now writing advertising copy for a cosmetics firm at three times my salary. I often think of her. And of Mattie, who was in graduate school with me, and who is teaching at Willowdale Academy, holding seminars on James Joyce under the philosophic maples. And I think of you, in a far away town, walking serene in daylight from Monday to Friday, and I think I must be crazy to stay on here. And yet—there is a certain phrase we have, a kind of in-joke: "Let it be a challenge."

There goes the bell. Or is it only the warning signal? The bells have gone berserk. I now go to check the PM attendance in my homeroom—Admiral Ass says it prevents escapes.

Love,
Syl

P. S. Did you know that according to the Board of Education's estimate it would cost the city $8 million to reduce the size of classes "by a single child" throughout the city?

PART II

From
The Calvin Coolidge
Clarion

Calvin Coolidge
∽◎ CLARION ◎∾

September

INTERESTING INTERVIEWS:

Miss Sylvia Barrett, the new English teacher, is not
only everybody's choice "Audrey Hepburn" of Calvin
Coolidge but is also a very attractive young woman of
whom we are so very proud. The interview found her
to be 5 feet 4 inches in her stocking feet, with brown
hair and blue-gray eyes and very pleasant to talk to. She
received her B.A. degree with Phi Beta Kappa and
Magna Cum Laude (It's Greek to us!) and her M.A.
(Miss America?) with highest honors. (Boy! What a
record!)

Listed among her favorites are Chaucer the poet (That's
Greek to us too!) and reading books. She is also partial to painting in her spare time (Don't go up and pose
for her, boys!) and bicycling (built for two?), whipped
cream (Oh, those calories!) and swimming (Yummm!);
and she likes to visit different places like everyone else.
She visited some places in Mexico last summer (Habla

49

Espanol?). She feels that teaching here will be a real challenge to her.

Glad to have you at Coolidge, Miss "Audrey" Barrett, and hope you stay awhile.

~~~~~~~~~~~~~~~~~~~~~

A MESSAGE FROM OUR PRINCIPAL:

Your education has been planned and geared to arm and prepare you to function as mature and thinking citizens capable of shouldering the burdens and responsibilities which a thriving democracy imposes. It is through you and others like you that the forward march of democracy, spurred and fortified by a thorough and well-rounded education, will move on to greater triumphs and victories. We have no doubt that our aims and efforts in this direction will bear fruit and achieve the goals and objectives set forth, for in the miniature democracy of our school you are proving yourselves worthy and deserving of our trust and expectations.

Very sincerely yours,
Maxwell E. Clarke, Principal

~~~~~~~~~~~~~~~~~~~~~

COMPLIMENTS OF VANITY CORSET CO.

~~~~~~~~~~~~~~~~~~~~~

THE CORNER COFFEE SHOPPE:
   "WHERE FRIEND MEETS FRIEND"

~~~~~~~~~~~~~~~~~~~~~

HOW TO AVOID FRESHMAN FOLLY———

SOPHOMORE SLUMP----

JUNIOR JITTERS----

SENIOR SORROWS:

JOIN YOUR G.O.!!! GET YOUR G.O. BUTTONS
WHILE THEY LAST!!! GO, GO, G.O.!

SCHOOL SPIRIT, ANYONE?
COME AND ROOT FOR YOUR TEAM!
SCHEDULED BASKETBALL GAMES:

SEPT.   CALVIN COOLIDGE VS. MANHATTAN MUNICIPAL
OCT.   CALVIN COOLIDGE VS. (?) UNSCHEDULED
NOV.   CALVIN COOLIDGE VS. (?) UNSCHEDULED
DEC.   (?)

~~~~~~~~~~~~~~~~~~~~~~~~~~~~~~~~~~~~

Dr. Maxwell E. Clarke
James J. McHAbe
Mary Lewis
SylVia Barrett
Ella FrIedenberg
Paul BarriNger

Beatrice SchaChter
Charlotte WOlf
Frederick LoOmis
Henrietta PastorfieLd
Marcus ManheIm
SaDie Finch
Frances EGan
Samuel BEster

~~~~~~~~~~~~~~~~~~~~~~~~~~~~~~~~~~~~

FACULTY FLASHES

The teacher the girls would like to be on a desert island most with: MR. PAUL ("POET") BARRINGER

The teacher readiest with unselfish helps: MRS. BEATRICE ("MOM") SCHACHTER

The teacher who makes lessons most like games: MISS HENRIETTA ("PAL") PASTORFIELD

Most absentminded teacher: MR. MARCUS ("H$_2$O")
MANHEIM

Most glamorous teacher: MISS SYLVIA BARRETT

THE CALVIN COOLIDGE CLARION is "The Voice
of Your School." Please subscribe and solicit ads to keep
it "talking"!

We wish to express our gratitude to Miss Mary Lewis,
Faculty Advisor to *The Clarion*, who so unstintingly
gave of herself to us.

Sept. 25

Dear Ellen,

It's FTG (Friday Thank God), which means I need not set the alarm for 6:30 tomorrow morning; I can wash a blouse, think a thought, write a letter.

Congratulations on the baby's new tooth. Soon there is bound to be another tooth and another and another, and before you know it, little Suzie will start going to school, and her troubles will just begin. Though I hope that by the time she gets into the public high school system, things will be different. At least, they keep *promising* that things will be different. I'm told that since the recent strike threats, negotiations with the United Federation of Teachers, and greater public interest, we are enjoying "improved conditions." But in the two weeks that I've been here, conditions seem greatly unimproved.

You ask what I am teaching. Hard to say. Professor Winters advised teaching "not the subject but the whole child." The English Syllabus urges "individualization and enrichment"—which means giving individual attention to each student to bring out the best in him and enlarge his scope beyond the prescribed work. Bester says to "motivate and

54

distribute" books—that is, to get students ready and eager to read. All this is easier said than done. In fact, all this is plain impossible.

Many of our kids—though physically mature—can't read beyond 4th or 5th grade level. Their background consists of the simplest comics and thrillers. They've been exposed to some ten years of schooling, yet they don't know what a sentence is.

The books we are required to teach frequently have nothing to do with anything except the fact that they have always been taught, or that there is an oversupply of them, or that some committee or other was asked to come up with some titles.

For example: I've distributed Shakespeare's *Julius Caesar* to my 5th term class of "slow non-readers." (Question: How would "fast non-readers" read?) This is in lieu of *The Mill on the Floss*. I am supposed to teach *Romeo and Juliet* OR *A Tale of Two Cities* (strange bedfellows!) to my "low-normal" class, and *Essays Old and New* to my "special-slows." So far, however, I've been unable to give out any books because of problems having to do with Purloined Book Receipts, Book Labels without Glue, Inaccurate Inventory of Book Room, and Traffic Conditions on the Stairs.

But I have not let it discourage me. I've been trying to teach without books. There was one heady moment when I was able to excite the class by an idea: I had put on the blackboard Browning's "A man's reach should exceed his grasp, or what's a heaven for?" and we got involved in a spirited discussion of aspiration vs. reality. Is it wise, I asked, to aim higher than one's capacity? Does it not doom one to failure? No, no, some said, that's ambition and progress! No, no, others cried, that's frustration and defeat! What about hope? What about despair?—You've got to be practical!—You've got to have a dream! They said this in their own words, you understand, startled into discovery. To the young, clichés seem freshly minted. Hitch your wagon to a star!

Shoemaker, stick to your last! And when the dismissal bell rang, they paid me the highest compliment: they groaned! They crowded in the doorway, chirping like agitated sparrows, pecking at the seeds I had strewn—when who should materialize but Admiral Ass.

"What is the meaning of this noise?"

"It's the sound of thinking, Mr. McHabe," I said.

In my letter-box that afternoon was a note from him, with copies to my principal and chairman (and—who knows?—perhaps a sealed indictment dispatched to the Board?) which read (sic):

> "I have observed that in your class the class entering your room is held up because the pupils exiting from your room are exiting in a disorganized fashion, blocking the doorway unnecessarily and *talking*. An orderly flow of traffic is the responsibility of the teacher whose class is exiting from the room."

The cardinal sin, strange as it may seem in an institution of learning, is talking. There are others, of course—sins, I mean, and I seem to have committed a good number. Yesterday I was playing my record of Gielgud reading Shakespeare. I had brought my own phonograph to school (no one could find the Requisition Forms for "Audio-Visual Aids"—that's the name for the school record player) and I had succeeded, I thought, in establishing a mood. I mean, I got them to be quiet, when—enter Admiral Ass, in full regalia, epaulettes quivering with indignation. He snapped his fingers for me to stop the phonograph, waited for the turntable to stop turning, and pronounced:

"There will be a series of three bells rung three times indicating Emergency Shelter Drill. Playing records does not encourage the orderly evacuation of the class."

I mention McHabe because he has crystallized into The Enemy.

But there are other difficulties. There are floaters floating in during class (these are peripatetic, or unanchored teachers) to rummage through my desk drawers for a forgotten Delaney Book. (I have no idea why it's called that. Perhaps because it was invented by a Mr. Delaney. It's a seating-plan book, with cards with kids' names stuck into slots.)

There are questionnaires to be filled out in the middle of a lesson, such as: "Are there any defective electrical outlets in your home?"

There is money to be collected for publications, organizations, milk, G.O. (the General Organization), basketball tickets, and "Voluntary Contributions to the Custodial Staff." The latter is some kind of tacit appeasement of Mr. Grayson, who lives in the basement, if he exists at all; he is the mystery man of Calvin Coolidge.

There is the drilling on the street below that makes the windows vibrate; the Orchestra tuning up down the hall; the campaigners (this is the election season) bursting into the room to blazon on my sole blackboard in curlicued yellow chalk:

HARRY KAGAN WINS RESPECT
IF YOU WILL HIM FOR PRES. ELECT!

and

GLORIA EHRLICH IS PRETTY AND NICE
VOTE FOR GLORIA FOR VICE!

And the shelter area drills, which usually come at the most interesting point in the lesson. Bells clanging frantically, we all spill out into the gym, where we stand silent and safe between parallel bars, careful not to lean on horses, excused, for the moment, from destruction.

Sometimes the lesson is interrupted by life: the girl who, during grammar drill, rushed out of the room to look for her lost $8.70 for the gas and electric bill, crying: "My mother will kill me, for sure!" And for sure, she might. The boy who apologized for not doing his homework because he had to go to get married. "I got this girl into trouble all right, and we're Catholics, but the thing is, I don't *like* her."

Chaos, waste, cries for help—strident, yet unheard. Or am
I romanticizing? That's what Paul says; he only shrugs and
makes up funny verses about everyone. That's Paul Barringer—a writer who teaches English on one foot, as it were,
just waiting to be published. He's very attractive: a tan crew
cut; a white smile with lots of teeth; one eyebrow higher
than the other. All the girls are in love with him.

There are a few good, hard-working, patient people like
Bea—a childless widow—"Mother Schachter and her cherubs," as the kids say, who manage to teach against insuper-
able odds; a few brilliantly endowed teachers who—unknown
and unsung—work their magic in the classroom; a few who
truly love young people. The rest, it seems to me, have either
given up, or are taking it out on the kids. "Those who can,
do; those who can't, teach." Like most sayings, this is only
half true. Those who can, teach; those who can't—the bitter,
the misguided, the failures from other fields—find in the
school system an excuse or a refuge.

There is Mary Lewis, bowed and cowed, who labors
through the halls as overloaded as a pack mule, thriving on
discomfort and overwork, compulsively following all direc-
tions from supervisors, a willing martyr to the system. She's
an old-timer who parses sentences and gives out zeros to
kids who chew gum.

There is Henrietta Pastorfield, a hearty spinster who is
"married to the school," who woos the kids by entertaining
them, convinced that lessons must be fun, knowledge sugar-
coated, and that teacher should be pal.

There is Fred Loomis, a math teacher stuck with two
out-of-license English classes, who hates kids with a pure
and simple hatred. "At the age of 15," he said to me, "they
should all be kicked out of school and the girls sterilized so
they don't produce others like themselves." These were his
words. And he comes in contact with some 200 children a
day.

The school nurse, Frances Egan, wears white space shoes
and is mad for nutrition; Mrs. Wolf, the librarian, cannot

bear to see a book removed from its shelf; and Miss Ella
Friedenberg, an ambitious typing teacher promoted to Guidance Counselor, swoops upon the kids and impales them with
questions about masturbation. She has evolved a PPP (Pupil
Personality Profile) into which she fits each youngster,
branding him with pseudo-Freudian phrases. She has most
of the teachers bamboozled, and some of the kids terrorized.

My other colleagues I know just by sight: Desk Despots,
Blackboard Barons, Classroom Caesars and Lords of the
Loose-Leaf, Paul calls them. He has the gift of words. Lyrics
are his forte; he composed an amusing song about our principal: "Hark, hark, the Clarke/ At heaven's gate . . . something—something," I forget. He wrote a verse about me too:
rhymed me with "14 carat." Very attractive man.

McHabe, of course, is the kind of petty tyrant who flour-
ishes best in the school system, the army, or a totalitarian
state. To me he personifies all that is picayune, mean and
degrading to the human spirit. I've had a head-on clash with
him over one of my boys, Joe Ferone, whom he had accused
of theft—unjustifiably, as it turned out; and he has alluded
darkly to the danger of my getting a U (Unsatisfactory)
end-term rating.

I don't know why I am championing Ferone, who is the
most difficult discipline problem in the school, except, perhaps, that I dimly sense in him a rebelliousness, like mine,
against the same things. When he is in school, which isn't
often, he is rude and contemptuous; hands in pockets, toothpick in mouth, rocking insolently on his heels, he seems to
be watching me for some sign.

Most of the time, I am still struggling to establish communication. It is difficult, and I don't know whom to turn to.
Dr. Clarke? I don't think he is aware of anything that is
going on in his school. All I know about him is that he has
a carpet in his office and a private john on the fourth floor
landing. Most of the time he secludes himself in one or the
other; when he does emerge, he is fond of explaining that
education is derived from "e duco," or leading *out* of. He is

also partial to such paired pearls as: *aims and goals; guide
and inspire; help and encourage;* and *new horizons and
broader vistas;* they drop from him like so many cultured
cuff links.

And Dr. Bester, my immediate supervisor, Chairman of
the English Department, I can't figure out at all. He is a
dour, desiccated little man, remote and prissy. Like most
chairmen, he teaches only one class of Seniors; the most experienced teachers are frequently promoted right out of the
classroom! Kids respect him; teachers dislike him—possibly
because he is given to popping up, unexpectedly, to observe
them. "The ghost walks" is the grapevine signal for his visits.
Bea told me he started out as a great teacher, but he's been
soured by the trivia-in-triplicate which his administrative
duties impose. I hope he doesn't come to observe me until
I get my bearing. I'm still floundering, particularly in my
SS class of "reluctant learners." (Under-achievers, non-aca-
demic-minded, slow, disadvantaged, sub-paced, non-college-
oriented, underprivileged, non-linguistic, intellectually deprived, and laggers—so far, I've counted more than ten
different euphemisms for "dumb kids"!)

But I am busiest outside of my teaching classes. Do you
know any other business or profession where highly-skilled
specialists are required to tally numbers, alphabetize cards,
put notices into mailboxes, and patrol the lunchroom?

What a long letter this has turned into! I've quite lost
touch with the mainstream, you see, isolated as I am in 304,
while bells ring, students come and go, and my wastebasket
runneth over.

Write, write! And tell me of the even tenor of your days.
If things get too rough here, I might ask you to move over.

Love,
Syl

P. S. Did you know that in New York City high school
teachers devote approximately 100 hours a year to homeroom

chores? This makes a grand total of over 500,000 hours that they spend on clerical work. That's official school time only; the number of extracurricular hours spent on lesson plans, records, marking papers, and so on is not estimated.

S.

Facatty Conference minutes

NOTES FOR FACULTY CONFERENCE MINUTES

MET: On Monday, Sept. 28
At 3:06 P.M.
In: School Library
Attendance: 100%

Dr. Clarke's after-summer greeting: "Shoulder to wheel & nose to grindstone"   1½ min.

Bea Schachter brought up urgent problems left over from last term: the burden of the teaching-load and of clerical work, and inadequate facilities   1 min.

Above problems postponed for time being. Two Feuding Floaters sharing same room were given floor:

Floater #1: When enters classroom, finds writing on blackboard with "Do not Erase" over it; feels it's unfair usurpation of valuable blackboard space.

Floater #2: Desk dictionary found in back

of room; obviously taken by kid! *Dictionary not to be removed from desk at any time!*

Floater #1: No room left in left-hand desk drawer.

Floater #2: Left-hand drawer not #1's but #2's.

Subcommittee of Grievance Com. on Rotation of Teachers to more Equitable Room Assignments formed to look into above.   6 min.

Bea Schachter raised question of student dropouts.

McHabe: Must stick to mimeographed procedure.   ½ min.

Main topic for discussion: Marks to be entered on the left or the right side of blue line on PRC?

Various Pro's and Con's. Which is best way to *save time?*

Committee formed to look into.   8½ min.

Barringer suggested abolishing afternoon homeroom.

Vetoed by McHabe   ½ min.

Discussion on School Aides:

Aides were finally assigned to us to relieve teachers of non-teaching chores, but now teachers have been assigned *other* non-teaching chores. Also, Aides turned out to be in the way: they are not allowed to take over a class; not allowed to work on records; not allowed Late Room or Health Room. Also, cafeteria workers resent them for just sitting around.

Conclusion: School Aides to guard exits of building and challenge visitors.   10½ min.

Problem raised re dope addiction among students, and "pushers" in school area.
>   Shelved for lack of time.   ½ min.

McHabe warned re smoking in lavatories.
Urged rereading of Smoking Circular.   1½ min.

Manheim: re inadequate Science Lab. equipment. Had made several requisitions.
>   McHabe: Must go through channels.   ½ min.

Miss Egan (School Nurse): Urged imporportance of hot breakfasts. Start day by stoking engine. Affects marks.
>   Dr. Clarke: "Mens sana in corpore sano."   1 min.

Mrs. Wolf (Librarian): When return books to library shelves, put in straight. Otherwise wastes time. Warn kids re crooked placing of books.   2 min.

Teacher (? gray suit, mustache): suggested adjourning.
>   McHabe: Not time yet.   ½ min.

Bea Schachter: re problems of integration. Dr. Clarke: Due and orderly process. Patience and Fortitude. Professional Dignity. Brother's Keeper. The Constitution.   2½ min.

Mary Lewis: re plaster falling from ceiling of her room. Grayson not cooperative.
>   McHabe: Must go through channels.   ½ min.

McHabe: Urged cooperation on lateness. Epidemic of. Strict observance late procedures. Parents to be notified by Letter #3. "Academic marks are affected when report cards are distributed" (sic).   8 min.

Miss Finch (School Clerk): "Teachers should function according to instructions."
>   Means: Hand in on time!   1 min.

Miss Friedenberg (Guidance Counselor):
Need more accurate CC's on PRC's.
(Means: "Capsule Characterizations" for
each student entered by teacher on Per-
manent Record Card.) One phrase
enough, provided it's *in depth*. Example:
"Latent leader; needs encouragement."
Study previous PPP's (Pupil Personality
Profiles).   3½ min.

Barringer: Suggested abolishing morning
homeroom.
Vetoed by McHabe.   ½ min.

Mary Lewis: Now that reading from Bible
on assembly days has been declared un-
constitutional, any objection to a minute
of silent prayer?
McHabe: OK if word "prayer" is not mentioned, and if don't move lips during.   1 min.

Teacher (? gray suit, mustache): suggested
adjourning.
McHabe: Not time yet.   ½ min.

Displaced Teachers: Because Fire Dept.
found 5th floor Science Office a fire hazard, it was moved to 3rd floor Math Book
Room and math books were left in Shop
Closet for time being, while Shop Teachers' Supplies were moved to 2nd floor Stor-
age Closet, the contents of which were
moved to Main Office for time being. In
the shuffle, 5th floor Social Studies Teachers who used Science Office for marking
papers, etc. were displaced. Where can
they go? Committee formed to look into.   5 min.

Dr. Clarke's conclusion: Education is necessary for growth in democracy.   2 min.

Problems of instructional load, burden of
  clerical work and inadequate facilities
  were postponed for lack of time.   ½ min.

Teacher (? gray suit, mustache) suggested
  adjourning.   ½ min.

Faculty Conference adjourned at 4:06 P.M.
                                          _____
                            TOTAL: 60 min.

(Rewrite, type up in triplicate, and respectfully submit)

11 *Pupil-Load*

Oct. 2

Dear Ellen,

Another FTG; another week. Time collapses and expands like an erratic accordion, and your letters bring order, sanity and remembrance of things past to my disheveled present. I envy you your leisure to browse and putter and to enjoy your family in peaceful suburbia. As for me—as for me . . .

The cold war between the Admiral and me is getting warmer; tension between Ferone and me is getting tenser; Miss Finch, the school clerk, floods me with papers from the giant maw of her mimeograph machine, and I'm not at all sure that I will last in the school system.

In my homeroom, I'm lucky if I can get through the D's in taking attendance. Admiral Ass lurks outside in the hall, ready to pounce at the first sign of mutiny. Or perhaps he watches through a periscope from his office.

In my subject classes, we are still juggling books. *Essays Old and New* was changed by the powers that be to *The Odyssey* and *Myths and Their Meaning*. I have only two weeks in which to teach my SS class the mythology of the race and Homer's great epic, since other teachers are waiting for these books, since they must be read before the Mid-

67

term Exams, since questions on them will appear on the Midterms, and since the Midterms must be scheduled before Thanksgiving to enable the teachers to mark them during the holidays.

I keep looking for clues in whatever the kids say or write. I've even installed a Suggestion Box in my room, in the hope that they will communicate their feelings freely and eventually will learn to trust me.

So far, most of them are still a field of faces, rippling with every wind, but a few are beginning to emerge.

There is Lou Martin, the class comedian, whose forte is facial expressions. No one can look more crestfallen over unprepared homework: hand clasped to brow, knees buckling, shoulders sagging with remorse, he is a penitent to end all penitents. No one can look more thirsty when asking for a pass: tongue hanging out, eyes rolling, a death-rattle in the throat, he can barely make it to the water fountain. No one can look more horrified at a wrong answer issuing from his own traitor lips; or more humble; or more bewildered; or more indignant. I know it's not in the syllabus, but I'm afraid I encourage him by laughing.

I'm beginning to learn some of their names and to understand some of their problems. I even think I can help them —if they would let me. But I am still the Alien and the Foe; I have not passed the test, whatever it is.

I'm a foe to Eddie Williams because my skin is white; to Joe Ferone because I am a teacher; to Carrie Paine because I am attractive.

Eddie uses the grievance of his color to browbeat the world.

Joe is flunking every subject, though he is very bright. He has become a bone of contention between McHabe and me because I believed in his innocence in the stolen wallet incident. I trust him, and he—he keeps watching me, ready to spring at the first false move I make.

Carrie is a sullen, cruelly homely girl, hiding and hating behind a wall of fat.

Harry Kagan is a politician and apple-polisher. He is running for G.O. president, and I'm afraid he'll be elected.

Linda Rosen is an over-ripe under-achiever, bursting with hormones.

And pretty Alice Blake, pale with love, lost in a dream of True Romances, is vulnerable and committed as one can be only at 16. She feels deeply, I'm sure, but can translate her feelings only into the cheap clichés she's been brought up on.

Then there is Rusty, the woman-hater.

And a quiet, defeated-looking Puerto Rican boy, whose name I can't even remember.

These children have been nourished on sorry scraps, on shabby facsimiles, and there is no one—not at home, not in school—who has not short-changed them.

You know, I've just realized there is not even a name for them in the English language. "Teen-agers," "Youngsters," "Students," "Kids," "Young adults," "Children"—these are inappropriate, offensive, stilted, patronizing or inaccurate. On paper they are our "Pupil-load"; on lecture platform they are our "Youngsters"—but what is their proper name?

The frightening thing is their unquestioning acceptance of whatever is taught to them by anyone in front of the room. This has nothing to do with rebellion against authority; they rebel, all right, and loudly. But it doesn't occur to them to think.

There is a premium on conformity, and on silence. Enthusiasm is frowned upon, since it is likely to be noisy. The Admiral had caught a few kids who came to school before class, eager to practice on the typewriters. He issued a manifesto forbidding any students in the building before 8:20 or after 3:00—outside of school hours, students are "unauthorized." They are not allowed to remain in a classroom unsupervised by a teacher. They are not allowed to linger in the corridors. They are not allowed to speak without raising a hand. They are not allowed to feel too strongly or to laugh too loudly.

Yesterday, for example, we were discussing "The fault, dear Brutus, lies not in our stars/ But in ourselves that we are underlings." I had been trying to relate *Julius Caesar* to their own experiences. Is this true? I asked. Are we really masters of our fate? Is there such a thing as luck? A small boy in the first row, waving his hand frantically: "Oh, call on me, please, *please* call on me!" was propelled by the momentum of his exuberant arm smack out of his seat and fell to the floor. Wild laughter. Enter McHabe. That afternoon, in my letter-box, it had come to his attention that my "control of the class lacked control."

But I had made that little boy think. I started something in him that emerged as an idea. I got him excited by a concept.

Sometimes, of course, I am misled by their eagerness. There's a girl who never takes her eyes off me. This morning, when I asked a question about Brutus, she flung out her hand, pleading to be recognized. When I called on her, she said: "You wearing contack lens?"

It's a good thing Bester wasn't there to observe me. Yet there's more to that man than meets the eye. I'm impressed by his masterly handling of what's known hereabouts as "a discipline problem." He had stepped into the Early Late Room (don't ask me to explain what it is, nor why I was there) and asked one of the boys for his program card. "Aw, go jump in the lake," said the boy. The class sucked in its breath. With icy courtesy, Bester asked the boy to repeat what he had said, please. The boy did. "What were the first two words?" Bester asked, exquisitely polite. "Aw go." "Would you say that again, please?" "Aw go." "What was it again?" "Aw go." "Would you mind repeating the next word?" "Jump." "Again, please?" "Jump." "Again?" "Jump." Do you know how absurd the word "jump" can begin to sound after a while, when spoken solemnly by a boy standing among his peers? The boy was licked, and he knew it; the snickering class knew it; Bester knew it; and as he left, he said, with the same impeccable courtesy: "I'll be glad to recommend you for a remedial speech class."

I wish I could learn his assurance. It's in my homeroom that I feel such a failure. They are still suspicious of me. They are still trying me out. One girl, shy and troubled, did reach out. She asked to see me after school last Monday.

She was apparently afraid to go home. Unfortunately, it was the day of the Faculty Conference, which is sacrosanct; attendance is compulsory. Perhaps I could have helped her. She hasn't been in school since. Truant officer reports she has run away from home.

At the Conference (we're supposed to sit it out for one hour each month; anything less, I believe, is unlawful) I watched my brothers and sisters, resignation or indifference settled like fine dust upon them—except for a few nervous souls who kept stirring up the soup. As a new teacher, I understood the protocol: I was not to speak. I was, however, asked to write up the minutes. I took notes, which I must now type up, and I timed the meeting: 60 minutes to the second!

All our hours and minutes are accounted for, planned for, raced against. Preparations are already afoot for Open School Day and the Xmas Faculty Show, and there are strange portents in the air and on the bulletin board. Only this morning a cryptic notice appeared over the time clock: "Advanced Algebra will be offered next term until further notice." I don't know what it means, either; nor what "minimal standards and maximal goals" means—it's a problem of communication.

Communication. If I knew how to reach them, I might be able to teach them. I asked them to write for me what they had covered so far in their high school English, and what they hoped to achieve in my class. Their papers were a revelation: I saw how barren were the years they brought me; I saw how desperately they need me, or someone like me. There aren't enough of us. Yet—with all my eagerness to teach, teaching is the one thing Calvin Coolidge makes all but impossible.

To the outside world, of course, this job is a cinch: 9 to 3, five days a week, two months' summer vacation with pay, all legal holidays, prestige and respect. My mother, for example, has the pleasant notion that my day consists of nodding graciously to the rustle of starched curtsies and a chorus of respectful voices bidding me good morning.

It's so good to have *you* to write to!

Love,
Syl

P. S. Did you know that in New York City there are more than 800 schools, over 86 high schools, and about one million pupils? And that out of every 100 children who start school, only 15 go on to receive a college diploma? For most, this is all the education they'll ever get.

S.

12 *A Doze of English*

In answer to your question what we got out of English so far I am answering that so far I got without a doubt nothing out of English. Teachers were sourcastic sourpuses or nervous wrecks. Half the time they were from other subjects or only subs. One term we had 9 different subs in English. Once when Dr. Bester took our class I got a glimpse of what it's all about but being the Head he isn't allowed to teach.

Also no place to learn. Last term we had no desks to write only wet slabs from the fawcets because our English was in the Science Lab and before that we had no chairs because of being held in Gym where we had to squatt.

Even the regulars Mrs. Lewis made it so boreing I wore myself out yawning, and Mr. Loomis (a Math) hated teaching and us. Teachers try to make us feel lower than themselves, maybe this is because they feel lower than outside people. One teacher told me to get out of the room and never come back, which I did.

A Cutter

What I got out of it is Litterature and Books. Also some
Potery. And just before a test—a doze of English. Having Boys in class dis-tracks me from my English. Better
luck next time.

                                          Linda Rosen

In Miss Pastorfeilds class I really enjoyed it we had
these modren methods like Amature Hour and Gussing
Games in rows with a scorekepper and to draw stick
figures to show the different charactors in the different
books and Speling Hospital and Puntuation Trafic and
Sentence Baseball with prizes for all thats the way to
really learn English.

                                          A True Student

I only learned one thing and that is a "quotion mark"
I know a "quotion mark" upside down and that's all this
one teacher thaught. I had one well not to mention no
names and she was mad for "grammar" mistakes, Miss
Lewis loved to pick on me! With Pasterfield we "dramatized" everything in sight and my last was a bug on
"Democricy", we spent all our time voting on what to
do and no time to do it.
     Only once I had a teacher that was any good but she
got "sick" and left. I hope this term with you will be
good because you seem to be "alive" though it's too
early to tell.

                                          Chas. H. Robbins

I hate to think back on all my English years except
one teacher I will never forget because when my note
book wasn't so good (it was mostly in pencil) instead

of telling me to do it over in ink she just told me to put renforcements on the holes and that will be enough. The next day she asked me did I put renforcements in. When I said I did she didn't even look she just said she'd take my word for it. That gave me a warm feeling inside because it was the first time a teacher took a pupil's word without asking to see if it was true. Most of the time they don't even know your name.

Me

In two years of H.S. Eng. I learned
1. How to read a newspaper
   A. Headlines
2. How to outline
3. Comparises of
   authors (Hawthore)
4. And S. Marner

They shouldn't give S. Marners out. We would prefer a teen age book like Lollita better.

Teenager

During my many years of frequenting school I was well satisfied with my instruction. English is a very important language to study, especially if it's the language we speak daily. Since most of us are in High School, we are interested in getting an English education. I believe English to have been of grave importance to me and I will try in my next future to increase my knowledge. English outshines all my other subjects. I've always had good marks because I am a worker and I feel that anything a teacher tells me is of benefit to me. Speaking, which is my specialty, composition, which also attracts my attention, writing perfect sentences with punctuation where it really belongs, and many

others which are of grave importance have been taught
to me with excellent results. I was likewise impressed
by the good work of my classmates. I hope to achieve
further progress in my chosen program of study with an
excellent teacher like yourself.

                              Harry A. Kagan
                              (The Students Choice)

Being your new around here you should know I made
a bargian with all my teachers, if I don't bother them
they won't bother me. So from now on I'm not writting
any more for you.

                                        the Hawk

In my 16 year life span so far I've had my share of
almost every type of teacher but one I shall ne'er forget
was in elementary (6th grade) because with her I had
to watch my peas and ques. She was so strict she gave
us homework every night and tried to pound it into our
heads but it's the way she did the pounding that makes
her different. She took a real interest and brought out
our good and bad points. She stayed in every day after
school so we could come in and ask her questions about
the work. She militarized us and sometimes whacked us
but for all her strictness a strange thing happened at the
end of the term: every one gathered around her and
kissed her.

But high school seems harder, speeches, speeches,
that's all we hear.

                                        Dropout

What I learned in English is to doodle. It's such a boring subject I just sat and doodled the hours away. Sometimes I wore sunglasses in class to sleep.

Doodlebug

I don't look at a teacher as a thing but as a person like myself & I accepted many teachers with their faults & tried to conscentrate on their Dr. Jekile side. But some are just not cut out to be teachers—too old and nervous & the way she taught you just couldn't understand it. She was the talker. If she didn't talk about her sisters or next door neighbors she talked about the generation of today & we couldn't get a word in edgewise. She was one of those that make big plans at the beginning of the term & never get around to it. They act like they're doing you the greatest favor, with sarcastic remarks like "The nerve of some peoples children!" The answer was actually scared out of us even if we knew it. When we did answer she gave us no credit but said "It's about time you learned something!" Whenever I laughed or excuse me burped in class quite acidentally I would be pulled out to sit in some remote corner of the school.

A Bashful Nobody

I had Dr. Bester for one week while my regular teacher took a rest cure and we liked him but I feel he developed a false character to cover up. This false character consisted of a stern face and remarks but every one saw a good teacher shining through the false window of sterness. He roused our somewhat hidden interest in English and we all worked our head off for him.

Carole Blanca

I once had an English teacher in another school that not only treated me as a student but as she would her own sons. She gave me clothes that her son had outgrown. The clothes that were given to me were in good condition.

Frank Allen

In Junior High we had a brand new teacher of English, he was so young he couldn't manage the class at all, we didn't listen to a word he said even when he shouted. One day while he had a chalk fight with a kid the kids all left the room one by one. Well, instead of going out to the hall to see if we were there he put on his coat, took his umbrella swung it over his shoulder and marched out of the room whistling. He didn't say a word to us. You can probably guess that we were replaced by a new teacher.

That is the one English that stands out in my head.

The only teacher I had who didn't make us feel so bad about ourselves. That's Mrs. Schachter. She was plain with us and she made everything seem easy which it isn't. She even liked us. Every since I have pleaded on bended knee to get her back but to no availl. I wish I went to a school with big sunny windows with trees in them and no one talks behind your back. Where the teacher would be more of a friend and not have favorites just because some one is better.

Vivian Paine

As long as you asked here is my list:
Miss Pastorfield lets us walk all over her
Mrs. Lewis they should retire her
Mr. Barringer is a big show off
Mrs. Schachter OK
Miss Barrett should be a movie stare
Mr. Loomis ignorammis
You may not agree but that's my opion.

Mr. X

While attending Jr. H.S. I ran across a teacher who enjoyed himself and didn't mind being a teacher. His way of teaching was simple, he taught with pride and always understood his pupils even if they couldn't explain themselves. He wasn't a dictating teacher but in some magic way we always behaved ourselves. I learned everything I know about English from this nobel man. He made me feel the earth around me, he was like wine except that he didn't give high marks. I frequently went to his room during lunch, we played darts, we ate lunch he brought for us and he would help us with what he could even in other subjects like science. In the summer we went to the park with him and played baseball. This teacher and I still correspond with each other by writing letters.

grateful student

English is a personal subject that should be taught
by men. Too many females in the schools and they're
all no good.

                                                    Rusty

———————————

In my other school I was more of a Majority because
the Whites were only these few kids but the education
they dished out wasn't so good. Here they tried to
integrate me but it didn't take.

I'm not what you call an "A" student but I don't mind
school at lease it takes me away from home but the
teachers are too prejudice they are mostly Whites and
I never got a fair mark out of them.

I'm not exacly a book reader but I didn't mind it so
much untill the teachers started in they ruined it for me.
I got no advantage out of diograms and spelling words
to write ten times only a waist of good paper. Semicol-
lons also don't stick to my head. It's not right to be pick
on all the time!

                                    Edward Williams, Esq.

———————————

What I learned. What I hope to achieve.

So far I've learned words with meanings, words without meanings, oral words, spelling words, parts of
speech and a test every Friday. I hope to achieve a
grasp on literature and life.

                                                Sophomore

———————————

A kaleidoscope. A crazy quilt. An ever-shifting pat-
tern. Shapes and shadows that come and go, leaving
no echo behind, no ripple on the water where no stone
was ever dropped. Such is my remembrance of the lost

and vanished years of English, from whence I arise, all creativity stifled, yet a Phoenix with hope reborn each term anew. Will it be different this term? Will I be encouraged, guided, inspired? The question, poised on the spear of Time, is still unanswered. (I was supposed to be in Mrs. Schachter's Creative Writing class but because of a conflict with Physics 2, I couldn't get in.)

Elizabeth Ellis

Its not necesery to study english because, what's the use of it big deal so we never make society so what? We're still living aren't we who needs it. studing another langage it would be much better. for example take books it's alright when you see it in the movies. and the words oh, they really get me. It's a bunch of nonsence.

(Frankly I would perfer a teacher freely telling me I'm no good in english then giving me dirty looks in the hall.)

Disgusted

Dribs & Drabs, McBeth one week Moby Dick next, a quotation mark, oral debates on Should Parents be Strict? Should Girls Wear Jeans? The mistakes I made in elementery school I still make. I hope to achieve correction.

Stander

I think after you learn to speak English in kindergarden the subject should be droped. Ha-ha! Grammer should be outlawed! Coma sentences should be bared from the language! Oral talks are to embarassing for those not gifted with "gab". Writen work causes many errors in gr. & sp! Reading books are to hard to answer questions on it! (I like English with no strain on my brain!) Also on the dislike side of English I can put the constant anoyance of certain students who horsed around. I can put myself in that catagory because I horsed around and I didn't benefit myself one bit and probly anoyed the class! However we must take the good with the bad and know our whole life will not be a bed of roses!

                                                    Lou Martin

---

Grammar & Shakes. – Phooey!
Essays – a lot of gossip.
Ivanho is for the Birds.
George Elliot stinks, even though he is a lady.

Why did you ask this question? To show that *you* can do the job better? You teachers are all alike, dishing out crap and expecting us to swallow it and then give it back to you, nice and neat, with a place in it for the mark to go in. But you're even phonier than the others because you put on this act—being a dame you know how—and you stand there pretending that you give a damn. Who you kidding?

We're dirt to you, just like you're dirt to the fatheads and whistle-blowers who run this jail, and they're dirt to the swindlers and horn-tooters who run the school system.

Except for one man in this whole school no one has ever given a damn about me, and it's the same at home and in the street outside. You probably don't care for my language, so you can give me a zero in Vocabulary.

Anyhow I'm quitting at the end of this term and joining the dogs eating dogs eating other dogs in the great big lousy world you're all educating us for. I sure as hell got myself an education. Though it's not in any syllabus. But you're the one who's stuck here. Don't worry, you'll find plenty of others willing to play your game of baah, baah, little lost lambs, come back to school. But trot in step, double file. And you'll get your nice clean diplomas served on crap. Yummy.

I trust this answers your question.

Joe Ferone

Joe – Though your vocabulary is colorful, certain words would be more effective if used sparingly. You express yourself vividly and well, and your metaphors—from dogs to lambs—are apt. I would tend to give you a considerably higher mark than you give yourself, and I am not speaking of English.

There is some truth in what you say, but you are far too intelligent to cling to a view as narrow as yours. As for your indictment of me—in this country one is innocent until proved guilty. Why not give me the chance any suspect gets? I think we should have a talk. Can you see me after school today?

S. Barrett

I don't understand them big words you use, and I'm busy after school. Every day. You'll have to prove yourself on your own time.

Joe

(P.S. I wish I could believe you.)

13

Enrichment Etc.

Dear Miss Barrett,
 Here is a copy of the English Syllabus; let it be your
Bible. It discusses various ways to provide enrichment,
etc.

Samuel Bester
Chairman, Language Arts Dept.

* * *

A GUIDING PRINCIPLE TO BE CONSIDERED IN ALL CLASS-
ROOM PROCEDURES IS THE PROVISION FOR INDIVIDUAL
DIFFERENCES AND NEEDS OF PUPILS. THE TEACHER
SHOULD DISCOVER EACH PUPIL'S ATTAINMENT IN SKILL
AND KNOWLEDGE—REGARDLESS OF GRADE PLACEMENT
—AND THEN LEAD HIM FORWARD FROM THAT POINT.

* * *

THE DEVELOPMENT OF A READING HABIT BASED ON A
LOVE OF READING MAY WELL BE THE MOST IMPORTANT
CONTRIBUTION THE SCHOOL CAN MAKE.

* * *

SPECIAL ATTENTION SHOULD BE GIVEN TO MAKING THE
ENGLISH CLASSROOM AS ATTRACTIVE AS POSSIBLE.
THERE SHOULD BE SHELVES AND TABLES FOR THE CARE
AND DISPLAY OF A WIDE VARIETY OF BOOKS AND PERI-
ODICALS. MOVABLE CHAIRS AND DESKS PROMOTE INFOR-
MALITY AND FACILITATE GROUP WORK. PROVISION FOR
THE USE OF A SCREEN AND A PROJECTOR, A TAPE-RE-
CORDER, AND OTHER AUDIO-VISUAL AIDS IS DESIRABLE.

PART III

Persephone

Mon., Oct. 5

Dear Ellen,

White brick sounds splendid for your fireplace, but I know nothing about flues except that they make me uneasy.

As a matter of fact, I'm also uneasy about teaching. Rumor has it that the ghost walks this week: Bester is on the prowl and is likely to observe my class. What will I do if he comes to see my Special-Slows?

Today, in connection with our study of Myths, I put on the board Edna Millay's "Prayer to Persephone." * Do you remember it?

> Be to her, Persephone,
> All the things I might not be;
> Take her head upon your knee.
> She that was so proud and wild,
> Flippant, arrogant and free,
> She that had no need of me,
> Is a little lonely child
> Lost in Hell,—Persephone,
> Take her head upon your knee;
> Say to her, "My dear, my dear,
> It is not so dreadful here."

* From *Collected Poems*, Harper & Row, Publishers. Copyright 1921, 1946 by Edna St. Vincent Millay. By permission of Norma Millay Ellis.

At the sight of a poem, they groaned—it's the thing to do. Yet when I asked who was speaking (lover about a loved one? mother about a child?), Vivian Paine raised a timid hand: "Maybe a teacher?"

There is a need for closeness, yet we can't get too close. The teacher-pupil relationship is a kind of tightrope to be walked. I know how carefully I must choose a word, a gesture. I understand the delicate balance between friendliness and familiarity, dignity and aloofness. I am especially aware of this in trying to reclaim Ferone. I don't know why it's so important to me. Perhaps because he, too, is a rebel. Perhaps because he's been so damaged. He's too bright and too troubled to be lost in the shuffle.

I want to get to know him—all of them. One way is to help them say whatever is uniquely theirs in their own words, for words are all we have. I am eager to read their compositions, to empty the Suggestion Box, to listen.

You ask the silliest questions, darling! What do you mean, why must I float?—Because Mary Lewis uses my room for two of her classes. Why doesn't she use her own?—Because another floater uses hers. We share the bulletin board and blackboard 50–50. I'm always curious to see what she's got on her half.

She says she prefers my room because it has movable chairs—the kind with an arm rest for writing surface. Her room still has the small desks attached to the floor, from the days when the building was an elementary school. There is the problem of where to fit the students' knees.

You want to know about Paul.

So do I. He's clever and quick and, of course, marvelous looking, with that eyebrow. But there's something about him that—eludes. He even hates to be touched by the kids; it's almost a phobia he has about being jostled in the halls. He always waits until the hall traffic subsides before he leaves his room.

He has a devastating effect on the girls. "What I like about him," one of my homeroom girls said, "is the way he always leans against his desk and sometimes he sits on top of it instead of behind it."

That may be it.

You and Mother are my most faithful correspondents. She worries about my living alone in the big city, without a real kitchen. And she keeps sending me clippings from the Johnstown, Pa. papers: rape, assault, murder. With one stark warning scribbled in the margin: "Be careful!" Only in school, she feels, am I safe.

I wonder.

Much love,
Syl

P. S. Did you know that only 21% of New York City's budget goes for education, compared with as much as 70% in small communities?

S.

From Miss Barrett's Wastebasket

15

Scratch Paper   English 33 SS
by Chas. H. Robbins   Miss Barrett

My Best Friend
Chapter 1

My "best friend" is considered by what we do for each other. Of all the "friends" that I have only one (1) is my best friend and his name is "Tony" but I call him "Corkey". When we go somewheres we are all ways together no matter where the place is. There are many things between he and I. If ever I would loose this "friend" I wouldn't know what to do. Many boys and girls call us "brother" meaning that we never part with each other and are all ways together. That is why he is my "best friend". (100 words exacly)

* * *

My Best Friend. Scrap paper, don't count!
I have many best friend. One of who is Johnny. Johnny is 15 yrs. of age, about 5 ft. 4¼ in. has a charactor which consists as follows, he is smart, a fair player, never fights with his best friends. He wears glasses and is a rather cleancut boy. By cleancut I mean dresses very neat. Why I like him is because we're great friends.

92

INTRASCHOOL COMMUNICATION

FROM: B. Schachter
TO: S. Barrett

Dear Syl—Let's go *out* to lunch and *splurge* at Schraffts!
Forget your Super-Slows and shake the chalk dust off
for half an hour. I'm tired of coffee that tastes of paper.
Here I sit in this draft, like Cerberus at the Gates of
Hell—guarding what? And from whom? I'll swap my
Lobby Duty for your Hall Patrol any time! Say yes to
the cherub who delivers this note, and let's eat like
ladies!
(I understand you may be observed this morning—
Give them something to write, like "My Favorite Sport,"
or "Sea Thoughts," and relax!)

Bea

* * *

Dear Bea—Can't make it today—sorry. Parent arriving
lunch per. to ask why son got 35% on spelling test. Must
answer him. How?

Syl

* * *

Dear Syl—Don't try. There's no communication; no one
really listens. Every man is an island. Give him a con-
tainer of coffee instead.

Bea

* * *

Scr. Paper Outline

Hi there, "the sound echod mysterously in the crowded
street", as my hand was grabbed by the familar hand
of *My Best Friend Mike*", how is every old thing Bill?

r

Fine, "I replied in answer. I was suprized, for I didn't

expect it. It was a clear winter day with sparkeling

snow sparkeling on

● ● ●

Lesson Plan

Eng. 33 SS
Comps. wr. in class; approx. 100 wds: My Bst. Fr.
Emph. brevity & clarity
First draft on scrap paper; hand in cl. cpy
Remind: Topic Sent. & Concluding Sent.
On Blackbd: Impt. of Friendship:
    I. Personal enrich.
      A. Give & Take
      B. Another's pt. of view
      C. Vs. loneliness
   II. Social
      (Man – gregarious animal)
  III. Biz.
  IV.

● ● ●

My Best Friend

Friendship is important. It gives us personal enrichment and it gives us the give and take of another persons point of view. Friendship is also vs. loneliness and
social. Friendship is important because man is an animal in our society and in biz.
        only 43 words, need 57 more

● ● ●

My best friend is Me, Myself and I. I say this because
you can't trust any one. They tell you they're your best

friend and behind your back they call you names like fatso. This is why I have Me, Myself and I and I don't care. I lost 4 lps. and I don't even bother with the other girls because they're all catty. I love Me, Myself and I for a friend.

* * *

MY BEST FRIEND

~~Everybody/in/the/whole/world/has/one/friend/who/~~
~~we/all/feel/deeply~~
~~The/best/thing/in/human/nature/is/to/have/a/best~~
~~we/all/need/a/friend/for/business/and/social/reasons~~
~~I/must/tell/you/about/a/wonderful~~
Man is a gregious animal.

* * *

Dear Sylvia—
The Ghost Walks today! Quick—put something on board & make sure there are no paper scraps on floor & that windows are open 4 inches from top! He's just been in to observe me—I started a Punctuation TV Panel but it got out of hand. And I forgot to put assignment on board. Why don't you let them write a composition in class? He gets bored & leaves. Pass the word. Remember *windows* & *enrichment!*

Henrietta

* * *

Composition. Should Cap. Punishment Be Abollished? Scrap P.
I will write on this topic we discused very much in Soc. Studies and I think it should because what good is an El. Chair after the murder is allready too late to do any good and sets a ~~bad~~ good example for other crooks.

Pass to Lavatory—10:08 A.M.

                                                        S.B.

Returned to class: Only wooden passes honored.
                                                    JJ McH

*   *   *

Memo: Due before 3: (*Gen. Office*)
       Attendance repts, Truant slps, Absentee cards
       Alph. list homeroom stdnts
       Health cds (Vaccin. & Dental)
       (*Eng. Dept*)
       Number F's last term
       % Repeating Eng.
       Raising standards (means of)
       Switch *Macbeth*???

*   *   *

In Memory of Those Who Died Waiting for the Bell

Did you do Math?

Stop it, Stupid!

Drop Dead!

You to!

* * *

Dear Dr. Clarke, justly
~~As/you/have/pointed/out,//teaching/here~~
~~should/be/a/dedic~~ ∧
It seems to me that ~~the/burden/of/the/clerical~~
much valuable teaching time is wasted on

* * *

Admit to class—9:01 A.M.
Lateness Unexcused
Claims books fell on subway tracks.

JJ McH

* * *

SCRAP PAPER

MY FAVORITE COMPANION. FIRST DRAFT. 103 WORDS.

I wish to state that my favorite companion is Munro. The real reason why I have attemted to choose him as my favorite companion is he knows how to conduct his self. He has no propensity to fight and he is the type of boy I can take over my house and not be ashamed of him. Every avarage boy has a propensity for a companion which he prefers and he will always try and get one well I have just finished writing about. P.S. In my opinion I think we should have less composition and more lunchroom. Also go home earlier.

CIRCULAR # 28
PLEASE KEEP ALL CIRCULARS ON FILE, IN THEIR ORDER
TOPIC: MAXIMAL GOALS
TO DEVELOP DEEPER UNDERSTANDING OF THE SPECIAL
FUNCTIONS OF SECONDARY EDUCATION AND TO EN-
LARGE THE TEACHER'S CONCEPT OF THE MEANING OF
EDUCATION IN OUR DEMOCRACY; TO ASCERTAIN AND
BRING ABOUT NEEDED CHANGES THAT WILL FACILITATE
THE IMPROVEMENT OF TECHNIQUES OF TEACHING AND
COORDINATION OF INSTRUCTION; TO DIRECT EXPERI-
MENTATION IN PURPOSEFUL AND CONCOMITANT LEARN-
INGS; TO MAKE USE OF ALL ANCILLARY AGENCIES AVAIL-
ABLE TO SCHOOL AND COMMUNITY; TO MEASURE THE
RESULTS OF TEACHERS' ACTIVITIES IN TERMS OF PUPIL
GROWTH TOWARD APPROVED GOALS.

* * *

My best friend is my dog. A dog is a man's best friend.
They are loyal and devoted all his life through thick
and thin even though he can't talk. No more ink in
my fou

* * *

Dear Dr. Clarke,
        I don't wish to sound
     as a member of a profession which
        As you know, most of our students are
underprivileged and deprived, they desperately need

* * *

My best friend is a TV and if it every gets out of order
I don't know what to do with myself. Like all normal
teenagers I have my specialities but I have so many different programs I can't begin to talk about them all.
They are too many but all are my best. When I sit
around the house I am never lonely with TV.

Motivate Comp. Lesson:
  Impt. of Communication
    A. Need to express selves and be understood
    B. Language as a tool of communication
Put on blackbd:
"What oft was thought but ne'er so well expressed"
(Pope?)
"Le style est l'homme"
Carfare .... .15
Newsp. .... .10
Coffee .... .10
Tuna sand. .... .60
Coffee .... .10
Teachers' Interest Com... 1.50
                        ‾‾‾‾‾
                        2.55 (so far)

*   *   *

Admit to class—8:39 A.M.
Disciplined by me for whistling in the hall.

                                    JJ McH

*   *   *

Dear Miss Barrett,
    Remember me? I was in your class the first week of
school and tho I never came back due to moving I think
I will never forget you and the time you talked to me
on the subway. Altho english was not my best subject
everything we did was nice and you were the only one
who took an interest. You never made any bad remarks.
How's the old Alma Mater? How's Dr. Clarke? Is he
still a Dr? Well, lots of luck. Say hello to everybody
for me and take care of yourself.

                        Your former loving pupil,
                                    Iris Lefferts

The ghost walks! He's in Rm. 301 now. Heading
due north. Looks grim. *Open your windows!*

* * *

CIRCULAR # 27
PLEASE KEEP ALL CIRCULARS ON FILE, IN THEIR ORDER
TOPIC: ADDENDUM TO PUPIL PERSONALITY
    PROFILES
TO SECURE A MORE COMPREHENSIVE EVALUATION OF
PUPIL ORIENTATION TO HIS ENVIRONMENT, ADDITIONAL
SPACE HAS BEEN PROVIDED ON THE ENCLOSED CHARAC-
TER-ATTENDANCE RATING SHEETS IN ORDER TO INCLUDE

* * *

My best Friend. Well, well! Right of the bat, as soon
as we sit down, our teacher Miss Baret gives us a composition to write! Well, well! to be frank with you, I
do not like it. I do not like to write compositions when
we could be discussing. Or dramatize or a speling bee,
but not so much composition! It's not fair to the Union!
Ha-ha, joke!

* * *

MY BEST FRIEND

Last summer I visited my Ant on the beach. My ant
has a cottach on the beach and every summer she invites me to visit her and I did. I had fun on the beach
swiming and handball and getting the healthy benefit
of the sun and broadwalk. I gained and went on the
loop. I hope my Ant invites me again next summer.

* * *

Late Pass:
    Admit to class—8:32 A.M.
    Unexcused—Claims alarm didn't go off.
                                            JJ McH

TO: Custodian
Dear Mr. Grayson—
My window-pole seems to be missing. Room 304.
Urgent! 2nd request.

S. Barrett

No one down here. Try after lunch.

* * *

ENGLISH DEPARTMENT MEETING AT 3 P.M. IN SCIENCE
LAB 309 ON:

SELECTION OF MATERIALS OF INSTRUCTION FOR EN-
RICHING THE TOTAL EXPERIENCE OF THE PUPIL:

SHOULD <u>MACBETH</u> BE TAUGHT IN THE 6TH TERM IN-
STEAD OF THE 4TH?

* * *

Dear Mrs. Barnett,
Please excuse my son Arnold for not doing his English homework. He got in trouble with the Police last
night and they kept him in the Station House. Hoping
you will excuse him, I remain

Mrs. Rose A.

* * *

Scrape paper
A) My B. Freind
1. Name adress
2. What we do togeather
3. Why I like my b. freind
4. Why my b. freind likes me
5. Hobies
6. Concluding sent.
7. Man—gregarous animal

* * *

Dear Dr. Clarke,
I know how busy you are, but I feel
you are, undoubtedly, aware of the discrepancy existing

My best friend is my imaginary twin sister. She does
everything I tell her. She is beautifull and obeys me
freely. We share and share alike (beautifull dresses,
etc) Her name is Roseanne. We are closer than any
body even if she is only in my mind. She is my twin
and she never talks back.

*   *   *

BOOK ROOM
REQUISITION SLIP

Need   40 *Syntax & Style* for Eng. 33 SS
                             (Register—46
                             (Chronic truants—7
          79 *Romeo & Juliet* for Eng. 52 & 56
                             S. Barrett—Rm 304

We have only 4 Syntaxes & 26 Romeos in Bookroom.
Can you use Ivanhoes instead? There are 160 copies
here.

*   *   *

major, and won my Master's degree with first honors for my
thesis on THE FRENCH INFLUENCE IN THE OCTOSYLLABIC COUPLET
OF CHAUCER"S "BOKE OF THE DUCHESSE." I hold a license in
English in the New York City Secondary Schools and am at
present teaching at Calvin Coolidge High School.
        In/order/to/supplement/my
        If there is a teaching vacancy in your evening or
summer session, I should appreciate hearing from you.

                             Sincerely yours,
                             Sylvia Barrett

*   *   *

My best friend is my boy-friend and he is tall, rich and
handsome, he has a twotone Caddy convertable with
white leather seats of genuine white leather and takes

me danceing every night in nightclubs ect. He gives me orhcids and jewlry ect. and has a big yahct. He lives on Park ave with servants of which I will be mistress of and a ranch type house in Bev. Hills with a swimming pool ect. That is why I hope to meet him.

* * *

FROM: DR. SAMUEL BESTER
        CHAIRMAN, LANGUAGE ARTS DEPT.
TO: MISS BARRETT

Dear Miss Barrett,

Please announce to your students the New York Chamber of Commerce Essay on: PRESERVING HISTORIC BUILDINGS IN NEW YORK.
    Encourage all students to participate.

S. Bester

* * *

May I borrow your window-pole? Please give to bearer.

S.B.

Dear Syl— Someone has swiped mine. There's a run on window-poles today. And on pole-bearers!

Bea

* * *

Late Pass:
    Admit to class: 8:36 A.M.
    Unexcused: Claims IRT stuck.

JJ McH

* * *

My Best Friend

My best friend is Miss Barrett, our English teacher. Although this is the first term I have met Miss Barrett, she is pretty, a good dresser, a good marker, and fair in

her attitude. She is the type teacher every student likes.
For the reasons above mentioned I choose Miss Barrett.

* * *

DEAR (SIR
      (MADAM
                    I AM (PLEASED TO INFORM YOU THAT
                         (SORRY
YOUR (SON'S   WORK HAS SO FAR
     (DAUGHTER'S

* * *

My best friend is a good book. I enjoy good books
that are educational very much. Books help your grammer and spelling. Also increase your vocabulary. I am
a great reader of books. My best favorite is "Antony and
Cleopatra" by Shakespear. In this book I like the part
where the author tries to show love. Where Elizabeth
Taylor and Richard Burton make love which I like. I
like other good books too, mostly classical.

* * *

Memo: Return *English as a Communications Art*.

* * *

I have some best friends and also some worst friends
but its hard to write down, its hard to explain what I
really want to say about friends and others its hard to
explain to anybody I often wisht I had a friend thats
understanding. But its very hard.

* * *

```
Dear Dr. Clarke,
     Since I began teaching, I have felt a lack of
```

*   *   *

Please admit bearer to class—
    Detained by me for going Up the Down staircase
    and subsequent insolence.

                                        JJ McH

*   *   *

My best friend

I believe my Mother to be my best friend because. She
always listens to my troubles and trys to comfort me.
She has been sacraficing all her life so I could be a
credit to her and not a bum and all I did since born is
cause her trouble by shooting pools and doing such
things. I am apoligizing in this letter. Very truly yours.

*   *   *

```
Dear Dr. Clarke,
```

JJ's Lament

INTRASCHOOL COMMUNICATION

FROM: Paul Barringer, Room 309
TO: Sylvia Barrett, Room 304

Sylvia!

Where did you disappear after dinner last night?

Was I that blotto?

Must be the latest rejection slip. The tone is not only polite but patronizing: Why don't I write of something familiar to me?

The school system is familiar to me.

Am I to write of kids sprawling in classrooms? Yawning in assembly? Pushing through the halls? (You know I never venture forth in hall traffic.)

Am I to write of teachers marking papers? Of Mc-Habe's circulars? (You know I have a low boredom-threshold.)

The only thing I can do with him is give him a song to sing. I call it *J.J.'s Lament:*

> The ceiling fell? The ink ran dry? A student dared
> to smile?
> Of every new disaster

I prove myself the master
By sending out more circulars, more circulars to file!

A missing kid? A kissing kid? A paper on the floor?
For every major crisis
One remedy suffices:
More circulars, more circulars to put into a drawer!

A crowded cafeteria?
A substitute's hysteria?
A visitor from Syria?
A missing Book Receipt?

I merely send out circulars
To add to other circulars
To add to other circulars
Numerical and neat!

I want him to star in the Faculty Show, but he has another commitment. I'd like to write him a splendid aria, entitled: "It Has Come to my Attention That."

Why do you refuse to be in the Show? You are wasting yourself in the classroom.

Why do you refuse? You are wasting yourself.

A girl who is patient like patient Griselda
Will find all she's getting is elder and elder.

Meet me for lunch?
Meet me at three?
Meet me this evening? I promise to stay sober.

Paul

I wish other teachers would be brave like you and put in a Suggestion Box. They're always telling us what's wrong with us, what about the other way around? Boy, would I like to tell them off. But you're OK even if you are a teacher.

>   (You said we don't *have* to sign our name)

Scram! Hit the road! Leave town! If you know what's good for you! (You asked for it!)

>   A Well Wisher

Don't think you'll get off so easy just because you speak nice and you don't seem scarred of us, last term we had a man teacher and we made him cry.

>   Yr. Enemy Enemy

Not enough boys and too many girls in the room. But that's not your fault. Also some schools they have danceing in the cafeteria and they put on different things, why not? You only live once.

Linda Rosen

It was very interesting of you to give the compositions on My Best Friend, there are quite a few persons you've helped. Keep up the good work.

Harry A. Kagan
(The Students Choice)

Being you're so young don't be so leniant, we take advantage, especially Joe Farrone, he must be your pet because he gives you so much trouble. Also give out more up to date books then the Oddesseys. They should rewrite the Oddessey over with more up to date incidence.

Failing

Can you make the chalk stop from squeeking?

Nervous

Please tell Lou Martin to quit showing off, he thinks he's so comic well I don't.

Signed — Serious Student

Fuk. Screw. Crap. Goddam. Nerts to you.

Unsinged

You ask for revelant matters only. Assemblys too boring. I always know what he's going to say (Clark).
Show movies instead.

                                                    Mr. X

Don't try so hard, you'll live longer, sit down & relax
when you teach.

I have many problems but won't burden you with them
in this Box. They're not fit for human ears. Though you
seem to be a very understandable person. By that I
mean you understand us being not so old yourself. Too
bad you're a teacher and pretty like my sister. I wish
you were a plain person then we could be close.

                                                    Vivian Paine

---

Sitting near the window in this room I have caught a
cold because there's a hole in it. Well life is like that,
you have to pay for your pleasure, with cash or otherwise.

                                                    Fifth Row Last Seat

This school is run like a Army. The least little thing he
(McHaber) get excited. He better watch his step, after
all I pay his sallary with taxes!

Tax Payer

Linda Rosen—sex pot, Alice Blake—stuck up, and you
like Joe Feroni, he's just asking for attention.

Neglected

You're lucky you're a women teacher, if it was a man he
would of walked into something he didn't see coming
his way, with a women my temper is controlled but a
man doesn't last long. (This is the last time I am
writting!)

the Hawk

Dont call the Roll so early.

Late Bird

In the past I always looked forward to my English
classes with regret but when I entered your room, low
and behold, I saw your cheerful countenence standing
in front of the class & I got really interested in the subject. You seem to mean it when you smile.

A Bashful Nobody

Homer is not a very good writer.

Reader

Everybody is always picking on me because of prejudice and that goes for everybody. Mr. Machabe realy
has it in for me just because I am color. I have allready
fill a complain to Dr. Clark.

Edward Williams, Esq.

Clean up the slums! Before you go to the moon! And
stop the Atomb Bomb! Before its too late! As far as
school, without us there could be no school, ha-ha! And
no futures!

Lou Martin

How about a date? I'll fix you up like you never had it
before.

Loverboy

Throw out myths. Throw out old teachers and put in
new. Throw down this delapidated school and build a
clean one, more moderner, like my other was. With
Loud Speakers in every class room where they told you
over the Loud Speaker about personal hygene and for-
est conservation and things like that even if it came in
the middle of a lesson. With telephones inside the rooms
where if a teacher forgot a pencil she could call up to
find out if it's there and later go get it. The traffic in the
halls was more roomier and the cafeteria wasn't in the
basement. You could sit down and eat. But I couldn't
stay.

Stander

Don't start up with me!

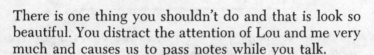 Poisen

---

There is one thing you shouldn't do and that is look so beautiful. You distract the attention of Lou and me very much and causes us to pass notes while you talk.

Anonimus

Is it possible to change my seat to next to Linda Rosen because of my eyesight?

Frank Allen

What makes you think you're something? You're only a female and I can't stand females. I got enough trouble at home I don't need school.

Rusty

You're a good teacher except for the rotten books you have to teach like the Oddissy. I wouldn't give it to a dog to read.

Disgusted

I suggest you and other teachers get a raise in salary so they can live right. I'm sorry I talk out of turn during your teaching, I admit it.

Loudmouth

Parents are too pushy.

Doodlebug

I want to thank you for giving me your time after school, for encouraging me to write, for trying. But with 40 others in the class, whose problems are so different, I realize how little you can do, and I feel we are both wasted.

Elizabeth Ellis

Teach more interesting stories that are hopeful. How in Pygmalian and Galatea the statue got human for the marriage.

Yours for Happy Endings

I am not a good penman but I must tell some one. I put this in the Suggestion Box for the record. Today is my birthday. Happy Birthday!

Me

INTRASCHOOL COMMUNICATION

FROM: 508
TO: 304

Dear Syl—

I'm returning window-pole. Thanks.

Just now, a former student dropped in to see me. "You still teaching?" he asked. Turns out he's making more money than you and I together, playing saxophone in a band. Flunked English, I think. His PPP wasn't so hot, either. Why didn't they give me piano lessons? Why did I ever learn to read?

It must be Indian summer that's making me so droopy—or the quiz on *Hamlet* I've been marking. Sample: "Mr. Hamlet, Sr. appears to Mr. Hamlet, Jr. as a dead ghost and bids him revenge."

Bea

115

INTRASCHOOL COMMUNICATION

FROM: 304
TO: 508

Dear Bea— I've been wading through a pile of "Due before 3" mimeos—but now at last I know what to do with them: into the wastebasket! I'm also hep to the jargon. I know that "illustrative material" means magazine covers, "enriched curriculum" means teaching "who and whom," and that "All evaluation of students should be predicated upon initial goals and grade level expectations" means if a kid shows up, pass him. Right?

I'm a bit nervous about Bester's visit. He tells me he plans to "drop in" again, and suggests that this time I do not give "a written lesson on friendship" (!)

Would you let me know what you think of the enclosed lesson plan on book reports? I wish I'd had real training instead of a few Ped courses and six months of pupil-teaching. I feel so inadequate!

Are there any compensations?

Syl

*   *   *

INTRASCHOOL COMMUNICATION

FROM: 508
TO: 304

Of course there are! I invite you to visit my Honors class in Shakespeare, or my Creative Writing class— you wouldn't believe you were in the same school. Actually these kids would do well on their own. To me there are greater compensations when a slow student glimpses an idea, when an apathetic or hostile kid raises a faltering hand.

Don't underestimate Bester. Behind the pedagese language is a man who knows all about teaching; you would do well to attend to what he says when he comes to observe you.

Your lesson plan is excellent—except for the Emily
Dickinson line: "There is no frigate like a book." The
sentiment is lovely, the quotation is apt—only trouble
is the word "frigate." Just try to say it in class—and your
lesson is over.

Bea

*   *   *

INTRASCHOOL COMMUNICATION

FROM: 304
TO: 508

Dear Bea— Thanks for the tip on frigate. How about:
"There is no *steamship* like a book"? I myself have already vetoed Channing's: "It is chiefly through books
that we enjoy intercourse with superior minds."

In the meantime, I've been filling out follow-up slips
on my Joe Ferone: Truant Officer reports there's no
such address as the one he has given. Ella Freud says
he never showed up for interview. Subject teachers
claim he's been cutting classes. Nurse says he's on Dental Blacklist. And McHabe floods me with warnings.

But I'm not discouraged. I think the problem is not
unreachable kids but unteachable teachers.

The Board of Ed has been Sir-or-Madaming me with
the enclosed:

ELIGIBILITY TO QUALIFY FOR SALARY INCREMENT IN
STEPS C1, C2 AND C6 DEPENDS ON SUCH IN-SERVICE
ALERTNESS COURSES AS MAY BE REQUIRED TO QUALIFY.

Please translate.

Syl

*   *   *

INTRASCHOOL COMMUNICATION

FROM: 508
TO: 304

Dear Syl—
Looking alert won't help. If you want a raise, take a
course. No coursie, no money. A First Aid course will

do. You don't even have to take it—just ask the nurse to
give you a paper saying you know how to apply tourni-
quet. Do you? Because you may need to!

   As far as kids are concerned, you're on right track,
but don't misjudge teachers—they're not so much unteachable as unrewarded. And even McHabe has his
uses—before he came to Coolidge there was Chaos.
He's trying to create order the only way he knows how.
His pupil-load is 3,000 kids!

Bea

(Henrietta is looking high and low for Paul; dying to
be in Faculty Show; wants him to write some lyrics for
her. Do you know where he is? He looked a bit fuzzy
again yesterday.)

B.

❂   ❂   ❂

INTRASCHOOL COMMUNICATION

FROM: 304
TO: 508

Dear Bea—

   I don't know where he is; he has an unassigned 1st
period, but he never appears until the 2nd. Someone
punches him in—right under Sadie Finch's nose. Hope
she doesn't find out.

   I'm treasuring her latest: "Teachers must not punch
each other out."

   Just saw Grayson scuttling through the main floor;
so he *does* exist! Ferone was with him. What goes on?

Syl

❂   ❂   ❂

INTRASCHOOL COMMUNICATION

FROM: 508
TO: 304

Dear Syl—
Ferone is not the only boy in Grayson's stable. I know
several who make periodic visits to the basement. What

goes on could be anything: Hashish—Racing forms—
Orgies. They don't appear to be any the worse for it.

Bea

* * *

INTRASCHOOL COMMUNICATION

FROM: 304
TO: 508

Dear Bea—

Letters from the Board becoming more pressing. Now
they want money from me. This is from Payroll Division:

> DEAR SIR OR MADAM:
> AN EXAMINATION OF THE PAYROLL RECORDS SHOWS THAT
> YOU RECEIVED A SALARY OVERPAYMENT IN THE AMOUNT
> OF $2.75 FOR LAST JUNE.

I wasn't even teaching in June, and I certainly don't
have $2.75. Apparently they don't know I'm file # 443-
817 and have got me confused with another—possibly
443-818?

Syl

* * *

INTRASCHOOL COMMUNICATION

FROM: Mrs. B. Schachter, Lobby
TO: 304

Dear #443—

The Board moves in a mysterious way. Always did.
In my day—the Depression Years—they failed a bril-
liant girl who would have made a great teacher—on
the oral exam, for something they called "lateral emis-
sion"! They almost got *me* on the "sibilant S" (that was
the year they were after the S's): My Waterloo was:
"He still insists he sees the ghosts."

And a friend of mine, a Millay scholar, was failed for poor interpretation of a sonnet by Millay. Her appeal was not granted, even after Edna Millay herself wrote a letter to the Board explaining that was exactly what she had meant in her poem. My friend did establish a precedent, I believe: ever since, candidates for the English license have been given poems by very dead poets, long silent in their graves.

Now, of course, things are different: they thrust the license upon anybody who can stand up and use a board eraser.

The Aide didn't show up and I'm stuck in the lobby again. Send down some cheery news!

                                                             Bea

* * *

INTRASCHOOL COMMUNICATION

FROM: 304
TO: Mrs. B. Schachter, Lobby

Dear Bea—
    Cheery? I feel lost and a bit absurd—as if I were tilting at windmills which aren't there, or shouting in an empty tunnel. I keep trying to remember who I am. The Board of Ed has the same trouble.
    Now they inform me that "A teacher who has exhausted his cumulative sick leave may borrow up to 20 days of additional sick leave."
    Who's sick? I don't mind their lack of faith in my health; it's the Dear Sir or Madam I mind. How do I convince them I'm a Madam?

                                                             Syl

* * *

INTRASCHOOL COMMUNICATION

FROM: Mrs. B. Schachter
TO: 304

Dear Syl—
    Play it cool. They'll catch on.

                                                             Bea

INTRASCHOOL COMMUNICATION

FROM: 304
TO: 508

Dear Bea,

Today I must return *Odyssey* and *Myths & Their Meaning;* someone else needs crack at them. I've had only ten school days on them, in my slow class, with half of students absent or truant, and not enough books to go around, and no help from librarian—whose note is enclosed:

My dear Miss Barrett,

I am forced to cancel the library lesson you had planned for your 3rd term students in connection with their study of mythology. Sending them here six at a time creates havoc and disorder. They have already misplaced *The Golden Age of Greece* and have put Bullfinch on the Zoology shelf, besides talking. Two of your students took out books indiscriminately, that had nothing to do with the assignment. I cannot allow them the facilities of the school library until they learn the proper respect for the printed page.

Sincerely,
Charlotte Wolf, Librarian

Do you know Paul's song about her: "Who's Afraid of Charlotte Wolf"?

I think I really got the kids interested; I made myths live for them by linking them with their own lives and with the present. To find out how much they've actually absorbed, I'm giving them a quiz next period. I've armed myself with a red pencil (over McHabe's dead body!) for correcting content, and a blue one for mistakes in spelling, grammar, etc. The two-tone correction was the idea of a Ped Prof of mine in college.

What I had attempted to do was to convey the comedy of the gods against the tragedy of mortals—

Syl

INTRASCHOOL COMMUNICATION

FROM: 508
TO: 304

Dear Syl–

   That may be the only way to convey tragedy: through comedy. Humor is all we've got.

                                                          Bea

ENGLISH 33 SS
ANSWER BRIEFLY:
WHY DO WE STUDY THE MYTHS AND THE ODYSSEY?

Because we want to talk like cultured people. At a party how would you like it if some one mentioned a Greek God and you didn't know him. You would be embarrased.

_____

We study myths like Orpheum & his girl friend because it takes place in the Greek Underground. We want to know how our civilization got that way.

_____

Myths are everywhere. Many everyday things like thunder are based on myths. It helps increase our vocabulery in words like Volcanno and By Jove! and to gain experience for future behavior.

_____

The reason we study it is because it shows the kind of writting they went in for in days of Yore. If this isn't the right answer well I don't know.

The Odessye I've just read helped me an awful lot in my life.

We study myths to learn what it was like to live in the golden age with all the killings.

I'm sure there are many reasons why we study these things but I missed it due to absense. I brought a note.

We study myths so we may comprehend in a superior fashion the origines of many idiocyncracies of our language throughout the decades, constant references to mythologic occurances have spawned such sparkling gems as Jumping Jupiter. By aquaintance with sundry gods and their female counterparts one might discover the birthplaces of such phrases of which we speak.

Diana ruled the moon and fell in love once with a mortal and because of its outcome she never again did so.

If it wasnt for Myths where would Shakesper be today?

Well, for students going to colledge even if they don't go to colledge everybody needs a certain amount of literature in their backround.

To me the "Odyssey" was just another Ethan Frome or Silas Marner.

It's hard to avoid reading because every wheres we go reading is there.

My own opinion is that I hated the Odessy.

I dont know why we read them but I can tell about it. Pyramid and Thisbe are next door neihgbors who like Romeo and Juliette were caused to die by their parents. They saw each other thru a hole in the wall. After a while they couldnt stand it and decided not to meet by the hole any more. So they met by a tree. Thisbe runs away at the sight of a lady lion who's mouth is dripping blood. She dropped a clothe which the lady lion only picked up and thats all. Pyramid walks over and sees the clothe full of blood. He became agrieved and slewed himself. She then walks over and seeing her lover laying on the ground she couldnt stand the sight of him and likewise slewed herself. The blood of them both joined and changed the white flower to purple. How beautiful is love.

It developes our
        (not finished)

We dove deeply into the Odessey to get what we can out of it. I think it's valuable to us. It's very difficult to understand the English of before.

_____

Mythology is studied in the school system because most of us come from it.

_____

My opinion about the Oddysey is ridiculous. I don't want to hear about some one's troubles.

_____

The reason we study mythology is to gain tolerance for others even if they don't deserve it.

_____

I didn't know we'd have a quizz on it so didn't study for it, but I imagine we read it to be a round person.

_____

What you may call it felt that the people of the earth should have fire and he stole it from Ollympus and took it to earth. He was then punished by being tied to a mountain top and have his liver eaten out every day by a Vultur.

_____

Once a person studies myth's they look on life a little different. I know I do.

_____

Why do we study the Odyssy? Because everybody in high school at one time or another read it and now we have to read it because it's our turn.

_____

The Trojan horse was used as a spy of today. Gods were used as dictators and Penelpe still walks the streets of modern society.

If the odessy is of no value to me its probly because I didnt put myself into it to begin with.

Just about all myths are based on Love and that is why.

We read myths for learning about the gods and godesses and their affairs.

We read it because it's a classicle.

PART IV

FTG again—Oct. 9

Dear Ellen,

Your letter gave me the lift I needed; I was beginning to think I wasn't communicating with *anyone!* My students have come to me so empty-handed that I don't know where to start, or what to give them, or how to fill in the gaps.

The other day Bester popped into my SS (special-slow) class, and I gave an emergency composition to be written in class. The topic was "My Best Friend," and as I read the papers, I wondered: How do I correct them? What do I correct? Spelling? Punctuation? The inarticulate loneliness between the lines? I don't know where to start, or whether to laugh or cry. Perhaps the two are the same.

And I'm not communicating literature to them either. I saw that when I gave a quiz on mythology.

That leaves just you and me. I loved your account of the painters redecorating your bedroom. Certainly, you should stand pat on pale blue and mauve; don't let them get away with buff!

In the same mail came a letter from Mattie, telling me of a February vacancy at Willowdale. Very tempting. It's a small college where I could get an appointment even with-

131

out a PhD. Trouble is—I *like* high-school kids; I chose to
teach them; I feel they need me. Especially a boy like Ferone.

I look up his PRC. That's the Permanent Record Card
kept for each student throughout his years in high school;
it includes marks, IQ tests, aptitude tests, personality ratings,
teachers evaluations, percentile curves, notes, letters, affi-
davits, interviews, truant officer's reports—the history of a
child encapsuled in a folder.

His IQ is 133; his marks last term: 65, 20, F, 94, 45. The
94 is in Social Studies. The 20 is in English. I marvel: why
20? why not 18? or 33? or 92? Is it based on his thinking,
feeling, punctuation, absence, self-expression, memory, insolence? And where on the percentile curve does he fit? Or
a girl like Alice? Or a boy like Eddie? What mark does Eddie
get for the way the white world has treated him? Or Alice—
for the fantasies the movies have fed her? Or I—or even I?

On the left of the blue line are Attitude Ratings for Citizenship, Cooperation, Cleanliness, Leadership Potential—to
be marked from 1 to 5. Ferone's average is 1½. Getting along
with Peers=Good; Getting along with Teachers=Poor.

Next to that—"Disciplined on the following dates," and a
long list, ending with "Obscene language in auditorium."

On the right of the blue line are the CC's—Capsule Characterizations. At the end of each term, each teacher enters
a succinct phrase for each student. "Should try harder" is
the favorite.

I glance through other PRC's.

"fine boy"
"fine boy"
"should try harder"
"fine boy"

This is the defeated looking Puerto Rican boy whose name
no one remembers and who signs himself: Me. (He wished
himself a happy birthday in my Suggestion Box.) I make
sure of his name: Jose Rodriguez.

The CC's are followed by the PPP's—Pupil Personality
Profiles—devised by Miss Friedenberg—a self-appointed
Freud. These are based on her interviews with the kids, and

are phrased in pseudo-analese. Ferone "should channel his libidino-aggressive impulses into socially acceptable attitudes." Vivian Paine "suffers from malfunctioning of the ego due to compulsive obesity." Lou Martin "exhibits inverted hostility in manic behavior-patterns." Eddie Williams "must curb tendency to paranoia due to socioeconomic environmental factors." Rusty, the woman-hater "shows signs of latent homosexuality induced by narcissistic mother and permissive masturbatory practices." Alice Blake "is well balanced and integrated."

Occasionally, among the inanities in the PRC's, are sudden entries of teachers with insight and a desire to help; entries of after-school conferences with kids, home visits, extra tutoring, honest attempts to deal with their problems. But they are rare.

Right now, I feel, is the most critical time in the children's lives—their last chance to turn into what they will eventually be. And so many are lost to us forever! Statistics on dropouts are staggering. What has become of those kids, and where are they now?

Ferone isn't a statistic. Eddie Williams isn't a statistic. Jose Rodriguez (I remembered his name!) isn't a statistic. And there isn't much Calvin Coolidge is offering them.

Under Reasons for Dropouts, teachers have written:

"Business opportunity."

"Financial need."

"Further development of experiential possibilities."

But I went directly to the source: I asked my own students to write me honestly why they wanted to leave school. I am enclosing a few of their notes:

I dont go for school, if you're a color person its all a lot of lies, nobody does like they do in books. At lease in my experience. And teachers, they're no better than parents, either too busy or yelling their heads off. And all prejudice.

Edward Williams, Esq.

I know school is supposed to help me with my life, but so far it didn't.

Rusty

When I turn 17 my father says why should he feed an extra mouth. Ha-ha, that's me!

Lou Martin

We must look "behind the books" in school. This shows we "American boys" are concerned not with "swalling" things they way they are given to us without looking at the contents of the bottle and seeing what it contains. In these "atomic days" you never know when "America" will call on its young men so we must learn to think for themselves. Not being "hoodwinked" like our forfathers in the war. But mine wants me to stay in school.

Chas. H. Robbins

The more time in school the less time to make $.

Dropout

To be honest I tell you I have more trouble with my mother because she is a sick lady and there is no one to take care of her untill I come home from school. She's got heart trouble so she can be here today and gone tomorrow thats why there isn't much use for me to do a lot of school work because there other things in life like a job for a living. After all some day I'll get married and I have to take mother to live with me and my wife so what's the use of school.

Failing

The teachers hate me.

Vivian Paine

I know my father passed away a year ago and my mother is of course nervous about it so I want to make plenty of it to be my own boss.

Ambitious

I'm nobody especial so nobody knows me, maybe I'll be somebody with a job.

Me

Give me one good reason why I should stay.

Joe Ferone

I, too, want to look "behind the books." I want to give Ferone several good reasons why he should stay. And I understand that when Vivian says the teachers hate her, she means that she hates the teachers—or rather, herself. The PRC tells me nothing. The kids do. Let me tell you about Jose, for example.

Myths and their Meaning polished off, my SS class was given a collection of simple contemporary short stories; fortunately, there was a surplus in the Book Room. The first one dealt with a child who was allergic to sweets, his mother, who had admonished him never to eat them, and a goodhearted but misguided neighbor who believed the child's stories about his cruel mother and his deprivations, and who fed him sweets until he became violently ill. The mother threatened to sue the neighbor. End of story.

The discussion I started in class—about good intentions and responsibility—proved so lively, that I decided to follow it up with a dramatization. I asked them to come prepared the next day to transform the classroom into a courtroom; we would plead the case, as a sequel to the story. Reminding them to familiarize themselves with the people and the situation in the story and to remain in character during the improvised court session, I assigned the roles: mother, father, neighbor, child, prosecuting attorney (Harry Kagan, of course!) defense attorney, witnesses for the defense and the prosecution, even the doctor. I realized that we had left out the judge. Through one of those swift moments of inspiration, I turned to Jose Rodriguez and asked him to be prepared to act the judge. A few in the class snickered; Jose nodded; and I myself had no idea what to expect.

The following day he appeared in class in a cap and gown —a black graduation gown and mortar-board, borrowed or rented at what trouble or expense I could only guess, and a large hammer for a gavel. He bore a look of such solemn dignity that no one dared to laugh.

He sat at my desk and said: "The court clerk is supposed to say they gotta rise."

There was such authority in his voice that slowly, one by one, the class rose. It was a moment I don't think I will ever forget.

The class was directed to sit down, and the wheels of justice proceeded to turn. The prosecution and the defense testified; witnesses were called, examined, cross-examined; excitement ran high. When anyone spoke out of turn, Jose would pound on the desk with his hammer: "This here court will get quiet. Call the next witness. You keep quiet, or you'll be charged with contempt."

He overruled every objection: "Maybe I'm stupid, but I'm the judge and you gotta listen."

And when Harry Kagan challenged him on court procedure, he said, with quiet assurance: "I ought to know. *I been.*"

The court ruled for the defense.

When the bell rang, Jose slowly removed his cap and gown, folded them neatly over his notebook, and went on to his next class; but he walked as if he were still vested in judicial robes.

I don't think he will ever be quite the same.

And that's it; that's why I want to teach; that's the one and only compensation: to make a permanent difference in the life of a child.

The Willowdale offer is not so tempting, after all.

Love,

Syl

P.S. Did you know that out of the 77,000 dropouts in New York City 90% are Negroes and Puerto Ricans?

S.

21

Bulletin Board,
Room 304

MISS BARRET'S CLASSES
(USE LEFT SIDE OF BULLETIN BOARD ONLY)

"THOSE WHO EDUCATE CHILDREN WELL ARE MORE TO BE HONORED THAN PARENTS, FOR THESE ONLY GAVE LIFE, THOSE THE ART OF LIVING WELL."

ARISTOTLE

LOST & FOUND

LOST: Green plad jacket, tore lining broke zipper. Urgent need!

Lou Martin

* * *

LOST: Make Up kit imitation red aligator.

Linda Rosen

138

LOST: "Hollywood Horoscope of Stars" magazine. Reward . . . .

Alice Blake

* * *

LOST: (Or *stole*! ! !) My left lense from my eyeglases between here and History.

Edward Williams, Esq.

* * *

LOST: Poster, printed with Indian Ink, saying that *Government of the Students, by the Students, for the Students, shall not perish from Calvin Coolidge.*

Harry A. Kagan
The Students Choice

* * *

FOUND:

* * *

BEST STUDENT SAMPLES:
"The Theater of the Absurd and All the Angry Young Men"

A Comparative Study

by Elizabeth Ellis

If there is a connection between absurdity and despair, and I believe there is, then Edward Albee, John Osborne, Harold Pinter and Arthur Kopit are all brothers trapped under the same skin. In examining both the symptoms and the more obvious manifesta—

(cont. on next page)

Excellent, as always!

SPELING QUIZ — 100%
Vivian Paine

1. accept
2. acquainted
3. advice
4. artichoke
5. ascend

"READING MAKETH A FULL MAN, CONFERENCE A READY MAN, AND WRITING AN EXACT MAN."

SIR FRANCIS BACON

HUMOR

St. Peter: "Who is knocking at my gate?"
Voice: "It is I."
St. Peter: "Go away, we don't need any more school teachers here!"

Teacher: "There are two words in the English language
you must never use. One of them is *swell* and
the other is *lousy*."

Pupil: "What are they?

JOB OPPORTUNITIES

Experienced Baby Sitter. Apply Office 211.

MISS LEWIS' CLASS:
(USE RIGHT SIDE OF BULLETIN BOARD ONLY)

THE 3 C's: CHARACTER + CONFLICT = CLIMAX
THE 5 E's: EXAMINE, EVALUATE, EXPRESS, ELUCIDATE, END
"CUE" = COHERENCE, UNITY, EMPHASIS

BEST STUDENT SAMPLES:
TRUE OR FALSE TEST — 100%
Kurt Werner

1. T
2. F
3. F
4. T
5. T
6. F
7. T
8. F
9. F
10. T

Very Good!

COMMITTEE CHAIRMEN:

Paper Distribution Committee—Luis Ramos
Blackboard Committee—Judy Thornwald
Sanitary Committee—Sybelle Klopotkin
Room Traffic Committee—Wong Gee

CLASS ACHIEVEMENT GRAPH:

22

A Probing Question

INTRASCHOOL COMMUNICATION

FROM: 304
TO: 508

Dear Bea—

Thank you for letting me observe your Senior Honors and Creative Writing classes; it was worth giving up my unassigned and lunch periods to see! How wonderful to hear a discussion of Hamlet's relationship to Ophelia on such an adult level! Their insights, their involvement, their comments on their outside reading were a revelation to me. And your Creative Writing class made me aware of how much is going on inside them; how serious and yet how touchingly young they are. I wanted to hug each and every one of them. And you.

I realize these are specially selected groups, the cream off the top, but at least I know that this kind of student exists, and this kind of teaching is possible.

Can we meet for a few minutes? I'm bursting to talk to you about it!

(You promised to let me see the paragraphs they were writing in class.)

Enviously,
Syl

INTRASCHOOL COMMUNICATION

FROM: 508
TO: 304

Dear Syl,

Never mind the cream; it will always rise to the top. It's the skim milk that needs good teachers.

Enclosed are a few of their papers; I haven't corrected them yet.

Sorry can't meet you now: Am with child.

Bea

* * *

MRS. SCHACHTER'S CREATIVE WRITING CLASS
ASSIGNMENT:
Write one paragraph, asking a probing question on any topic you wish. Give it a suitable title.
Remember what you've learned about the use of imagery in conveying emotion.

THE WORLD'S INDIFFERENCE

Stink and stench assailled his nostrils as he reeled drunkenly into the room. The whisky lay heavy in his gut. His belly rumbled. "I think I'll puke", he thought. But by then they had him. Handcuffs, the works. "*Why?*" he shouted from his very gut. "*Why me?*" But the world kept rolling along.

SPRING REMEMBERED

I remember Spring. The lilacs and the stars. The rose and the dew. You and the night. I remember. I remember holding hands beneath the moon which was suspended like a silver locket upon a chain of stars from the neckline of a cloud. I remember the leaves whispering like lacy gossips in the trees. I remember the lake lapping. I remember how sharp like a thorn was love. Why do I not remember your Name?

IMAGES

Look, the cat! The cat is on the mat. I can spell cat. But what is cat? That is the question! The cat is a fog or smudgey smoke from a cigarette or a purry furry ball or a tiger ready to spring at you. You never know.

LIFE, BE NOT PROUD

Life, be not proud, thou hast made many mistakes tho thou hadst had a chance to be beautiful, yet thou hadst fouled it up. Why is there sufering and troubles galore? Why is there man's inhumanity to man? Why is there prejudice between all the races? Why is there jails and hoor houses and lynches and unemployment? Why is there death? Life, be not proud!

SNOW

The snow lies on mountain and dale like a naked woman exposing its glistering white body voluptously and proud of her nakedness under the warm sun. Soon the warm sun will melt it. What then?

THE SUBWAY

The subway is a monster giant snake that crawls inside the Bowels of the Earth, emerging to vomit forth its food at the different stations. It then swallows another belly full of us to crawl into the Bowels where darkness dwells. Who knows when it will re-emerge again?

WHY DO I LOVE?

Brown throated is my love and potent are his groins
and laughing are his long lashed eyes. The songs he
sings are many. His lips, insistent with passion's flame,
are smooth upon my young mouth. Although my love
doth walk with feet of clay upon my heart, I do not
care: I love. Why do I love? I know not. I only know
I love.

LIFE REFLECTED IN THE TELEVISION EYE

I see the television eye. It does not see me albeit I
scream jump laugh weep rant rage stick out my tongue
at it. Within the television eye, among the shadows and
the horizontal streaks the little people live and love and
eat and die interupted by commercials. While I, yes I,
posess the power to turn them off whenever I feel like
it. Just so to God are we as they, for Lo! He can stop
our mouths while in the middle of a sentence and snap
our hearts in twain. His Eye sees us albeit we do not
see Him. What is God?—God is the Universal Antenna.

THE FUTURE?

The question I ask can never be answered while in the
proccess of being asked. For I inquire about the Future.
And only the Future can tell about itself. Is it there for
us? We're a fast breed because we don't know if there
is time ahead or total anihilation of Man. I sometimes
wonder, what will become of me and my forthcoming
children?

ACENTUATE THE POSITIVE

Who?
  What?
    When?
      Where?
        Why?
          How?

O foolish *?* mark, it doesn't matter. What matters is the *!* To *?* is to be told how bad you are and various problems better not to know. So only live with *!*

TO WHAT SHALL I COMPARE THEE TO?

You are to me a Sunday morning smelling of frying bacon and promises of more. You are to me a racing car at 95 miles per hr. that no one else has. You are to me a lazy curtesan in her feminine bed room with ostrich feathers fanning her brow. You are to me a fresh meadowland. You are to me the sounds of the City that spell a band of gypsies with tamburines and hunking cars and tooting trucks' symphony or the hot beat of Rock n Roll that jerks a thousand feet. You are to me the end of the line. But what am I to you?

INTEGRATION

They speak of Integration. It's a word. What does it mean: a bus? a cop? a school? a headline? a tomstone? a neighbor's fight? a parent's yells? a speech? a boycot? a politician? It's all the same to me for words are only words. Yet deep and dark, deeper than any well and darker than any skin something lies and slumbers. Unburry it and hearken what it says. A simple truth: My brother.

UNTITLED

To be
Or not to be—
By this
I mean:
    To be myself?
    (Who am I though?)
Or else to be
What my parents
    (Alas, poor Yorik, I knew them well!)
Would like me to be
Because
Of their own regrets
Or
What the World expects?
    (The choice is tough)
        The rest is silence . . . .

THE OLD MAN

The old man just stood there. Just stood. There. Where I was. A reproach? To my youth, perhaps. To my good health. His chest was sunk. His hands shook with palsy. Finished. Through. Finis. His sands of time had run. But mine had just begun. Someday I too. Not now. Not yet. Why, then, do I feel so guilty?

THE MURDERER

I saw him scuttling like a crook, making his fearful way, stelthy among the dirty dishes crustied with grease in the sink, bearing a morsle of food to his secret sons behind the drain board. How fearful were his eyes. Shall I kill him?
(Mrs. Schachter—Is it clear I am talking about a cockaroach?)

MONTHLY REPORT ON PHYSICAL CONDITION OF ROOM

ROOM: 304
TEACHER: S. BARRETT   OCT. 13

Door off hinge
Sliding wardrobe panel doesn't close; blackboard on it
can't be used.
Book closet, back of room, broken; shelf splintered.
Window in back, right, broken.
Teacher's desk missing two drawers.
Radiator keeps clanging.

> (*Same conditions prevail as in last month's report*,
> with addition of radiator. Hole in window getting
> bigger, though. Wind and rain blowing in. Also,
> glass crunching underfoot.
>
> S. *Barrett*

• • •

Dear Miss Barrett,
    You have neglected to send in attendance sheet for
today.

Sadie Finch
Chief Clerk

149

Dear Miss Finch,

The reason is that Linda Rosen chose to wear a pink sweater and fuchsia stretch pants to school this morning. She was seen by Mr. McHabe, who invited her to cool her heels in the office. She was also seen by the boys in my homeroom, who migrated en masse to her vicinity. Since we had no quorum, I couldn't take attendance. I will do so this afternoon—unless they have followed her like lemmings into the sea and are all drowned.

S. Barrett

*   *   *

FROM: James J. McHabe, Adm. Asst.
TO: Miss S. Barrett

Dear Miss Barrett,

All out of board erasers. All out of red pencils. Requisition for window-poles has been sent to the Board last spring—we must be patient.

There has been an epidemic of chalk-stealing. Please keep chalk under lock except when in use.

Can you use some posters? Still have left-over yellow on green TRUTH IS BEAUTY, also some black on white LEARNING=EARNING.

JJ McH

(A frivolous attitude and levity of tone towards attendance taking are unsuitable to the high seriousness of our profession.)

JJ McH

*   *   *

INTRASCHOOL COMMUNICATION

FROM: 304
TO: 508

Dear Bea—

Fired by my visit to your classes, I asked Dr. Bester if I might observe other English teachers, to learn more about techniques. Stony silence. I guess no one else is willing to be seen. (I was particularly eager to discover how Henrietta teaches Punctuation Traffic. I understand she uses a system of signals such as Stop, Go, Curves Ahead. . . .)

Had another run-in with J.J. McH., in connection with my levity. But I've got to hold on to my sense of humor—which is really a sense of proportion.

"You and Mrs. Schachter are the only teachers with humors in the entire school," a student said to me. "You see the funny sides, which makes it easier."

It makes it much easier. How can I take seriously such mimeographed absurdities as "Lateness due to absence," "High under-achiever," and "Polio Consent slips"?

Syl

* * *

INTRASCHOOL COMMUNICATION

FROM: 508
TO: 304

Dear Syl,

I'll match yours any day with: "Please disregard the following."

Bea

* * *

FROM: James J. McHabe, Adm. Asst.
TO: all teachers

YOUR WHOLE-HEARTED COOPERATION IS ESSENTIAL IN DISCOURAGING ILLEGITIMATE LATENESSES, SINCE THEY TAKE AWAY TIME FROM VALUABLE SCHOOL TIME. PENALTIES FOR INFRACTIONS MUST BE FOLLOWED THROUGH.

JJ McH

Admit to class: 9:30 A.M.
  Lateness unexcused. Claims got lost in transit.

                                              JJ McH

*   *   *

CIRCULAR # 59

PLEASE KEEP ALL CIRCULARS ON FILE, IN THEIR ORDER

TOPIC: TEACHERS' WELFARE

THE PRESIDENT OF THE UNITED FEDERATION OF TEACH-
ERS HAS ASKED THE BOARD OF EDUCATION TO SUPPORT
LEGISLATION FOR HIGHER DEATH BENEFITS AND PEN-
SIONS FOR TEACHERS WHO DIE OR ARE HURT IN THE
LINE OF DUTY. YOUR SUPPORT OF THIS MEASURE IS
NEEDED.

*   *   *

Miss Barrett,
  Joseph Ferone of your official class was absent from
Math this morning. He claims he was working for Mr.
Grayson. Please discipline and enter on PRC.

                                    Frederick Loomis

*   *   *

FROM: JAMES J. McHABE, ADM. ASST.
TO: ALL TEACHERS

SINCE SCHOOL AIDES HAVE RELIEVED TEACHERS OF
MANY NON-TEACHING ASSIGNMENTS, TEACHERS ARE RE-
QUESTED TO REPORT TO THE OFFICE FOR FURTHER
ASSIGNMENTS.

                                              JJ McH

*   *   *

Dear Miss Barrett,
  Joseph Ferone missed an important Physics test today because he was with Mr. Grayson. If you arrange
for him to see me, I'll be glad to make out another test
for him.

                                    Sincerely yours,
                                    Marcus Manheim

INTRASCHOOL COMMUNICATION

FROM: P. Barringer, 309
TO: S. Barrett, 304

Sylvia!

Sorry I couldn't keep our date last night.

I enclose a peace-offering:

In a few days you'll be exposed, for the first time, to Open School.

It's an experience.

Model parents will visit model teachers in model classrooms.

Let's sing this to them, with apologies to Gilbert & Sullivan:

> I am the very model of a modern teacher, *well* aware
> Of all the new developments from Iowa to Delaware;
> I've information sundry on my many students various
> On all the graded levels of their tabulated areas.
> I go to lectures numerous to hear what all the rumor is
> My back is full of callouses from my psychoanalysis;
> My head is full of insights and devoid of common fallacies.
> The truant and the super-slow have my attention dili-gent;
> I even have some time to give the normally intilligent!

There is more, but I'm due at rehearsal.

Last call: Will you, at least, join the chorus? Help with makeup? Sew costumes? Paint props?

Meet me, same time, at The Tavern?

Paul

*   *   *

TO: ALL TEACHERS

I HAVE NOTED AND OBSERVED IN ASSEMBLY THAT A NUMBER OF OUR STUDENTS SEEM UNCERTAIN OF THE WORDS OF OUR ALMA MATER SONG, "THE PURPLE AND

GOLD." THERE SEEMS TO BE CONFUSION IN THE FIRST
STANZA PARTICULARLY. TEACHERS ARE ADVISED AND
URGED TO GO OVER THE WORDING WITH THEIR STU-
DENTS SO THAT THE SONG MAY BE SUNG AT THE NEXT
AND SUBSEQUENT ASSEMBLIES WITH THE RIGHT AND
PROPER FEELING AND ENUNCIATION. THE WORDS ARE
AS FOLLOWS:

> Ye loyal sons and daughters
> Whose hearts will ne'er grow old
> As long as ye are true to
> The purple and gold.

MAXWELL E. CLARKE,
PRINCIPAL

* * *

CIRCULAR # 61

PLEASE KEEP ALL CIRCULARS ON FILE, IN THEIR ORDER

TOPIC: HOMEWORK ADDENDUM

WE HAVE HAD AN EPIDEMIC OF UNPREPARED STUDENTS.
A STUDENT UNPREPARED WITH HOMEWORK MUST SUB-
MIT TO HIS TEACHER, IN WRITING, HIS REASON OR REA-
SONS FOR NEGLECTING TO DO IT. PLEASE KEEP THESE
HOMEWORK EXCUSES ON FILE IN THE RIGHT-HAND
DRAWER OF YOUR DESK.

JAMES J. MCHABE
ADM. ASST.

From the Right-Hand Drawer, Room 304

I know homework is essential to our well being, and I did it but I got into a fight with some kid on the way to school and he threw it in the gutter.

My dog chewed it up.

I didn't know we were supposed to do it.

I fell asleep on the subway because I stayed up all night doing my homework, so when it stopped at my station I ran through the door not to be late & left it on the seat on the subway.

The cat chewed it up and there was no time to do it over.

Why I Didn't Do It. When you tell us to bring a book report I do not like it because I have to go to the library and get a book to read it. It will take me about two month or more to read it and I have to owe money to them and it adds up. It isn't fair to the pocket, Haha! In those hours when I have to read the book I can watch TV or play around or shoot a couple.

As I was taking down the assignment my ballpoint stopped.

I had to study French so didn't have time to study English.

I did it but left it home by mistake.

If a teacher wants to know something why doesn't she look it up herself instead of making we students do it? We benefit ourselves more by listening to her, after all, she's the teacher!

The baby spilled milk on it.

My brother took "my" homework instead of "his."

I have to work after school and they kept me til midnight.

The page was missing from my book.

Even though I brought in a legal note for absence he sent me back. That's why I'm unprepared.

I had to take care of my three siblings because my mother is in the hospital.

I lost my book & just found it.

There's no room in my house now my uncle moved in and I have to sleep in the hall and couldn't use the kitchen table.

Some one stole it.

I was sick and had to go to bed.

What homework?

My dog pead on it.

PART IV

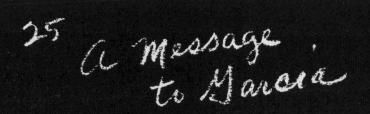

25 *A Message to Garcia*

TO: ALL TEACHERS

FOR THOSE WHO MISSED LAST MONDAY'S ASSEMBLY BE-
CAUSE OF THE CONFUSION RESULTING FROM SWITCHING X2·
AND Y2 SECTIONS, A COPY OF DR. CLARKE'S ADDRESS TO
THE HONOR STUDENTS IS ENCLOSED.

I AM PLEASED AND PRIVILEGED TO SALUTE AND
CONGRATULATE THOSE OF YOU WHO HAVE THROUGH
YOUR OWN DETERMINATION AND STICKTOITIVENESS
ACHIEVED AN HONORED AND ENVIABLE PLACE ON THE
HONOR ROLL. YOU HAVE BEEN GIVEN THE OPPORTU-
NITY OF LEARNING FROM AND CONTRIBUTING TO THE
CULTURAL HERITAGE OF THE GENERATIONS BEFORE
AND AFTER YOU AS THEY HAVE LEARNED FROM AND
CONTRIBUTED TO YOU. NOW YOU MUST DRAW UPON
THE RICH WAREHOUSE OF SKILLS YOU HAVE ACQUIRED
AND KNOWLEDGE YOU HAVE WON AND CONTINUE TO
FACE THE FUTURE, TO GO ONWARD TOWARDS VEN-
TURES EVER NEW, FORWARD TOWARDS HORIZONS
EVER WIDER. AS THE GREAT POET SO WELL PUT
IT: "SAY NOT THE STRUGGLE NAUGHT AVAILETH."
IT AVAILETH; IT AVAILETH INDEED; FOR NOTHING

LASTING OR WORTHWHILE WAS EVER WON WITHOUT
IT. YOU WHO HAVE THUS FOUGHT AND STRUGGLED
TO ACHIEVE THE SPLENDID DISTINCTION OF A PLACE
ON THE HONOR ROLL KNOW FULL WELL THAT THIS
IS SO, AND AS I LOOK UPON YOUR PROUD AND HAPPY
FACES, I AM REMINDED OF THE YOUNG MAN WHO, IF
YOU RECALL, HAD SO ZEALOUSLY AND SO SELFLESSLY
CARRIED THE MESSAGE TO GARCIA.
AND YET, THOSE OF YOU WHO HAVE NOT ACHIEVED
SUCH A PLACE ON THE HONOR ROLL MUST NOT FEEL
THAT YOU HAVE FAILED. ON THE CONTRARY, IT IS YOU
WHO ARE THE BACKBONE AND THE REAR-GUNNERS
FOR THOSE WHO HAVE FORGED AHEAD, FOR WITHOUT
YOU AND YOUR CONTRIBUTION, THEY COULD NOT
HAVE ACHIEVED WHAT THEY DID. IN A LARGE MEAS-
URE OR SMALL, WE EACH AND ALL OF US ARE CON-
TRIBUTING TO THE GOOD OF THE WHOLE, THOSE BE-
HIND THE THRONE AS WELL AS THOSE ON THE
THRONE, WHICH IS THE ULTIMATE AIM AND GOAL OF
DEMOCRACY IN ACTION. ANYONE WHO HAS HAD THE
GOOD FORTUNE TO ATTEND OUR G.O. MEETINGS
KNOWS THAT DEMOCRACY CAN AND DOES WORK, AND
IT IS UP TO EACH AND EVERY ONE OF US TO PASS IT
ON INTO THE FUTURE.

*   *   *

Sylvia!
No chance to stop by today.
My classes are being covered while I'm in auditorium,
presumably blocking out Faculty Show. Actually, I'm
writing my own version of Calvin Coolidge Gilbert &
Sullivan. It will never pass by the censors, but may win
a smile from you. Which is all I ask.
Teachers will play kids. What do you think of this
number, for instance—played by our talented trio: Henrietta Pastorfield, Mary Lewis, and Charlotte Wolf?

> Three little maids from school are we,
> Nourished on heroin and "tea,"
> None with a Phi Beta Kappa key—
> Three little maids from school!

Three little maids from Calvin Coolidge,
Giggly and wiggly and young and foolidge,
Out to avoid a little schoolage—
Three little maids from school!

In counterpart, the boys—played, I think, by Loomis,
Manheim and McHabe:

Three little lads from school are we,
Beatniks, repeatniks, as you can see
(If you peruse our PPP)—
Three little lads from school!

Junior delinquents, always truant,
Each with an officer pursuant,
And a vocabulary fluent
Having to do with school!

Loomis: I keep on learning less and less, and
McHabe: I am what's known as quite a mess, and
Manheim: I am a problem adolescent—
Three little lads from school!

It's good to get out of the classroom, away from vapid
faces blinking at me. You have one of them in your
homeroom—Alice something—who bathes me in long,
liquid glances. Lord preserve me from puppy crushes.
My taste runs more to Chaucerian-scholar types.

Meet me at The Tavern after school? I need to get
blotto. Got another "Thank-you-for-letting-us-see-your-
clever-manuscript-unfortunately" letter. My characters
are too improbable, they tell me. My setting, too exotic.
Well, why not? One must escape.

This is no job for a man—or woman, either. Unless,
like Clarke, you can spend the day sitting and knitting
your brows. Here's one for him:

When I was a lad I went to school
And copied on the board the Golden Rule;
Each day I copied in a Palmer hand—
Not a word that I was writing did I understand!
I copied on the board so carefully
That now I am the Principal of Calvin C.!

I would have included his Message to Garcia speech,
but the only rhyme I could think of was Marsha. And
I don't know who she is. Too bad. It's a memorable
speech, an apt commentary on school. Everyone rushes
urgently around to get the message in on time. But no
one knows what the message is.

Why do you refuse to be in my show? You don't
even have to sing.

Paul

❖ ❖ ❖

FROM: JAMES J. McHABE, ADM. ASST.
TO: ALL TEACHERS

Do not accept lateness excuses due to fire on the
BMT today. This was checked by me with the Transit
Authority. There was no fire on the BMT today.

JJ McH

❖ ❖ ❖

TO: ALL TEACHERS

Polio Consent slips are due in Health Office before
3 P.M. today.

Frances Egan
School Nurse

❖ ❖ ❖

CIRCULAR # 42

PLEASE KEEP ALL CIRCULARS ON FILE, IN THEIR ORDER

TOPIC: PPP AND EMOTIONAL PROFILE EVALUATION

TO ENABLE THE TEACHER TO GAIN A MORE PROFOUND
INSIGHT INTO THE EMOTIONAL PROBLEMS OF EACH STU-
DENT AND TO ACHIEVE A GRASP, IN TOTO, OF THE
SOCIOECONOMIC FACTORS SHAPING HIS CHARACTER DE-
VELOPMENT AND PERSONALITY GROWTH, THE GUIDANCE

OFFICE, AS A RESULT OF THOROUGH DEPTH-INTERVIEWS,
HAS EVALUATED THE WHOLE CHILD IN RELATION TO
ALL HIS AREAS IN THE PPP ON EACH PRC.

Ella Friedenberg
Guidance Counselor

* * *

FROM: The Health Office
TO: Miss Barrett, Room 304

CONFIDENTIAL MEDICAL REPORT

Copy to: Mr. McHabe
Miss Finch

Rosen, Linda, of your official class, will be out of
school until cleared by the Board of Health. Wasser-
mann positive. She is to be carried on your register
under Temporary Suspension.

Lazar, Evelyn, of your official class, deceased two
days ago, of infection following a self-induced AB,
as attested by the Medical Examiner. She is to be taken
off your register permanently.

Frances Egan
School Nurse

Touch Wounds

Oct. 16

Dear Ellen,

Evelyn Lazar is dead. That's the girl who asked to see me the day of the Faculty Conference. Perhaps if I had, she would be alive today. She died of an infection following an abortion she had tried to induce with a knitting needle, after she had run away from home. Now she's but a name to be removed from the homeroom register. Permanently.

Paul says: "Sauve qui peut! Think only of yourself. Getting involved does them no good."

Bea says: "You're not God. Nothing is your fault, except, perhaps, poor teaching."

Henrietta says: "If you've kept them off the streets and given them a bit of fun for a while, you've earned your keep, such as it is."

Sadie Finch says: "Hand in before 3 locker number and book receipts for Lazar, Evelyn."

Ella Freud says: "Environmental influences beyond our control are frequently the cause of emotional disequilibrium."

And Frances Egan, the school nurse, left her nutrition charts long enough to tell me there was nothing that could have been done. "Evelyn had a rough time with her father," she said. "Once she came in beaten black and blue."

"What did you do for her?"

"I gave her a cup of tea."

"Tea? Why tea, for heaven's sake?"

"Why? Because I know all about it," she flared, shaking with anger. "I know more than anyone here what goes on outside—poverty, disease, dope, degeneracy—yet I'm not supposed to give them even a band-aid. I used to plead, bang on my desk, talk myself hoarse arguing with kids, parents, welfare, administration, social agencies. Nobody really heard me. Now I give them tea. At least, that's something."

"But you're a *nurse*," I said helplessly.

She showed me the Directive from the Board posted on her wall: THE SCHOOL NURSE MAY NOT TOUCH WOUNDS, GIVE MEDICATION, REMOVE FOREIGN PARTICLES FROM THE EYE . . .

Are we, none of us, then, allowed to touch wounds? What is the teacher's responsibility? And if it begins at all, where does it end? How much of the guilt is ours?

There was a discussion in the Teachers' Lunchroom about it.

Mary Lewis was shocked at the moral laxness of young people today. Surely, she said, the overworked teachers couldn't be expected to add chaperoning to their long list of chores. Henrietta Pastorfield had nothing against sexual freedom—provided it was in the open. Had the girl been in her class, this wouldn't have happened; her kids confided in her because she spoke their language. Fred Loomis said—sterilization—that's the answer. Sterilize them and kick them out of school. Bea Schachter spoke of love; that's what these children were starved for. Paul Barringer disagreed. They can't handle love, he said; they know nothing about it. Amused detachment is the only way to remain intact. But we cannot remain intact if we teach, Bea said. And we must teach—against all odds, against all obstacles, in the best sense of the word. Nuts, said Loomis; kids don't belong in school.

There we sat in the jungle of a white porcelain table with an artificial rose in a plastic vase upon it, and a sign on the wall advising us to remove trays before leaving, each stalking his own path through the underbrush. After a while only Mary, Henrietta, Paul and I were left in the lunchroom. I tried to speak, but Mary cut me short:

"I started out like you, too, but I found there's nothing you can do, so you may as well give up. Just wait till you've been here as long as I— You work yourself to the bone, and no thanks from anyone. The more you do, the more they expect of you, and it's the same in other schools, believe me. Here at least we have Sadie Finch and a couple of Aides to help, but no one really cares, and they just pile more and more on you. I've got no blackboard and they never fixed my radiator, and they stuck me with three preparations and Remedial Reading, and with the Late Room and the Junior Scholastics; and they made me volunteer to be Faculty Advisor to *The Clarion,* and I have to travel from the 3rd to the 5th floor with my varicose veins. In 23 years I've never been a minute late; I'm always the first to hand in reports —ask Finch—and I never complain; I just do my work, though everyone knows I have the worst homeroom kids in the school, and it takes all my energy just to keep them quiet—before I even *start* teaching!"

"If they're restless," Henrietta said, "I kid them out of it. It doesn't matter how much they learn as long as they enjoy coming to school; at least, they're *exposed* to learning. And they know they're free to discuss anything with me—sex, anything. The kids feel I'm one of them; I'm pretty hep for an old maid."

"It's nothing to joke about," said Mary. "We make everything too easy for them. They're so used to sugar-coating, they come to me with no idea about how to study or what a sentence is. How can they learn a foreign language if they don't even know their own?"

"The ones that want to, learn," Henrietta said. "Take Bob —the best English student in the school. Writes like a dream —won the interscholastic essay contest—handsome, polite, a joy in the classroom. I don't have to teach him to parse sentences."

"Because I did," said Mary. "It's your kind of newfangled pussy-footing and side-stepping that makes them illiterates. With me they get a solid foundation, the disciplines of learning. In my class they don't get away with hot-air discussions and exchanging their opinions and describing their experiences. What opinions can they have? What have they experienced? What do they know? That's an affront! They learn what I know!"

"Trouble is," Paul smiled his most charming smile, "a teacher has to be so many things at the same time: actor, policeman, scholar, jailer, parent, inspector, referee, friend, psychiatrist, accountant, judge and jury, guide and mentor, wielder of minds, keeper of records, and grand master of the Delaney Book."

"Perhaps you have a rhyme for this?" Mary inquired politely.

"Certainly," said Paul, striking a pose. "Listen:

We should be versed in Psychology,
In Theory and Technique;
Our devastating smile should be ready to beguile,
Our chalk should never squeak!
We must be learnèd as well as neat,
With high IQ's and unflattened feet;
We must be firm, yet we can't be rude—
And that must be our customary attitude!"

"Very amusing," said Mary. "This kind of thing must keep you busy; no wonder you're never here the 1st period. Who punches you in—Gilbert and Sullivan?"

But he had made his point, and when the bell rang, they were smiling.

Poor Evelyn Lazar—unwept, unsung, and lost in the bickering. Her death haunts me; I keep thinking—if only I'd been able to hear her cry for help! But we may not touch wounds—--

Evelyn is only one girl I happen to know about because she happened to be in my homeroom and because she happened to be traced and found. What of the countless others who drop out, disappear, or wrestle alone in the dark? Paul says that I make too much of it; that what she probably wanted to talk to me about was a change of locker or an extra-credit slip. But that isn't the point—that isn't the point at all.

Are we paid only to teach sentence structure, keep order and assign those books that are available in the Book Room?

Yet here is Henrietta, smacking her lips with spinsterish lasciviousness over her star pupil, Bob; and here is Paul, mocking the technicolor daydreams of little Alice; and here am I, jousting with McHabe for the soul of Ferone. I am still determined to reach him. He has been as insolent and wary as ever, refusing to see me after school, sauntering into class, toothpick in mouth, hands in pockets, daring me to— what? Prove something. Finally he did agree to have a talk with me. "You *sure* that's what you want? OK, you call the shots!" But before we could meet, he was suspended from school for two weeks for carrying a switch-blade knife. Suspension, you see, is a form of punishment that puts a kid out of our control for a specified period, to roam the streets and join the gangs.

When I tried to tell McHabe that it would have been more valuable to let Ferone keep his appointment with me than to kick him out, he let me have it:

"When you're in the system as long as I" (They all say that!) "you'll realize it isn't understanding they need. I understand them all right—they're no good. It's discipline they need. They sure don't get it at home. We've got to show them who's boss. We've got to teach them by punishing them, each time, a hundred times, so they know we mean business. If not for us, they'll get it in the neck sooner or later—from a cop or a judge or their boss, if they're lucky enough to land a job. They don't know right from wrong, they don't know their ass from—I beg your pardon. You're young and pretty and they flatter you and you swallow it, playing phonograph records, encouraging them to gripe in your suggestion box, having heart to heart talks. A lot of good it does. Sure, we've got to win their respect, but through fear. That's all they understand. They've got to toe the line, or they'll make mincemeat out of us. You ever seen their homes, some of them? You ever been in juvenile court? Hear them talk about us amongst themselves? These kids are bad. They've got to be taught law and order, and we're the ones to teach them. We're stuck with them, and they've got to stick out their time, and they better behave themselves or else. All you people who shoot off ideas—you just try to run this school your way for one day, you'll have a riot in every room. I'm telling you this for your own good, you've got a lot to learn."

I probably do.

I'm going to be observed by Bester this week. He was nice enough to warn me. I plan to teach an adverbial clause or a poem by Frost.

I didn't mean for this letter to be so long—but I am confused and troubled, and you are interested enough to listen. There are times when I feel I don't belong here. Perhaps I should be teaching at Willowdale. Perhaps I should give up teaching altogether. Or perhaps I should find myself a nice young man, one who talks in prose, and settle down, as the saying goes. *You* seem to have found the answer.

But I don't want to give up without trying. I think the kids deserve a better deal than they're getting. So do the teachers.

I might be able to reach them through their parents; we're having Open School Day in a couple of weeks. Wish me luck—and give Jim and the baby an *extra* kiss today.

Love,
Syl

P.S. Did you know that the State Department has started a course in elementary composition for its officers, who cannot understand each other's memoranda?

S.

CHAPTER 27: CLARIFICATION OF STATUS

BOARD OF EDUCATION OF THE CITY OF NEW YORK

TO: Miss S. Barrett
Calvin Coolidge High School
New York, N.Y.

DEAR SIR OR MADAM:

IN REPLY TO YOUR REQUEST FOR CLARIFICATION OF YOUR STATUS, PLEASE BE ADVISED THAT ALL MEMBERS OF THE TEACHING STAFF SHALL BE APPOINTED BY THE BOARD OF SUPERINTENDENTS FOR A PROBATIONARY PERIOD OF THREE YEARS, EXCEPT THAT A TEACHER WHO RENDERS ONE YEAR OF SATISFACTORY (S) SERVICE MAY OFFER, IN LIEU OF THE OTHER TWO YEARS OF PROBATIONARY SERVICE REQUIRED BY THIS SECTION, A TOTAL OF TWO YEARS OF SATISFACTORY SERVICE EITHER AS A REGULAR APPOINTEE OR AS A REGULAR SUBSTITUTE IN THE SAME RANK, SUBJECT, AND LEVEL OF TEACHING AS THE PERMANENT APPOINTMENT APPLIED FOR. FOR THE PURPOSE OF THIS SECTION NO PERIOD OF SUBSTITUTE SERVICE SHALL BE COUNTED AS EQUIVALENT TO PROBATIONARY SERVICE UNLESS IT CONSISTS OF NO LESS THAN 80 SCHOOL DAYS OF SERVICE IN ANY 90 CONSECU-

TIVE SCHOOL DAYS IN THE SAME SCHOOL; AND A CREDIT OF ONE YEAR SHALL BE BASED ON NOT FEWER THAN 160 DAYS OF ACTUAL SERVICE EXTENDING OVER A PERIOD OF ONE YEAR. <u>THIS DOES NOT APPLY TO UNSATISFACTORY (U) SERVICE.</u>

I HOPE THIS HAS ANSWERED YOUR REQUEST FOR CLARIFICATION OF YOUR STATUS.

DIVISION OF APPOINTMENTS & RECORDS

Dear Teacher, prefibly Dear Friend,
    All your doings are fair. I never found anyone like you anywheres at home or in school. (I lost 2 more lps)
                    Hoping to hear from you,
                    Vivian Paine

McHabe is a jailer they should do away with him. Warning! this is my possitively last time I am writting!

the Hawk

    I changed my mind, a teacher can be human. I suggest the Board of Education picks all young and pretty teachers like you, who really play ball with us, and not a bunch of old foggies.

Long live you!

Frank Allen

Abollish prejudice. Abollish Miss Freedernburgs inter-vews they make me sick to my stomache. Like when she ask am I ashame where I live?

Edward Williams, Esq.

In these "dread" times of "Atoms" you remind me of another "teacher" I once had in "elementery". She had the courage to laugh at a "joke" even if it wasn't funny.

Chas. H. Robbins

Too stuck up for your own good and have pets.

Yr ENEMY

You think it's fair when a teacher takes off 5 points on a test just because I mispelled his name wrong? (Baringor).

You said we should sign our name to show we're not afraid of our convinctions. Well I am.

Anonimus

I suggest only men teachers. There is one traight that overshadows all your good points and that is you are a female, and my natural instinct tells me there are no good females. The opposite sex and I have nothing in common whatsoever and I am very sorry you were not a man.

Rusty

I am only in your Home Room, but I wish I had you for English. You told us not to mention names of teachers, well I have Mrs. L-w-s, her voice is so grading it makes my ears squint. Last term was no better, we had M-ss P-st-rf--ld, we had to make believe we were a TV pannel or a football team. With you maybe I could learn something but I'm dropping out of school anyhow so it's too late.

A Former Student

You convinced us you're the teacher.

Experienced Student

I happen to have another teacher for English . . . I feel deep within me that there should be a deeper closeness between an English teacher and a pupil because the subject touches the very heart . . . I am sure you're a good teacher too and quite attractive to look at. (I like the silver pin you wear on your gray jersy)

Alice Blake

Linda Rosen's got the Clap!.

Guess Who

Continue teaching myths and books of all kinds. This is a good idea and I believe future generations will benefit by it. I wish also to commend you and to thank you for taking an interest in mine and the class as a whole's grammar.

Harry A. Kagan
(The Students Choice)

Federal Lunches are Lousy.

                                    Eater

You're a great dresser, you know just how to wear your cloths, especially your red suit. I have no other complaint.

Well, well! I don't mind bad teachers so much but some habbits they have drive me nuts! Like chewing their eyeglasses (Mr. Loomis) or snifling their nose (Miss Pasterfield) or wearing the same thing every day (Mrs. Lewis)! Don't forget we have to look at them all period! Present company excluded, Ha-ha! Teachers should have a mirror in the back of the room so they could see how they look to us!

                                    Lou Martin

No homework over week ends, s'il vous plais! From Friday to Monday I like to forget the whole thing!

                                    Votre Ami

Get lost & stay there.

                Poisen

Is it possible for you to teach Creative Writing next term?

You showed me that writing clearly means thinking clearly, and that there is nothing more important than communication.

                                        Elizabeth Ellis

I wish I had you for Math (my favorite subject). But alas, we can not have our cake & eat it too.

                                        A Bashful Nobody

J. J. McH.
Should go to H.

                                                    Poet

I'm getting behine because school goes to fast for me to retain the work. Maybe if they go more slower with the readings?

                                                Repeter

I suggest: I. free lunchs
            A. Air condition classes
            B. No home work
         II. a TV in every room
            A. Movie stars for teachers
        III. 6 mo. vacations, school 10 to 12, kids
             take over!

                                            Teenager

Don't worry—
We're behind you 85 %!

I like everything we do in class but I don't like reading books & myth too I don't like. P.S. I don't like grammer. Oral reports I don't care for. You forget we're not normal like the good schools.

A True Pupil

Lessons are pretty interesting, especially if you come to class. I suggest better attendance for me.

Absent

I can't take my eyes off you your so beautifull. You're just like my imaginary twin Roseanne. If I was a boy I wouldn't even care about English, I would just sit and stare at you. But I'm not a boy so I'll just have to suffer the consequents.

Your Unknown Admireress

Having sprained my ankle in handball the nurse gave me a cup of tea. Is that suppose to help my ankle?

Athalete

I got a lot out of Myths, they help us to better understand our fellows. Especially Narsissis, he was a lot like Mr. Barringer only he didn't get drowned.

Odyssus

Riding to school in the bus I'm all worn out from the housework and dishes and I wish the boys who fool around and so forth would one day give me their seat I'd drop dead of supprize. Can something be done?

The Fair Sex

<u>List of Goods:</u> 1. You're always willing to listen to
                      our side no matter what.
                   2. When you don't know something
                      you're not ashamed to say you
                      don't know something.
                   3. You're not afraid to crack a smile
                      when necessery.
                   4. You always look happy to see us
                      come in.
<u>List of Bads:</u> None.
 <u>Suggestions:</u> More like you.

Your Fan

My mother has been living with me for 16 yrs, but
she still insists on cross-examining me.

Doodlebug

When in Miss Lewis' class a pupil finds it necessary
to visit the men's room he is often denied that priviledge.

Sophomore

English would be much better off with more teachers
like you that take an interest in their pupils instead of
teaching just because they have to due to circumstances.
Well ever since you elected me judge, I, for one will
never forget you as long as I live. You made me feel
I'm real.

Jose Rodriguez

PART VI

29 *The Road Not Taken*

MODEL OUTLINE OF LESSON PLAN

1. TOPIC: "The Road Not Taken" by Robert Frost.
2. AIM: Understanding and appreciation of the poem.
3. MOTIVATION: INTERESTING, CHALLENGING, THOUGHT-PROVOK-
   ING QUESTIONS, RELATING TO THE STUDENTS'
   OWN EXPERIENCES.
   1. What turning point have *you* had in your life?
   2. What choice did you make, and why?
   3. How did you feel about your choice later?
4. ANTICIPATION OF DIFFICULTIES:
   Put on board and explain words: *diverged*
                                   trodden
5. FACTUAL CONTENT OF LESSON:
   Read the poem aloud:
   "Two roads diverged in a yellow wood
   . . ." etc.
6. PIVOTAL QUESTIONS, DIRECTED TOWARDS APPRECIATION OF
   HUMAN MOTIVES:
   1. Why did he make this particular choice of road?

183

2. Why does he say: "I shall be telling this with a sigh"?
   What kind of sigh will it be? One of relief? Regret?

3. This poem ends with: "I took the one less traveled by, And that has made all the difference."
   What difference do you suppose it has made to him?

4. Had he taken the *other* road, how would the poem have ended? (Elicit from them: The same way!)

5. Why does Frost call it "The Road *Not* Taken" rather than "The Road Taken"? (Elicit: We regret things we haven't done more than those we have.)

6. Based on this poem, what kind of person do you suppose Frost was? (Elicit: direct, simple, philosophical, man who loved nature and had eye for concrete things.)

7. What is his style of writing?
   ("multum in parvo" or "much in little": economy of language, yet scope of thought)

7. ENRICHMENT:
   Pass around photo of Frost.

8. SUMMARY:
   1. Blazing a trail vs. conformity.
   2. Regret inherent in any decision.

(NOTE: Remember summary on *board!*
   Windows!
   No paper scraps on floor!
   Try to get Eddie Williams to recite at least once.
   Don't let Harry Kagan do all the talking.
   Change Linda's seat—put her next to girl?
   If time, play record of Frost reading own poetry.)

FROM: Samuel Bester,
           Chairman, Language Arts Dept.
TO: Miss S. Barrett, Room 304

Miss Barrett,

The following suggestions are unofficial: they will not appear on my formal Observation Report. If you wish a personal conference, please see me.

1. Windows should be open about 4 inches *from the top*, to avoid danger of students leaning out.
2. Relating questions to the pupils' own experiences is first rate, but don't let them run away with you. They often do it to delay or avoid a lesson. Example: in connection with making a choice, the discussion of whether or not girl in 4th row should wear her print or her green chiffon Saturday night was interesting, but 6 minutes on it was excessive.
3. Don't allow one student (Kagan?) to monopolize the discussion. Call on the non-volunteers too.
4. Always ask the question first; then only call on a student by name, thus engaging the whole class in thinking. Avoid elliptical, loaded or vague questions, such as: "How do you feel about this poem?" (too vague) and "Do we regret what we haven't done?" (The answer the teacher wants must *obviously* be *yes!*)
5. Your unfailing courtesy to the students is first rate. A teacher is frequently the only adult in the pupil's environment who treats him with respect. Instead of penalizing suspended boy who came in late, with toothpick in mouth, you made him feel the class had missed his contribution to it. That's first rate! (He should, however, have been made to remove the toothpick.)
6. "Note the simplicity of Frost's language," you said. You might try the excellent device of pretending ignorance or surprise: "But I thought a

poem had to have fancy words!" or "But isn't an adverb supposed to end in *ly*?" or "But doesn't Mark Antony say *nice* things about Brutus?"

7. The boy next to me was doing his math. It is wise for the teacher to move about the room.

8. Immediate correction of English was effected. However, you missed:

   "He should of took the road . . ."

   "On this here road . . ."

   "He *coont* make up his mind."

9. Enthusiasm is contagious. I'm glad you're not ashamed to show you are moved by emotion or excited by an idea. Unexpected intrusion of outsiders (plumber, etc.) need not necessarily curb this enthusiasm.

10. The less a teacher talks the better the teacher. Don't feed them; elicit from them. Learning is a process of mutual discovery for teacher and pupil. Keep an open mind to their unexpected responses. Example: comment of boy doing math that man *has* no choice.

11. Don't allow the lesson to end on the wrong note. Example: your question "What kind of man was Frost?" elicited the answer: "The kind of man who likes to write poetry." Just then the bell rang and they were dismissed.

12. Your quick praise of pupil effort and your genuine interest in what they say are first rate! It's fine for the girls to emulate you and for the boys to try to please you. But there are certain hazards in looking *too* attractive.

There is no question in my mind but that you are a born teacher.

Samuel Bester

INTRASCHOOL COMMUNICATION

FROM: 304
TO: 508

Dear Bea—

We have met the enemy, and he is ours!

I knew I'd be observed today and was prepared. At least, I thought I was.

There is a heading: "Anticipation of Difficulties" in the model outline, but I had difficulties I hadn't anticipated.

A boy got hiccoughs and almost fell out of the window; there was a false emergency drill signal; McHabe came to make an announcement; and the plumber dropped in to hammer on the radiator.

Bester sat and scribbled away at the back of the room, while I tried to keep in mind simultaneously 39 kids, lesson-plan, room passes, boardwork, Frost, troublemakers, scraps of paper on the floor, correcting their English, and enlarging the scope of the lesson to include moral and ethical concepts.

I didn't have time to cover half of the things in my Plan Book, and I forgot Summary and Windows, but I did ask "pivotal questions," linking the poem to their own experiences. Bester says I'm a born teacher! Congratulate me!

Syl

* * *

INTRASCHOOL COMMUNICATION

FROM: 508
TO: 304

Dear Syl,

Of course you are. A born teacher, I mean.

Linking a lesson to their own experiences is fine if you can do it, but sometimes it's a strain. I recall a young teacher whose opening question on Wordsworth's poem to a class of tough city boys in a vocational high school was: "How many of you have seen a sea of daffodils lately?"

Naturally, congratulations!

Bea

◦　◦　◦

Dear Miss Barrett,

I'll be absent tomorrow due to sickness so please let some one else read these minutes I took on today's lesson.

It was a most interesting and educational English period. Miss Barrett collected money for the *Scholastics* and any one who doesn't bring it tomorrow won't get it. Miss Barrett read some notices about the G.O. and Mr. McHabe came in to speak about no sneakers on cafeteria tables. Miss Barrett sent Roy out of the room for spitting out of the window to cure hiccups and thought us a beautiful poem by Mr. Robert Frost. The title was called "The Road Not Taken". Dr. Bester visited us. He sat next to Fred.

We discussed our different turning points in life. Vivian's turning point was college or work after graduation? This was not a good example because she is only a soph. Linda's turning point was about which dress to wear Sat. night. Eddie's turning point was when he went to the cellar and got hit on the head. Lou had no turning point.

The poet tries to say that because he took the road this made a lot of difference. He tells about yellow wood. He decides to take a walk and takes a wrong turning point and gets lost and sighs. The moral is we can't walk on two roads at the same time. Some people in class disagreed.

The poet (Mr. Frost) teaches us about life and other things. He was simple. He was economical and died recently. He blazed a trial on a new road.

Miss Barrett passed around his picture but it got only to the first row because some wise guy hogged it and wouldn't pass it. Multim im parva means he says very little. Trodden means walk.

His style was very good. He had his eye on things.

In my last term's English class we had to put poems under different Headings like Poems of Love and Friendship, or Nature and God's Creatures, or Religion and Death, and say where they belong to, but I'm not sure where this one belongs to.

Respectfully submitted,
Janet Amdur, Class Secretary

30 The Author Tries to Say

Fri., Nov. 6

Dear Ellen,

I rejoice with you at the departure of the painters. What do you mean, it came out buff?

You're right; I *am* attracted to Paul. He's very attractive. But the surface is so highly polished, it's hard to get hold of it. One slips off. Our relationship is surface too: an occasional drink together, a dinner, a movie in my "spare time, Ha-ha!"—as one of my kids would say. I smile at his amusing verses and I listen to his amused complaints about editors and school and fate. He's a kind of charming Minniver Cheevy—without the bathos. I'd like to like him more.

As for your questions: Yes, Linda Rosen is back, presumably cured. So is Joe Ferone, presumably not. He has changed his mind about seeing me after school. "What's in it for you?" he asks.

The day he returned to class, with a Late-Late pass from McHabe, who detained him for coming late (do you follow me?) I was observed by Bester. I taught a poem. Or did I? I don't think I got through to them, in spite of all my careful paper-plans, in spite of all of Bester's paper-words.

The trouble is their utter lack of background. "I never read a book in my life, and I ain't starting now," a boy informed me. It isn't easy to make them *like* a book—other teachers got there before me. Henrietta with her games in teams, Mary with her outlines. Or perhaps it goes further back, to the 1st grade, or the 5th?

190

The important thing is to make them feel King Lear's anguish, not a True-or-False test on Shakespeare. The important thing is the recognition and response, not an inch of print to be memorized.

I want to point the way to something that should forever lure them, when the TV set is broken and the movie is over and the school bell has rung for the last time.

But what a book report means to them is: to tell an interesting fact about the author ("Poe was a junkie"); to complete: "This book made me wish/ wonder/ realize/ decide"; to recount one humorous/ tragic incident; or to engage in hokum projects such as designing book jackets, drawing stick figures, holding TV interviews with dead authors or imaginary characters, playing "Who Am I?," and pepping up the classics. In other words, saving the others the trouble of reading the book.

Sample:

LOU: My book is——
I: The book you read.
LOU: Yeah. The title is called *Macbeth* by Shakespeare.
I: Its title *is*.
LOU: *Macbeth.*
I: But wasn't it required reading for last term's English? I understand *Macbeth* was taught in English 2 last term. You were supposed to report on a supplementary book. That means, in addition to the required——
LOU: I ain't never read it before.
I: I've never read it.
LOU: Me neither. In this book the author depicks—
I: Depicts.
LOU: Depicks how this guy he wants to——
I: Who?
LOU: Him.
I: He.
LOU: Yeah. He potrays that this here——
I: He *says*.

LOU: Mrs. Lewis told us not to say say. She gave us a whole list like depicks and potrays instead.

I: Yes, Harry?

HARRY: Observes.

I: I beg your pardon?

HARRY: Remarks. Narrates. Exclaims. I've got it written down.

I: She probably wanted you to avoid repetition. There's nothing wrong with the word "says." What's the theme of the play, Lou?

LOU: Well, the author narrates this murder——

I: No, the theme, not the plot. Does anyone know the difference between theme and plot? Linda?

LINDA: The plot is what they do in the book and the theme is how they do it.

I: Not exactly. The theme——Yes, Vivian?

VIVIAN: The theme is what's behind it.

I: Behind what?

VIVIAN: The plot.

I: Frank?

FRANK: The lesson.

I: What lesson? Please answer in complete sentences.

FRANK: That the author is trying to teach. The morale of the book.

I: The moral. It need not——Yes, John?

JOHN: He's supposed to mention three incidents.

I: But we're talking about the——Harry?

HARRY: Personal opinion.

I: What?

HARRY: He didn't give his personal opinion.

LOU: I didn't even get to it.

I: We're still trying to determine the difference between plot and theme. Sally?

SALLY: One is real and one is made up.

I: Well, actually—Yes, Carole, what is it?

CAROLE: Oh, thank God! I thought you'd never call on me! The author tries to say——

I:	Tries? Doesn't he succeed?
CAROLE:	He tries to show——
I:	He shows.
CAROLE:	He shows how you mustn't be ambitious.
LOU:	Potrays.
I:	Does he say that ambition is bad?
CAROLE:	Yes.
I:	*Is* it? Isn't it good to be ambitious? Lou?
LOU:	It's good, but not too.
I:	Not too what?
LOU:	Not too ambitious is not so good.
I:	You mean, excessive ambition can lead to disaster?
LOU:	That's right.
I:	Why don't you say it? The theme of *Macbeth* is that excessive—or rather, ruthless ambition often proves disastrous. That's what words are for—to be used. What does ruthless mean? Eddie?
EDDIE:	Steps all over.
I:	Say it in a sentence.
EDDIE:	He steps all over.
I:	Rusty, you wanted to say something?
RUSTY:	Mrs. Macbeth noodges him.
I:	You mean nudges?
RUSTY:	Noodges. Being a female, she spurns him on.
I:	Yes, John, your hand is up?
JOHN:	I read the same book, but my theme is different.
I:	What is it?
JOHN:	The theme is he kills him for his own good.

Never mind. I may be reaching too high, I may stumble and fall, but I'll keep on trying!

Love,
Syl

P.S. Did you know that at the College Entrance Examination Board's Commission on English it was found that a third of high school English teachers were unfit to teach their subject?

S.

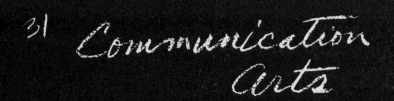

31

Communication Arts

FROM: CENTRAL CURRICULUM ADAPTATIONS COMMITTEE FOR APPRAISAL AND SELECTION OF INSTRUCTIONAL MATERIAL AND SPECIFIC DEVICES IN ORIENTATION AND MOTIVATION:

THE ORAL BOOK REPORT

FUNCTIONAL APPLICATION OF LANGUAGE SKILLS IN CONNECTION WITH A DEVELOPMENTAL PROGRAM OF READING MASTERY AND APPRECIATION, COMBINED WITH CONCURRENT TRAINING IN ORAL EXPRESSION CAN BEST BE ACHIEVED IN THE FORM OF THE ORAL BOOK REPORT INVOLVING ALL THE CONCOMITANT OBJECTIVES OF STIMULATING CONVERSATIONAL PARTICIPATION ON LEVELS OF SHARING OF INTELLECTUAL AND EMOTIONAL EXPERIENCES, WHICH IS THE CULMINATION OF THE COMMUNICATIONS ARTS.

PART. VII

32

Over the Time Clock

THE FOLLOWING TEACHERS ARE TO BE COMMENDED ON ACHIEVING 100% ATTENDANCE YESTERDAY:
None

THERE WILL BE A FIRE DRILL AT THE END OF THE FOURTH PERIOD TODAY; PLEASE DO NOT GIVE ANY TESTS.

CIRCULARS ON OPEN SCHOOL DAY HAVE BEEN PLACED IN YOUR LETTER-BOXES. PLEASE READ THEM CAREFULLY AND FOLLOW INSTRUCTIONS.

LOST & FOUND

LOST: Man's black umbrella, wooden handle—
      Ret. to M. Manheim
LOST: One galosha, black—
      Ret. to M. Manheim

LOST: Paperback book: "How To Stop Smoking in
        24 Hours."
        Ret. to F. Egan, Health Office

FOUND: Blue ball-point pen—doesn't write—
         Inq. office

TEACHERS WHO LINE UP IN FRONT OF THE TIME CLOCK
WAITING TO PUNCH OUT IN THE AFTERNOON CREATE
A CROWDED CONDITION IN THE DOORWAY. PLEASE WAIT
UNTIL DISMISSAL BELL RINGS BEFORE COMING DOWN.

                                              JJ McH

PLEASE DO NOT TAMPER WITH HAND ON THIS TIME
CLOCK.

THE OFFICE TELEPHONE IS NOT TO BE USED FOR PER-
SONAL CALLS. PLEASE USE THE PAY-TELEPHONE IN THE
BASEMENT.

TEACHERS' INTEREST COMMITTEE MEETING TODAY
DURING LUNCH PERIOD IN ROOM 404. PLEASE COME
PROMPTLY WITH YOUR LUNCH: LAST MONTH NO ONE
SHOWED UP!

PERSONALS

Mr. Draper lost his father; funeral tomorrow. We express our regret.

Mrs. Jane Tessler, on Maternity Leave, had a baby girl,
weight 6½ lbs. She is at Rhodes Hospital.

Zena Hall, graduate of Calvin Coolidge, is currently appearing in the chorus of the new musical revue, "Once
in Love."

Miss Sarah Daniels, who retired from school last year,
is eager to hear from members of the faculty. Her address: Midtown Hotel, Room 611

33

TO: PARENTS OF OUR STUDENTS

YOU ARE CORDIALLY INVITED TO VISIT OUR SCHOOL ON OPEN SCHOOL DAY, THURSDAY, NOVEMBER 12, FROM 1-3 P.M. AND FROM 7-9 P.M.

FOR YOUR CONVENIENCE, YOUR SON/DAUGHTER HAS PREPARED A COPY OF HIS/HER PROGRAM, GIVING THE NAME OF EACH OF HIS/HER TEACHERS AND THE ROOM WHERE THE TEACHER MAY BE FOUND. IF YOU ARE UNABLE TO VISIT THE SCHOOL, PLEASE ADDRESS YOUR QUESTIONS CONCERNING YOUR SON/ DAUGHTER TO THE TEACHER, ON THE ENCLOSED POSTAL CARD.

JAMES J. McHABE
Administrative Assistant

* * *

TO ALL PARENTS:

I AM CERTAIN AND CONFIDENT THAT YOU WILL WELCOME THE GOLDEN OPPORTUNITY FOR CLOSER COMMUNICATION AND RAPPORT BETWEEN THE SCHOOL AND THE HOME ON OPEN SCHOOL DAY. WE MUST ALL PITCH IN AND COOPERATE IN MAKING THIS A COMPLETE AND UNQUALIFIED SUCCESS, FOR ONLY THROUGH MUTUAL UN-

199

DERSTANDING BETWEEN PARENT AND TEACHER CAN
THEIR MUTUAL AIMS AND GOALS FOR THE HIGHEST
GOOD OF THE CHILD BE ACHIEVED.

MAXWELL E. CLARKE
PRINCIPAL

*   *   *

TO ALL TEACHERS:

I AM CERTAIN AND CONFIDENT THAT YOU WILL WEL-
COME THE GOLDEN OPPORTUNITY FOR CLOSER COMMU-
NICATION AND RAPPORT BETWEEN THE SCHOOL AND THE
HOME ON OPEN SCHOOL DAY. WE MUST ALL PITCH IN
AND COOPERATE IN MAKING THIS A COMPLETE AND UN-
QUALIFIED SUCCESS, FOR ONLY THROUGH MUTUAL UN-
DERSTANDING BETWEEN PARENT AND TEACHER CAN
THEIR MUTUAL AIMS AND GOALS FOR THE HIGHEST
GOOD OF THE CHILD BE ACHIEVED.

MAXWELL E. CLARKE
PRINCIPAL

*   *   *

FROM: JAMES J. MCHABE, ADM. ASST.
TO: ALL TEACHERS

BEFORE PARENTS ARRIVE, PLEASE MAKE SURE OF THE
FOLLOWING AND CHECK OFF EACH ITEM:

MATERIAL PLACED ON TEACHER'S DESK AS EVIDENCE
OF TEACHER ACTIVITY (BOOKS, ETC)
MATERIAL PLACED ON BULLETIN BOARD AS EVIDENCE
OF PUPIL ACTIVITY (100% TESTS, ETC)

ROOM DECORATIONS (UP)
WARDROBES (EMPTY)
FLOORS (CLEAN)
WINDOWS (OPEN OR CLOSED, ACCORDING TO WEATHER)
CHAIRS (IN EVEN ROWS)

IN ORDER TO SEE AS MANY PARENTS AS POSSIBLE, TEACH-
ERS WILL ALLOT NO MORE THAN 5 MINUTES TO EACH.
A LIST OF THE NUMBER OF PARENTS VISITING EACH

TEACHER WILL BE KEPT IN THE OFFICE: THE TEACHER WHO SEES THE LARGEST NUMBER OF PARENTS IS TO BE COMMENDED.

THE TEACHER REFLECTS THE SCHOOL.

JJ McH

* * *

TO: ALL TEACHERS OF ENGLISH

VISITING PARENTS SHOULD BE IMPRESSED WITH THE IMPORTANCE OF ENGLISH AS A COMMUNICATIONS ART.

EXHIBIT OF PUPILS' COMPOSITIONS, MARKED WITH TEACHER'S COMMENTS, IS SUGGESTED, AS WELL AS BLACKBOARD OUTLINE OF MEANINGFUL LESSON.

THE TEACHER REFLECTS THE DEPARTMENT.

SAMUEL BESTER,
CHAIRMAN, LANGUAGE ARTS DEPT.

* * *

TO: ALL TEACHERS

PLEASE REMIND THE PARENTS YOU INTERVIEW OF THE RELATIONSHIP BETWEEN NUTRITION AND ACADEMIC WORK.

FRANCES EGAN
SCHOOL NURSE

* * *

INTRASCHOOL COMMUNICATION

FROM: H. Pastorfield
TO: S. Barrett, 304

Dear Sylvia,

Can you let me have a few of your kids' compositions for my bulletin board? I haven't had time to assign any yet—Thanks loads!

Henrietta

INTRASCHOOL COMMUNICATION

FROM: 508
TO: 304

Dear Syl–

If you get into any difficulty, send me an S.O.S. You'll meet all kinds of parents. But the ones who *should* come, don't.

                                                    Bea

       * * *

INTRASCHOOL COMMUNICATION

FROM: M. Lewis, 302
TO: S. Barrett, 304

Dear Sylvia,

Do you happen to have a basin and a sponge? A rag will do. My clean-up monitor didn't show up and I have to do it all myself!

                                                    Mary

       * * *

INTRASCHOOL COMMUNICATION

FROM: P. Barringer, 309
TO: S. Barrett, 304

Sylvia!

If any parents do show up, try to get rid of them fast, and meet me at the usual place——

                                                    Paul

POST CARDS

Dear Miss Barett, I am the mother of Edward Williams but I can't come I've got my hands full his father is put away he's mental and it's very hard without more trouble from school. There's a lot of work for him to help out at home so can you let him out earlier?

                                        Mrs. G. Williams

Dear Miss Barrett,
My daughter Vivian wanted me to come but I have my
Monthly Social. You're her favorite subject. She tries to
copy you tho what good will it do the way she looks.
My other daughter is a completely different type. Please
don't let her eat so much sweets, it breaks out on her
skin and she gains and looks terrible. I keep telling her
but it just goes down the drain.

Sincerely yours,
Elsie Paine

*   *   *

Does the Board of Education know you let our children
read filthy books on the outside like Catcher in the
Rye? You should teach the Bible instead, but they outlawed it.

*   *   *

Dear Miss Barret,
   It's not my son's (Lou) fault he failed spelling, he
comes from a broken home. When he gets bad marks
it only discourages him more and he starts cutting up.
He's getting too big for the other kids in his class, so
all the teachers said they'll pass him on. After all, it's
only spelling.

Mrs. Bess Martin

*   *   *

My question is who is Linda running around with after
school? When I ask she snaps my head off, but I know
she runs around. Her father more or less beats her but
she still runs around. Her two sisters went bad too after
I sacrificed for them, so I'm worried. Can you do something?

Mrs. Lucile Rosen

Dear Miss Barrett,
   Alice didn't want me to come. I hoped to see your
face to make me feel better. I don't know why she's so
moody. I don't know how I failed her.

                                   Mrs. Marian Blake

* * *

My dear Miss Barret,
   There was no time to interview you because I was
interviewing other teachers. It would have been a
pleasure to make the acquaintance of such a lovely
teacher like you. Harry A. Kagan, my son, always talks
about you very well. I hope you continue to guide him
in his career.

                                   Very truly yours,
                                   Alberta Kagan

* * *

Miss B–
I see by my son's work school hasn't changed. I used
to hate it too but I know they need an education. I
don't understand why Charles got only 68 so far. He
needs at least an 85 average to get into the college
of my choice, even though he thinks he doesn't want
to go. As a tax payer, please look into it.

                                   Roger Robbins

* * *

Dear Miss Barnet, Thank you for the invite but I can't
come to visit you and talk about my son Jose being that
I'm on the night shift at the factory besides my day job.
His mother can't come neither being dead. I hope you
excuse it.

                                   Truly yours
                                   Raymond Rodriguez

34

You're the Teacher

Dear Ellen,

Just got home from Open School session—and I *must* talk to someone!

It was a fiasco, though I did everything I was told to do. I got fresh book jackets from the library to festoon the walls with and had my wardrobe cleaned out. (Why is it only *one* sneaker is always left on the closet floor? And the ubiquitous, tattered notebook? I found one belonging to one of my homeroom girls, Alice Blake, full of scribbles, doodles, and chaos.) I even made sure that the little flag stuck in the radiator, which we salute each morning before singing the Calvin Coolidge Alma Mater ("Ye loyal sons and daughters" —a substitute for the unlawful hymns), was tilted at the correct angle. (The other day Admiral Ass found it drooping disrespectfully.)

I see 243 kids daily: 201 in English (after dropouts and new registers) and 42 in homeroom—but only a few parents showed up; a few wrote cards; and the rest ignored the whole thing. The ones I had particularly hoped to see never came.

I don't know why they hold Open School so soon after the beginning of the term, before we've had time to get to know

all our students. The Delaney Book wasn't much help to me;
it showed days absent, times late, and some checks, crosses
and zeros—I'd forgotten for what. Unprepared homework?
An insolent whistle? A four-letter word?

One father came, in work overalls, hands patiently clasped
on the desk, out of some dim memory of his own school days.
The mothers—patient, used to waiting, careworn, timid, bewildered or just curious—sat clutching their pocketbooks,
waiting to plead, appease, complain or hear a kind word.
A few were hostile and belligerent; they had come to avenge
themselves on their own teachers of long ago, or demand
special privileges, or ask the teacher to do the job they had
failed to do.

And I—who was I to tell these grown-ups anything about
their children? What did I know? A few clichés from the
mimeographed directives: "Works to capacity, doesn't work
to capacity, fine boy, fine girl." A few euphemisms: "Seems
to enjoy school" (the guffawer); "Is quite active" (the window-smasher) . . .

For a moment, the notion occurred to me to try to match
the parent to the child; but they were strangers, looking at
me with opaque eyes.

MOTHER: How's my boy doing?
I: What's his name?
MOTHER: Jim
I: Jim what?
MOTHER: Stobart
I: Oh, yes. (Now, which one was he?) Well,
let's see now. (Open the Delaney Book with
an air of authority: a quick glance—no help.
Stobart? Was he the boy who kept drumming with a pencil on his desk? Or the short,
rosy one who reclined in his tilted chair
combing his hair all the time? Or the one
who never removed his jacket? I couldn't
find his Delaney card; perhaps his mother
would give me a clue.)

MOTHER: About that F you gave him.

I: Oh, yes. Well, he's obviously not working to capacity. (He must be the boy who got an F on his composition, on which he had written only one sentence: "I was too absent to do it".) He must work harder.

MOTHER: Pass him, and he won't do it again.

I: I'm afraid that's no solution. He simply isn't using his potential.

MOTHER: You mean he's dumb?

I: Oh, no!

MOTHER: He's afraid to open his mouth. Smack him, just smack him one.

I: He should volunteer more.

MOTHER: I tried my best. (Helplessness, shame in her voice—and were there tears in her eyes?) Do me a favor—pass him.

I: Why do you think he is doing so poorly?

MOTHER: *You're* the teacher!

I: He seems to be just coasting along.

MOTHER: He can't help it, he was born premature. He won't do it again.

I: Well, it's a good thing that we are both concerned; perhaps, with more encouragement at home? Can his father——

MOTHER: That son of a bitch bastard I hope he rots in hell I haven't seen him in six years (said in the same apologetic, soft pleading tone).

I: Well (five minutes are up, by my watch), it's been a pleasure to meet you. (But she doesn't go.) Is there something else?

MOTHER: (Those weren't tears; anger is filming her eyes.) What does it cost you to pass him? No skin off your hide!

I: I'm afraid his work doesn't warrant——

MOTHER: Do me a favor, at least keep him in after school. I can't take it no more.

I:	I'm afraid that's impossible; you see——
MOTHER:	But you're the *teacher!* He'll listen to a *teacher!*
I:	We can both try to make him work harder, but he has so many absences——
MOTHER:	Maybe if you made Physics more understandable to him he would come more.
I:	Physics? I teach English!
MOTHER:	How come?
I:	What room were you supposed to be in?
MOTHER:	306. Mrs. Manheim.
I:	I'm afraid there's been a misunderstanding. *Mr.* Manheim is the man you want to see. I'm Miss Barrett, Room 304.
MOTHER:	Well, why didn't you say so?

Still, I learned a few things. I learned that the reason a student failed to bring his father's signature is that the father is in jail; that the Federal Lunch the kids are always griping about is often the only meal they have; that the boy who falls asleep in class works all night in a garage in order to buy a sports car; that the girl who had neglected to do her homework had no place to do it in.

I have a long way to go.

In the meantime, write, write soon. You too bring me a glimpse of "real life." One can get as ingrown as a toenail here.

Love,
Syl

P. S. Did you know that due to the "high mobility" of families unable to pay rent, some schools have a turnover of 100% between September and June?

S

NOVEMBER 13

TO: ALL TEACHERS

YOU ARE TO BE CONGRATULATED AND COMMENDED ON THE COMPLETE AND UNQUALIFIED SUCCESS OF OPEN SCHOOL YESTERDAY. IT IS THROUGH PARENT-TEACHER CONFERENCES SUCH AS THESE THAT CLOSER COMMUNICATION BETWEEN THE SCHOOL AND THE HOME CAN BE EFFECTUATED AND ACHIEVED.

MAXWELL E. CLARKE,
PRINCIPAL

55

Please Do not Erase

Miss Lewis' Class

Whom did you see yesterday?
    ↳ object

John | did see | whom
              | yesterday
John - subject   ↳ adverb
he who
him - whom

Assignment for Monday:
Write a three paragraph composition
on one of the following topics. Under
line each subject once and each
object twice.

What It Means To Be An American
Sewage Disposal
Autumn Sunsets
Do No,   This Atomic Age
ERASE!!! The Family Garden

Miss Barrett's classes:

Do not ERASE !!!!

Miss B— I'm here so don't count me absent.
The reason I'm not here is
because I'm in the office.

Carole

DO NOT ERASE !!!!

Suggested Supplementary Reading Lists
are on my desk. PLEASE TAKE ONE
before leaving.

Doodlebug

Write a brief statement on
how you personally feel about
the problem of integration
in the schools.

DO NOT ERASE !

Integration

Although I personally am white and therefore out of this, I believe in integration. I think we should go along with the times and be more tolerant of other races. They have just as much right to be human. After all, they are voters too. The G.O. of which I am President of, is proud to live in a democracy.

Harry A. Kagan
(The Students Choice)

---

1. How stuppid can you get?
   A. Bussing kids to school miles away.
      1. Just to juggle it around.
      2. Then go back to the filthy slums.
         (After school)
2. Can't be juggle like diferent color marbles.
3. It takes time.
   A. Lincoln. (Slaves)
   B. Rome.
      (Wasn't build in a day)

Teenager

I'm proud to be of African decent but I can't stand the Portoricans.

Anonimus

Good morning, all of a sudden they woke up! It's about time! But they're doing it from the wrong end! Well, well, it's all in fun anyways and gives kids a chance not to do any work. They should give Boycotes every day to stay away from school! (Ha-ha, joke!)

Lou Martin

I think what they're afraid of is if we sit close to one another in school we'll intermarry and what about the color of the children. But that's dumb because it's all personal magnotism.

Linda Rosen

What's the good of it, there still prejudice on the outside, it's in the cards. At lease in my old school it was close to where I live so I could catch up on some extra sleep but got nothing out of it.

Edward Williams, Esq.

A lot of feeling is flying around loose and they've got to pin it down. It just let's off steam.

Doodlebug

This school is about 65–35 in favor whites but if the score was 50–50 and with more colored teachers then maybe it would tip the scale the other way, but if it gets to 35–65 in favor us then we got to start all over again to get it back on a even kiel.

Mr. X

We had a knifing on this subject on our block. It only makes us lose respect for school more and brings out more fuly words like nigger kike and spick which are not a good vocabullary.

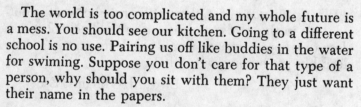

The world is too complicated and my whole future is a mess. You should see our kitchen. Going to a different school is no use. Pairing us off like buddies in the water for swiming. Suppose you don't care for that type of a person, why should you sit with them? They just want their name in the papers.

Stander

Why are there no Puerto Rican teachers? Why is there no Puerto Rican President? (the G.O.) Or Principle? The answer is Integration!

An American Citizen

Non whites
Also have rights
But not with fights.

Poet

People are inborn with hate for certain people and you can't force people to be more tolerant by legal laws, only by wishes. This country is a melting Pot with many opportunities to win respect from the class.

Jose Rodriguez

With the "bomb" going up and our "morals" going down what's all the fusst?

Charles H. Robbins

I think all whites blacks and browns and yellows should get together and intergrate against the reds (Commies) and pinkos.

Dropout

The trouble starts with where we live and not where we go to school. I mean crumby tennements.

Frank Allen

G.D. (a Negro in our Home Room) was huging J.N. (a White on the stairs) and C.B. (a Porto Rican) with C.R. (a White). I don't mind but my parents are against it.

Guess Who

Intergration is a Big Joke, who they think they kidding? What about Jobs? As far as the Future, forget it!

                                                    Minority

God made us all alike inside. It's only the skin that counts. We can all try to look better in spite of obstickles. Some races are more thinner than others. That's where a teacher comes in, to make us feel equal by looking up to her. The above is my reason for being an English teacher.

                                                    Vivian Paine

---

It's not up to me, I have enough problems without it.

                                                    Rusty

I have this colored friend Betty well, I never thought about it one way or the other until one day I went over her house for the first time and her father opened the door and I was surprized to see he was colored. Because, to me I was so used to her she always looked normal.

                                                    Lazy Mary

---

Compared to the school I came from which was Unintergrated it's like night & day here. We have teachers here that really try to teach you whenever they can and books they give out we can take home with us. And the classes in different rooms to go to, all the comforts of home.

                                                    Transfer

If they just leave it up to kids it wouldn't even arise.
                                Carole (used to be Carmelita) Blanca

---

They should keep themselves to themselves. We don't need them. We have our own life to live. We did without them for a long time, why should we change now? They only cause trouble.
                                                A Negro Student

---

In Social Stud. we discuss it to death, I'm sick and tired of the whole thing. Last time I'm writting!

the Hawk

Personaly I got intergrated a long time ago by swaping homework with all the kids in my class.
                                                        Failing

---

Can you guess by my handwriting if I'm white or not?
                                                A Bashful Nobody

PART VIII

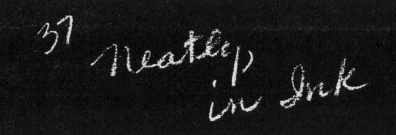

NOTE BOOK

Alice Blake   Calvin Coolidge High
Home Room Teacher: Home Room—304
 Miss Barrett

Keep *all* material in note-book. Write neatly, in ink.
1½ inch margins.

> "I'm a stranger and afraid
> In a world I never made"

How true, how true! How did the author know? . . . .

Correct the following for Fri.
  1. Rowing on the lake the moon was romantic.
Correction—While rowing on the lake the moon was
          romantic?
      Or—Rowing on the lake, the moon, was ro-
          mantic?
  2. Looking out of the window was a tree.
Correction—Looking out of the window a tree appeared
          in view.

3. I found a pencil loitering in the hall.
Correction—A pencil loitering in the hall was found by
      me.

Active vocabulary—Use three times to make the word
   yours.
Passive vocabulary—Don't use three times.

   Bring in own sentences illustr. vocab. words:
      enigmatic —She was very enigmatic.
      vindictive —She was very vindictive.
      vacillating—She was very vacillating.

Hand in tomorrow—History & Math
Look up and memorize dates & events leading up to war

Chapt. 14 Ans. quest. 1-10 back of book
May have test tomorrow. (*Be absent!*)

"April is the cruellest month mixing something and desire . . ."
Note to myself—Memorize all poetry lines Barringer
   reads.

   His voice . . . the way his eyebrow goes up . . .
      the hair on the back of his hands . . . it is too
      much . . . too much to bear . . .

Have Ma sign this—

PARENTS' CONSENT SLIP

I HEREBY GIVE MY SON,_____PERMISSION
              DAUGHTER,_____
TO PURCHASE TICKETS FOR _____. I UN-
DERSTAND THAT THIS PRODUCTION WAS INTENDED
PRIMARILY FOR ADULTS AND NOT FOR CHILDREN.

   SIGNATURE OF PARENT OR GUARDIAN:_____
   DATE:_____

Carole—Did you read Fanny Hill yet? Alice

I read Topic of Cancer, nothing to it. Carole

Let's see your Math. Alice

I didn't do it. I'm 4 days late and Frantick! Carole

Who you kidding? You're only a *virgin!* A.

That's what *you* think! Is this a long Home Room?
C.

I can't make out your handwriting . . . whisper instead of marking up my note-book. A.

Can't—Miss Barrett is looking this way! C.

She's alright. A.

I think you hate her. C.

You're nuts! A.

She likes Barringer. C.

You're nuts! A.

Do you think she's sexy? C.

She's not even married. A.

Don't be a dope! C.

She's cute looking. A.

You hate her. C.

You're nuts. I like the way she smiles . . . it's not put on. A.

You hate her anyway. Did you do ex. 9? What does X equal? C.

5.3 gallons. A.

How did you get it? C.

It's in the back of the book.   A.

Oh, my beloved . . . Only know me . . . Understand me . . . The first time I walked into 309 my heart told me it was fated to be . . . When you looked at me. . . . No one else in the World understands this feeling deep within me except you . . . my only love . . . If only . . . Last Sunday I took the subway to your

Carole—Do you like her dress? Miss Barrett's. The color.
                                                            Alice
It's sexy looking.   Carole

She uses too much make up.   A.

Only Lipstick. She likes Barringer.   C.

You're ruining my note-book. . . .   A.

You started it.   C.

Because we're sitting alphabetical . . . No one else is behind me.   A.

You must be a genius, you know Blanca comes after Blake!   C.

Whisper instead.   A.

Note to myself: Look up T. Elliot, a poet.
                         Look up word darkling.

Je veux tu veux il veut
nous voulons vous voulez ils

Assignments: Math—p. 51 ex. 3
                         p. 60 ex. 1, 7, 10
              French—Traduizes 2nd paragr. and review verbs for test (*Be absent!*)
              Physics—??? Manheim forgot to give assignment again!!!

(Put in my Diary about seeing Paul & Barrett in Coffee Shoppe & the anguish of it . . . Also how he held the door open for me and how his sleeve touched my arm . . . How to describe the ecstacy of it? . . . .)

Get—3 different note-books. In math he wants hard cover 6 by 4 .and with no lines and in pencil only. In Eng. must be loose-leaf 8 by 10 and French cahier she wants soft cover for verbs. In Soc. Studies—different color tabs.

"April is the cruellest month . . ." (Look up for myself & memorize)

$$A+ = 98\text{-}100 \text{ (Fat chance!)}$$
$$A = 94\text{-}97$$
$$A- = 90\text{-}93$$
$$D = 66\text{-}69$$
$$F = 0\text{-}65$$

When will the bell ring?   Carole

What's your hurry?   Alice

This Home Room is cruddy.   C.

You're nuts.   A.

This whole school is cruddy.   C.

The boys are cruddy. Especially Farone.   A.

He's crazy about Barrett.   C.

You're nuts. Don't scribble in my book.   A.

The books they make us read in school are cruddy!
Sale of Two Titties
Silly Ass Marner

Reminder: Open School Day Thurs. (Tell ma *not* to come!)

Did you ever think, like on a subway platform you see some one and maybe they're just the one for you but he's going the wrong way in the train? And you never meet?   Alice

Do you believe in Fate?   Carole

In Kismet I do.   A.

Me too.   C.

Conjugate
Ecrivez en francais
Look up & be prepared to discuss McCarran Bill

A̶l̶i̶c̶e̶ ̶B̶l̶a̶k̶e̶   —Marriage
P̶a̶u̶l̶ ̶B̶a̶r̶r̶i̶n̶g̶e̶r̶—Friendship

Love—Hate—Friendship—Marriage

Alice Blake—Marriage
Pauly Barringer—comes out Marriage too!!!

Mrs. Pauly Barringer. Alice Barringer
Mrs. Alice B. Barringer
Barringer, Alice

List of my Best Books:
    1. This is My Beloved
    2. Catcher in the Rye
    3. Love Poems of the Ages

4. Marriage Manuel
5. Zen

New moons, darks of the moon
Full moons—watch for full moon and write poetry!
My birthday—Taurus the Bull. Paul's birthday?
April birthstone—diamond. Flower—sweet pea.
May birthstone—emerald. Flower—lilly of the valley.

They're always interrupting when she talks to us. Are
you buying a ticket for the Thanksgiving Dance from
Kagan?   Alice

Who elected Harry Kagan anyhow? He's a pain in
the ass.   Carole

He's a fat pain in the ass. Are you going?   A.

He's a big fat pain in the ass. Frank is taking me. Are
you going?   C.

Every day you're ruining my note-book!   A.

You started it.   C.

$$\boxed{\text{ME}}$$

My height—5 ft. 2 in.
My weight—should be 110, is 112
Color hair—brownette
Color eyes—gray-blue or blue-gray
My name   My address   My telephone   My next of
kin   My school   My Home Room Teacher   My
blood type   My allergies   My favorite color   My
lucky number   My likes   My dislikes

Calories: Bacon 95 cal.
          hamburg 245
          baked pot. 145
          ice cream (vanilla) 200
          coke 80
          pizza—?

Note to myself—Improve posture. Look up <u>darkling</u>.

World's largest cities Tokyo   London   N.Y.
World's best dressed woman
World's best movie stars

Oh, my beloved, if you but knew . . . I am so near,
and yet so far . . . in this very room, a heart-throb
away . . . So ready . . . so ready for you & all you
stand for . . . Last Sunday I took the subway to your
stop (Your address is on the Time Card) and I walked
back & forth across the street from your house . . .
back and forth . . . just to see where you live. For a
moment I saw you in the window. . . . But perhaps
it wasn't even you. My heart was throbbing with love
and sadness . . . If I could die for you! . . . Like the
Lady of Shalot you read to us, floating dead on the river
under his window, and Lancelot never knowing . . .
never knowing . . . saying only "She has a lovely face,
the Lady of Shalot . . ."

I wonder if I'll ever dare to give you this letter . . .
for you to take into your hand . . . My *Real* Self in
your keeping . . . Maybe then you will look upon me
and know me . . . know me!!!! "Alice", you would
say—"lovely Alice, the first time you walked into Room
309 I felt it . . . It was meant to be . . ." Paul, my
beloved, I feel it too and my pulses are throbbing with
all that is inside me. Remember when you held the
door open for me and my elbow touched your suit?

Sometimes I feel I'm the only person in the World or
even the Universe . . . There's no one but I and I
want to jump up to the sky higher and higher and
throw my arms and yell like I'm crazy or maybe cry
and weep . . . I don't know what it is but I can't bear
it. "I am half sick of shadows, said the Lady of Shalot.
. . ." That morning when you were talking to Miss
Barrett in the Coffee Shoppe I wanted to die or kill her,
although she's a very nice teacher. In my bed at night

I pray to the ceiling, Dear Ceiling, make him love me or notice me in class where I sit . . . Make me worthy of him . . . Make him take me in his bold and throbbing embrace! . . . When I look at the cracks in the ceiling and how ugly everything is I think it's unreal, my house and my parents . . . Real life is someplace else . . . on moonlit terraces . . . in tropic gardens . . . foreign cities . . . darkling woods. . . . We are standing on a darkling hill together and your hungry lips seek

> Acetalyn in water plus what?
> Potassium
> Oxalic acid
> Boyles Law

> My Spelling Demons—
> Write in note-book three times, neatly in ink:
>> alright
>> alright
>> alright

Je me porte tres bien et vous?
Merci. Je aussi.

> Note to myself—Rewrite letter to Barringer on new pink stationary, use best handwriting and put in his letter-box. I *dare* me!

Tues. Assembly postponed to Wed. Music program. Listen courteously. No stamping of feet for applause.

> Quotation marks when talk to a person
> No quotation marks when talk to a thing (indirect)

Bring money for *Scholastic*. (Get from WHO?????????)

Carole—What did I miss yesterday?   Alice

Dr. God E. Clarke gave a speech. Same thing. And
Dr. Bastard observed us in English and we missed
half of Physics because of Shelter Drill. You didn't
miss a thing.   Carole

Guest Speaker on Vocations for Young People:
                    Archeology
                    Diatetics
                    Forestry
                    Law
                    Medicine
                    Millinery
                    Refrigeration
                    Religious Work
                    Teaching

Dearly Beloved . . . Last Sunday when I took the
subway to your stop, little did you know

Note to myself: don't forget skirt & shoemaker
                 Put letter in P.B.'s Box tomor-
                 row and *be absent!*

𝒜.ℬ.ℬ.

Alice Blake Barringer—A.B.B.
(A.B.—*same initials as before marriage!!!!*)

Carole—Did you do Totalitarian Countries?   Alice
    McHabe is a Dictator!   Carole
He's a crud.   A.
    Pastorfield is a crud. She's crazy about you know who!
                                              C.

But he's only a kid in her class!   A.

What the diff? She's *desparate!*   C.

I thought Bob was Linda's boy-friend.   A.

One of hers. She's crazy.   C.

She's alright.   A.

I think P.B. is crazy about S.B.   C.

You're nuts! And stop writing in my book!   A.

Dearest Beloved, My heart is throbbing with the loneliest

American Labor Party
Laissez-Faire Capitalism

If $X = \frac{2Y}{4}$ what does

Note to myself: Stop carrying it around and *Do It!!!*

Alice—What's the matter with you? Were you sick when you left the room?   Carole

I had to go down to the Letter Boxes & get something back.   Alice.

Did you?   C.   It was too late.   A.

Oh my God, dear God, what did I do! He's got my letter now . . . My soul lies naked in his hands . . . I'll die . . . I'll just die . . . .

Answer the following questions at the end of the chapter

Dear Mr. Barringer,

Last Sunday I took the subway to your stop having looked it up on your time card. I hope you don't mind the presumtion..... I walked back and forth across the street from your house. back and forth ... and I thought I saw you and my heart was throbbing with this love I bear for you.

I feel so deeply the Beauty and Truth of the poetry you read in class. I alone. especially such lines like "She has a lovely face, the Lady of Shalot......"

I think of you all the time .. at night, darkling, I pray to be worthy of you and all that you stand for...... I believe we understand each other and no one else ...... And if ever you need me to die for you I will gladly do so......

I hope you don't think me presumtious but I have to speak out the truth ..... the only truth ..

Sincerely yours,
Alice Blake

(marginal marks, left side: P, P, SP, cliché, omit, no caps, cliché, P, SP, word?, not clear, awkward construction, SP, P)
(marginal marks, right side: P, P, P, gr., P, P)

Alice—
Thank you for your note. Watch spelling and punctuation; you tend to use a series of dots to avoid it! Watch repetitions and clichés.
You might look up the spelling of the Lady in Tennyson's "Idylls of the King"—
P.B.

38

Unfortunate Incident

Dear Miss Barrett,

Thank you for everything .....
it's not your fault..... I wish
you all the happiness and
joy you ~~des~~ deserve.....
Some day they will
all know.... Be well
and take care of yourself.....
I hope I didn't inconvenience
you.

Alice Blake

233

INTRASCHOOL COMMUNICATION

FROM: H. Pastorfield, Room 307
TO: S. Barrett, Room 304

Dear Sylvia,
    Can you spare some chalk?
    What's all the commotion outside?

Henrietta

*   *   *

INTRASCHOOL COMMUNICATION

FROM: Mary Lewis, Main Office
TO: S. Barrett, Room 304

Sylvia—How awful! How perfectly awful! We've never
had anything like this since I've been here.
Where is Paul? His time card is punched in, but no one
can find him. How awful that it happened in his room!

Mary

(The office is Bedlam. Finch is in hysterics—never saw
her like this before!)

*   *   *

INTRASCHOOL COMMUNICATION

FROM: Marcus Manheim, Room 306
TO: Sylvia Barrett, Room 304

Dear Miss Barrett,
    They need me as a witness, although I didn't really
see it—I was just passing by 309. If you're not teaching,
can you cover my class for a few minutes while I sign
the papers and forms? Thank you.

S. *Manheim*

FROM: JAMES J. McHABE, ADM. ASST.
TO: ALL TEACHERS

ALL TEACHERS AND STUDENTS WILL PLEASE REMAIN IN
THEIR ROOMS, DISREGARDING THE BELLS, UNTIL THE
AMBULANCE ARRIVES.

JJ McH

* * *

Dear Miss Barrett,
    Please send down Health Card for Alice Blake—
Urgent!
    Do you have any blank Accident Reports? I'm all
out—Urgent!
    Do you know where Mr. Barringer is?—Urgent!

Frances Egan
School Nurse

* * *

INTRASCHOOL COMMUNICATION

FROM: 508
TO: 304

Dear Syl—
    It's ghastly, I know, but try to keep the kids busy.
    Can you reach Paul? It seems she left a letter for him
on his desk.

Bea

* * *

FROM: JAMES J. McHABE, ADM. ASST.
TO: ALL TEACHERS

AN UNFORTUNATE INCIDENT HAS OCCURRED. YOU ARE
REQUESTED NOT TO DISCUSS IT WITH ANY POLICE OFFI-
CERS IN THE BUILDING OR ANY OUTSIDERS. WE MUST
NOT ALLOW THE PUBLIC IMAGE OF OUR SCHOOL TO BE
DISTORTED UNDER STRESS.

JJ McH

Dear Miss Barrett,
    Please initial the entry: "Jumped or fell" over the red
line on the enclosed PRC for Blake, Alice.
    You will note that her CC's for the last 4 terms indi-
cate excellent adjustment:

                Term 1: Nice & helpful
                  "   2: Leadership potential
                  "   3: Reliable—blackboard monitor
                  "   4: Lovely girl—polité
It's most atypical for a girl with her stable PPP to
have done what she did, but there are factors beyond
our control.

                              Ella Friedenberg
                              Guidance Counselor

                    •   •   •

Dear Miss Barrett,
    Please fill out the enclosed Emergency Form:
    CHECK ONE: PARENT OR GUARDIAN
        REACHED
        NOT REACHED
                    BY TELEPHONE
                    BY TELEGRAM
    TO: PARENT OR GUARDIAN OF _____
    WE REGRET TO INFORM YOU THAT YOUR
        SON _____
        DAUGHTER _____

                    •   •   •

INTRASCHOOL COMMUNICATION
FROM: 508
TO: 304
Dear Syl—
    Anything I can do?
                                        Bea

FROM: James J. McHabe, Adm. Asst.
TO: all teachers

YOU ARE REQUESTED NOT TO OBSTRUCT ANY INFORMA-
TION THE POLICE WISH TO HAVE, PROVIDED YOU WERE
A DIRECT WITNESS TO THE OCCURRENCE, IN WHICH
CASE YOU ARE TO REPORT TO THE OFFICE AT ONCE.

JJ McH

❋ ❋ ❋

INTRASCHOOL COMMUNICATION

FROM: H. Pastorfield, Room 307
TO: S. Barrett, Room 304

Dear Sylvia,

What's the latest? Did Paul show up yet? I understand she left him a love letter! That's what happens
when sex drives are repressed. This whole business
should be aired out in the open!

Henrietta

❋ ❋ ❋

FROM: James J. McHabe, Adm. Asst.
TO: all teachers

THE NEXT TWO PERIODS WILL BE SHORTENED TO 38
MINUTES EACH, TO MAKE UP FOR THE LONG 1st PERIOD
DUE TO THE UNFORTUNATE INCIDENT.

TO PREVENT IRREGULARITIES IN THE FUTURE, TEACHERS
MUST REDOUBLE THEIR VIGILANCE AT ALL TIMES. NO
ROOM IS TO BE LEFT UNCOVERED AT ANY TIME, WHEN
NOT IN USE.

JJ McH

❋ ❋ ❋

Disregard bells.

Sadie Finch
School Clerk

TELEPHONE MESSAGE
FOR: Miss Barrett, 304

In answer to your call, Hospital called back to say
no change in condition.

* * *

Dear Miss Barrett,
    If you're free, can you relieve me in the Health Office
for a while? I must lie down someplace.

                                        Frances Egan
                                        School Nurse

* * *

INTRASCHOOL COMMUNICATION
FROM: Mary Lewis, Main Office
TO: S. Barrett, Room 304

Dear Sylvia—
    Paul just breezed in!

    Guess who's been punching him in every morning?
—Sadie Finch!

                                        Mary

* * *

Dear Miss Barrett,
    It has been a great shock to all of us, particularly to
those who, like you, knew the child. If you wish to be
excused from your classes, I shall be glad to take them
over.

                                        Sincerely,
                                        Samuel Bester

* * *

Sylvia!
    Just stepped into a hornet's nest.
    I am the villain of the melodrama.

Was I supposed to *encourage* a neurotic adolescent?

My real crime seems to be that I wasn't in my room the first period—even though I have no class. How could I know she would walk in and do it?

They tell me her fall was broken by the ledge below the window. Thank God for small mercies!

She left me a note full of dots and renunciation. It had to do with a love letter she had sent me, which I handled in the only way possible.

I can use a drink.

Meet me for lunch?

Paul

●　●　●

FROM: JAMES J. McHABE, ADM. ASST.
TO: ALL TEACHERS

LESSONS ARE TO PROCEED AS USUAL, WITH NO REFER-ENCE TO THE INCIDENT. TEACHERS ARE TO DISCOURAGE MORBID CURIOSITY ON THE PART OF THE STUDENTS.

JJ McH

●　●　●

Dear Miss Barrett, Is it OK if I start collecting money from the Home Room kids in my different subject classes to send flowers to Alice in the hospital? *If* she's OK. The thing is we always used to sit in front of each other.

Carole Blanca

39

Debits and Credits

Nov. 17

Dear Ellen,

So much has happened since the last time I wrote to you,
I don't know where to begin. Little Alice Blake threw herself out of a window, for the love of Lancelot. But instead
of floating, pale and lovely, past his window like the Lady of
Shalott (this was one of her fantasies I glimpsed when I
found her notebook), she is lying in splints and traction in
the hospital. She may need an operation on her hip bone,
her doctor tells me. She may limp for the rest of her life.
So far, she has refused to see anyone from school.

There has been a frantic spurt of directives.

McHabe advised us to keep our public image intact and
our students in their seats.

Bester reminded the English Dept. to open windows from
the top only. I said I would—except for my broken window,
which is broken from the bottom.

There has even been a circular from Clarke, addressed to:
Homeroom Teachers, Subject Teachers, Faculty Advisers,
Deans, Administrative Officers, Clerical Staff, Coaches and
Custodial Staff, urging us all to be aware of our responsi-
bility in a democracy.

Paul asks how *I* would have handled a love letter from
a student. I don't know—by talking, maybe, by listening.
I don't know.

How sad that we don't hear each other—any of us.

Major issues are submerged by minor ones; catastrophes by absurdities. There was a bit of a to-do about the school clerk who had been punching Paul's card in the time clock— a practice more honored in the breach. She, at least, proved her love in a practical manner. After a brief burst of unexpected emotion, she is spewing out mimeographs as impersonally as ever.

This was a week for erupting passions. Henrietta Pastorfield, hep spinster, good sport, pupils' pal, found her best student, Bob, in the deserted Book Room with Linda Rosen. She flew into a hysterical rage and had to be sent home. I don't know what she saw; apparently the kids had been "making out." What the exact boundaries of making out are I'm not sure. I'm not sure the kids are sure either. But it was enough to devastate poor Henrietta. "She can't even spell," she kept gasping between sobs. "He won the Essay Contest, and she can't even spell. . . ."

She hasn't been back since, and we have a young per diem substitute who had taught shoes in a vocational high school on her last job. Though her license is English, she had been called to the Shoe Department, where she traced the history of shoes from Cinderella and Puss in Boots through Galsworthy and modern advertising. "Best shoe lesson they ever had," she told me cheerfully. "Until a cop came in, dangling handcuffs: 'Lady, that kid I gotta have.'" To her, Calvin Coolidge is Paradise.

While Henrietta is recovering from her moment of truth and Alice is lying in the hospital, life goes on. We are now involved in preparations for the Midterm Exams and the Thanksgiving Dance.

But Alice's attempt to die was not in vain. Teachers are now more careful about punching in, and Paul has appointed a monitor to guard his room when he's not in it.

You ask about Ferone and Willowdale, in that order. I received a beautiful letter from the Department Chairman at Willowdale. He addressed me as if I were a lady and a scholar (hey, that's me!) and invited me to come for a personal interview in December.

And Ferone is still testing, testing me, with all the tricks of the trade. He pretends not to hear and keeps asking me to repeat. He drops books loudly, spends a long time picking them up, drops them again. He arrives late and stands gaping in the doorway. He answers me with false humility: "Yes'm, teach, you're the boss." He rocks on his heels, hands in pockets, the inevitable toothpick in his mouth.

"I got no homework."

"Why not?"

"I didn't do it."

"Why?"

"I just didn't."

"How do you expect to pass?"

"I'm supposed to accelerate at my own speed. I'm supposed to compete with myself. Well, I'm not so hot!"

Why do I bother? Because I feel something in him that is worth saving, and because once he wrote me: "I wish I could believe you."

Not that he's in class much; he keeps cutting to be with Grayson. I don't know what goes on down there. After the scandal about custodial misuse of funds, I look upon the whole Basement with a wary eye. There was, of course, a directive: STUDENTS ARE NOT TO USE STAIRCASE WHICH TERMINATES IN THE BASEMENT.

All staircases but one terminate in the basement.

But whenever I feel too frustrated to go on, I find an unexpected compensation: a girl whose face lights up when she enters the room; a boy who begins to make sense out of words on a printed page; or a class that groans in dismay when the end-of-period bell rings.

In order to remember the rewards when the going gets rough, I've made out a list of Debits and Credits:

DEBITS	CREDITS
Ferone (still unreached)	Jose Rodriguez no longer
Eddie Williams (" ")	signs "Me"!

Harry Kagan   (" ")

McHabe (!!!!!!)

Mild bladder symptoms (This is an occupational disease: there is simply no time to go to the bathroom!)

Clerical work piling up, up, *up!*

Nov. Faculty Conference: problems of overworked teachers, overcrowded classrooms, dropouts, integration, teachers' strikes, salary raises, teacher training, building scandals—were all "postponed for lack of time"—just as they were in Sept. and Oct.

Lunch hour at 10:17 A.M.

Not enough books, chalk, time to teach, endurance . . .

Etc., Etc., Etc.!

Vivian Paine losing weight; likes herself better.

Lou Martin, in the midst of clowning, raises a hand to answer a question!

Four kids took out public library cards for first time!!!

I may look forward to retirement after 35 years of service; at 70 it's mandatory!

Yes, Mother still sends me gory clippings. At the same time, she inquires delicately whether or not there is a young man in my life. I tell her there are many. Over a hundred.

I'm glad Suzie liked my birthday present. It's delicious to shop for a little girl of two. And please stop remonstrating —I may be a teacher, but I'm not *that* poor!

Tell me about your Thanksgiving. I was supposed to have dinner with Paul, but how can you wish on a turkey wishbone with a man who is capable of correcting a love letter?

Love,
                    Syl

P.S. Did you know that a third of all New York City teachers are substitutes?

                              S.

40

From the Suggestion Box

I suggest they do away with graff and coruption and make a school where we don't have to stand up in Assembly and Lunch! We should have a sit down strike but there's no place to sit, Ha-ha, joke!

Lou Martin

---

1. I like the way you "put it over" (Julius Ceazer)
2. Open School is a farse!
3. You didn't have to hush it up we knew all about it.
   A. Why she tried to kill her self!
      1. Misunderstandings of feelings between pupils and teachers.
      2. Misunderstandings of feelings between children and parents.

Teenager

You never call on me and if you do it's very seldom.

Cutter

Most fellows dislike their teacher not because the teacher is good or bad but just because the teacher is a teacher. You are different because you don't treat us like a teacher. Now coming down to the human side of things, you for one don't look like an old hag but beautiful every day. It slays me! Never in my life did I feel this in school. The way you walk up and down the isle really sends me and I hope you take it in the right spirit.

In these "distressful times" when any day the whole world can just as soon "blow up" I enjoy "poetry". The way your tone of voices make it sound in changing it to sadness or happiness or whatever it is suited for, depending on the "poem". I went to the school "librery" to look for more "Frost" but it was closed.

Chas. H. Robbins

If you could only be a man instead of a female I would say the only decent teachers in this school are you and Mr. Grayson and he's not even a teacher.

Rusty

I don't like the way you read, too emoting, and over our heads.

Yr Emeny

You gave me the courage to read a book.

                                                    Reader

When he said the fault dear Brutis is not in our stars meaning we got only ourselfs to blame he wasn't a color person.

                                        Edward Williams, Esq.

Don't ever change! There is a pleasing way in your manner of dressing (red suit) & shape. With you I could spend a whole day with nothing but English.

                                        A Bashful Nobody

For my money you stink.

                                                    Poisen

I never in my life used to have use for poems but when you read it aloud it makes the words come true. If every one would read it the way you do no one would be left hating poems. Can you recommend another poem?

                                            Jose Rodriguez

I have a math teacher for English and a typing teacher for Eco and you for Home Room and for French they keep changing around. I'm willing to do my best if they would only meet me ½ way.

                                        A True Pupil

Too much homework but I don't mind I don't do it anyway. And I'm possitively not writting any more for you.

the Hawk

What I like about you is you're brainy. In a nice way. I wish I could have you always but have to quit and go to work so must say a sincere goodbye.

                                        Dropout

If other teachers would be young and sexy looking like you they wouldn't have to snoop around and make trouble for couples that go steady. Snoopervisers make education hard to learn.

                                        Linda Rosen

Have Monday Orals on Tues. and Thurs. too. It pushes a lot of us out of our shyness when speaking in front of a crowd.

                                        Mark Anthony

I suggest more quiet classrooms because I like to sleep a lot.

Dead To The World

On Mondays what the hell do you think we are, Oraters?

Disgusted

Not enough men's rooms, a disgrace to mankind! A lavaratory centrally located would be a great comfort to all concerned.

Sophomore

Don't be so kind hearted because people take advantage. For instants, when I didn't do my homework and you gave me a break by letting me hand it in tomorrow, I felt I was a big shot and didn't have to do things til the last moment. Don't worry, I broke out of it very fast but with some one else it might have been bad for you. Well, don't take it so hard.

Mr. X

I am loosing weight rappidly just looking how slim you are in your red suit and others. You are much prettier than my sister. My goal is you.

Vivian Paine

(Did you notice how I wear my hair behind since you told me how you liked it?)

It is my considerable opinion that you are very well qualified. No matter how boring the lesson you always make it interesting. I suggest you continue your enjoyable and educational teachings.

> Harry A. Kagan
> (The Students Choice)

I'm not even in your class but hello anyway!

> Dr. Ben Casey

When you call on me to answer don't call on me when I don't know what the answer is, it makes me look dumb in front of the class. You always call on the others when they know what the answer is.

> Edward Williams, Esq.

I give the appearance of being mature but it's just the opposite.

> Doodlebug

I can honestly and truly say I disliked the book J. Ceaser by W. Shak. It has its good points but some how or another they didn't appeal to me. I suggest for J. Ceaser to have more humor to it, it's too sad.

> Disatisfied-with-Shak. Student

Miss P---ld and, Miss B--tt are in love with B-b and J-e
and Miss F---ch with Mr. B----er and Alice B. also, she
had his b-by, that's why.

                                                    Guess Who

---

You really made me get to the bottom of Julius Caesar.

                                                    Stander

We're behind you 95%. Don't worry.

How come Dr. Bester is so nice and different in class
than in his office, he's a good teacher but you'd never
know it looking at him?

                                                    Lazy Mary

---

They shouldn't allow bad morals in the Book Room.

                                                    Unsigned

You are the most understanding person I ever knew and
the best English teacher I ever had, and that includes
other subjects. This comes from the heart and not the
mouth.

                                                    Carole Blanca

---

Teachers are ruining America.

                                                    Zero

PART IX

41 Do You Plan to Indulge in a Turkey?

Sat., Nov. 21

Dear Ellen,

Yesterday was a day to remember. A day that ran a gamut. A day that provided what's known in Pedagese as "a spectrum of experiences." In the morning I found myself in the midst of a cafeteria riot which I had, somehow, instigated; in the evening I was dancing in the gym with the same boys who had been rioting a few hours earlier.

It began in my English class. Some of the kids had come to English straight from lunch, and I overheard them complaining about conditions in the school cafeteria. Since we were working on a letter-writing unit, I suggested that they compose a letter to the Board of Education, describing existing conditions and requesting better facilities. We had a preliminary discussion, and I realized that I had lifted the lid off long smoldering resentments: "We have to swallow lunch in 20 minute shifts . . ." "We have to eat standing up . . ." "Can't move . . . can't smoke . . . can't talk—only whisper". . ."Lousy food". . . ."They treat us like cattle . . ."

The next period—my unassigned—I passed through the Students' Cafeteria on my way to the Teachers' Lunchroom

253

next door for some coffee. The Aide assigned to the cafeteria
was not on duty. It was jammed with kids, half of them
standing; it was stuffy, noisy, messy with soiled trays on
wooden tables, paper bags, milk containers, coke bottles,
candy wrappers. Under a "No Talking" sign, leaning insolently against the wall, was Joe Ferone.

"You slumming?" he said.

"You could use some extra chairs," I said inanely.

"Plenty of chairs in the Teachers' Lunchroom," he said.
It was true. At that time of day, there were never more than
a few teachers there. "We're supposed to be as good as you?
Can we bring some of your chairs here?"

"Of course," I said. "Just be sure to return them at the end
of the period. Why don't you and a few of the boys——"

Before I could finish, there was a stampede to the Teachers' Lunchroom: boys shoving, pushing, shouting, dragging
chairs, waving chairs over their heads, fighting for seats,
yelling . . .

Suddenly—a shrill whistle: the Admiral himself.

"Silence! I want absolute silence!" He is furious. "There
is to be no talking here of any kind. Anyone opens his mouth,
you're in real trouble. I don't want to hear a *word* out of
you!"

They obey. All talking stops. Not a word is spoken. Then,
slowly, methodically, in ominous and terrible wordlessness,
they all rise, as if at a signal, and begin smashing dishes,
breaking bottles, throwing books, trays, papers on the floor,
flinging food against the walls; still silent, they march around
the room, weaving in and out and around the tables, a mob,
mute and inexorable; the only sound is the stamping of feet,
crunching of glass, breaking, cracking, splintering—punctu-
ated by McHabe's helpless whistle.

It was an extraordinary and terrifying sight. Who called
the cops, where they came from so quickly, I don't know—
but the moment they appeared, the mob turned into kids,
weaving back to their places in the same grim silence, and
waiting with vacant faces among the debris.

It was like something rehearsed, performed, and finished; so that when the bell rang, they left as if nothing out of the ordinary had happened.

"I'm afraid it was my fault, Mr. McHabe," I began.

"You're damn right it was your fault. I warned you. I told you what would happen if you run this school with ideas. You didn't believe me. Maybe now you will."

Then notes, circulars, directives began to fly fast and furious: "punitive action . . ." "firm measures . . ." "name of each student who was in the lunchroom . . ." "disgraceful exhibition of . . ." "to forestall future incidents . . ." until the inevitable "It has come to my attention."

And all through this avalanche, Ferone's mocking eyes seemed to follow me.

I tried to find out why conditions in the cafeteria could not be improved; the kids' complaints were certainly justified. Or why couldn't they eat out? Back to my source I went: the kids themselves. I'm enclosing some of their answers:

One term they alloud us in the lunchenette across the street and the drug store on the corner. But we were too much of a public nuisense and caused a disturbance to the peace of the other eaters. So they disalloud it.

If we get in an accident during school hours it's illegal. Supposing a car hits us while going to lunch? Last year the school got sued because this boy was sent with a pass from a teacher to buy her some aspirin & got runned over. Now we all must suffer for it.

It's expensive to eat out of school. Still, they should let us. After all we're human too.

So what if we knock a salt seller over or spill something by pushing each other or have a loud conversation
in a restarant? Does that make us Juvenile Delinquents
or sex manics?

Excuses and excuses and reasons and reasons is all
they give us but I don't buy it.

They tried to add on 10 extra minutes for each eating
shift to make it a real ½ hr lunch, but these minutes
they had to cut out off other periods and the teachers
said they couldn't afford to lose the 2 minutes off teaching time especially in Home Room.

One idea was brought out that when we brought
lunch from home to have us eat it in the auditorium.
But if we wanted to conclude our meal by bying milk
or ice cream we couldn't do it. Also the auditorium
usually shouldn't be as messy as a cafeteria. They would
have to get an extra teacher to watch that we didn't
get too messy.

What's the use of finding more chairs to eat when
there aren't enough tables?

I'm beginning to see some of the problems McHabe has
to face.
As a disciplinary measure, he wanted to call off the
Thanksgiving Dance scheduled that evening in the gym, but
the tickets had been bought, the school orchestra had been

rehearsed, the punch had been prepared, and he was made to see that punishing many for the misdeeds of a few was not only undemocratic, but was likely to lead to another "unwarranted outburst" on the part of the kids.

That afternoon I found on my desk a melting chocolate turkey and a card:

"A Happy Thanksgiving and many more
From the whole Room of 304."

And that evening, at the dance (I was one of the chaperones) I could hardly recognize in the scrubbed, combed, brushed, dressed up and oh, so polite kids the same ones who had left the cafeteria a shambles.

The gym was garlanded with festoons and balloons and crepe paper ribbons wound around basketball baskets and light fixtures. The parallel bars, the wooden horses, the mats were pushed against the walls; in one corner sat the school orchestra, each musician in a purple blazer with a gold CC on it, and a purple and gold satin CC draped around the drum; in another corner a table had been set up with a bowl of muddy punch, paper cups, and several packages of Lorna Doone cookies.

The other chaperones—Bea, cozy and beaming; Mary, harried by extra duties—were pouring the punch. Henrietta, who, I was told, had never missed a dance, was absent. So was Paul.

But it was the boys and girls who were a revelation to me. The boys especially, for many of the girls come to class with elaborate hairdos and makeup. It was the first time I had seen the boys dressed in suits, jackets, ties; shoes shined; faces stiff with decorum. Each had his name written on an orange paper pumpkin (left over from last year's Hallowe'en Dance) and pinned to his lapel; each said wih quiet solemnity:

"Good *evening*, Miss Barrett."

By far the most polite—and the shyest—was Lou Martin, the cut-up, the class comedian. He had approached to ask me for a dance, his body rigid and tilting slightly sideways with excess of politeness:

"May I please have the pleasure?"

He danced me off, holding me as if I were a soap-bubble, his hand barely touching my shoulder-blade. Perspired, committed, urging me with his face rather than his feet into a respectful two-step, he made gallant conversation:

"Do you plan to indulge in a turkey? . . . It's quite pleasant, the gym, the way they fixed it up. . . . Are you enjoying your teaching here? . . . You dance very excellently."

Ferone wasn't there, nor Eddie Williams, nor Vivian Paine; but Harry A. Kagan, the Students' Choice, was very much there, for the dance was sponsored by the G.O., of which he is president.

"These kind of affairs are rather childish, I think," he confided in me as he propelled me firmly around the gym, "but as long as it's for the G.O."

But when the kids danced with each other, they let go with wild gyrations, fast hops, twirls, pelvic twists, and rubber-kneed acrobatics. Lou Martin and Carole Blanca executed with abandon something known as "The Slop"; and Linda and Bob did an exhibition dance called, I think, "The Frug."

I loved them all last evening; especially Jose Rodriguez, who was not dancing, but who had paid his 75 cents for his ticket and had put on his best suit and had stood alone, waiting for an opportunity to speak to me. As he was about to leave, he took a deep breath, approached me, and said:

"I just want you to know how I feel about English. I think it's the greatest subject I ever had. I'm just— I just want you to know."

There are times when I wouldn't change places with anyone.

I'm exhausted—but have to save my strength for next week: Midterm Exams to take home and mark over the four-day Thanksgiving holiday.

A happy one to you—and many more—from Sylvia Barrett in 304.

Love,
Syl

P.S. Did you know that there are more school children in New York City than soldiers in the entire U.S. Army?

S.

42 I'm not Cheating, I'm Left-Handed

FROM: JAMES J. McHABE, ADM. ASST.
TO: ALL TEACHERS
RE: MIDTERM EXAMINATIONS

THE FACT THAT THANKSGIVING FALLS WHEN IT DOES THIS YEAR IS CAUSING DIFFICULTIES IN MIDTERM EXAMINATION SCHEDULES. SINCE THERE WILL BE NO FINAL EXAMS, MIDTERM MARKS WILL COUNT AS 2/3 OF THE FINAL MARK. IMPRESS UPON YOUR STUDENTS THE IMPORTANCE OF ACHIEVING AS HIGH A MARK AS POSSIBLE. VIGILANT PROCTORING DURING THE EXAMINATIONS IS ESSENTIAL TO PRECLUDE ANY TEMPTATION TO CHEAT.

PROCTORING INSTRUCTIONS:

1. ARRANGE SEATS IN EXAMINATION ROOM IN ALTERNATE ROWS, ONE SEAT DIRECTLY BEHIND THE OTHER. A SEAT NOT PROPERLY ALIGNED PRESENTS THE POSSIBILITY OF AN UNOBSTRUCTED VIEW OF ANOTHER'S PAPER.

2. STUDENTS ARE TO PLACE ON THE FLOOR IN FRONT OF THE ROOM ALL BOOKS, NOTEBOOKS, POCKETBOOKS AND PERSONAL POSSESSIONS.

3. PLACE EXAMINATION PAPERS FACE DOWN IN THE MIDDLE OF EACH DESK, AT RIGHT ANGLES TO THE BLANK ANSWER PAPERS, UNTIL THE BELL RINGS, AT WHICH TIME THE STUDENTS ARE TO TURN THEIR PAPERS OVER IN UNISON.

259

4. DO NOT ALLOW STUDENTS TO LEAVE THEIR SEATS FOR ANY REASON WHATSOEVER. THE PROCTOR IS TO APPROACH THEM AT THEIR SEATS TO DISTRIBUTE PAPERS AND TO ANSWER QUESTIONS.

5. NO QUESTIONS ARE TO BE ANSWERED BY THE PROCTOR.

6. IF A STUDENT DESIRES TO GO TO THE LAVATORY, THE PROCTOR WILL ESCORT THE STUDENT TO THE DOOR OF THE EXAMINATION ROOM AND SUMMON THE HALL PROCTOR, WHO WILL ESCORT THE STUDENT TO THE LAVATORY AND WILL REMAIN IN THE LAVATORY UNTIL THE STUDENT IS FINISHED. MALE TEACHERS WILL ESCORT BOYS, FEMALE TEACHERS WILL ESCORT GIRLS. THEN THE HALL PROCTOR WILL ESCORT THE STUDENT BACK TO THE DOOR OF THE EXAMINATION ROOM AND HAND HIM OVER TO THE ROOM PROCTOR.

7. PROCTORS ARE TO WATCH STUDENTS ACTIVELY THROUGHOUT THE EXAMINATION AND BE ON GUARD FOR THE FOLLOWING:
EYES ROVING
LIPS MOVING
LEFT ARM NOT COVERING PAPER
BENDING DOWN TO TIE SHOE LACE OR PICK UP FALLEN OBJECT
BLOWING NOSE, YAWNING OR SNEEZING TOO LOUDLY
REACHING INTO POCKET
CRUMPLING SCRATCH PAPER INTO A BALL
STRETCHING LEGS TOO FAR OUT
STUDYING NAILS OR INSIDES OF WRISTS

IMPRESS UPON STUDENTS THE IMPORTANCE OF HIGH ETHICAL STANDARDS: WHEN THEY CHEAT THEY CHEAT ONLY THEMSELVES. IF THEY ARE CAUGHT CHEATING, THE PROCTOR MUST BE BLAMED FOR LAX SUPERVISION.

INTRASCHOOL COMMUNICATION

FROM: Room 304
TO: Room 508

Dear Bea—

Just got Admiral's directive on Midterm proctoring
—with emphasis on marks and warnings against cheating. Cause and effect? I asked my kids to write down
how they feel about marks and exams; am eager to read
what they have to say. As for cheating, it seems to me
that—watched by hawk-eyed proctor—even if they had
no intention to cheat, they'd be tempted to outwit him.
Has anyone tried Honor System? I have a hunch that
if they felt they were trusted, they'd rise to that trust.

I have three room proctoring assignments. Thank God
I'm not a hall proctor!

What do I do if a kid is *not* covering with his left arm
a paper which is *not* at right angles to his desk?

                                                          Syl.

* * *

INTRASCHOOL COMMUNICATION

FROM: 508
TO: 304

Dear Syl,

You either kill the kid or yourself.

Honor System would never work here—too great a
premium on the Mighty Mark, which determines
whether or not a kid gets into college and causes parental pressures and senior breakdowns. This is true of
academic youngsters; non-academic ones cheat *pour le
sport*, as a matter of bravado, ingenuity or class status.
Not to try to cheat is square.

Trend is changing, though, from person-to-person
cheating to cooperative cheating and teamwork. Some
of the excuses they offer, when detected, are: altruism,

good sportsmanship, innocence: and "I'm not cheating, I'm left-handed!"

The kids put the burden on teacher: "What's the difference to you if you add another 10 points?" "Why did you fail me? I didn't do nothing!" The reply, of course, is: "That's just it."

I'd like to know if you get any insights from their own comments on marks. You're a brave girl; we who are about to die salute you!

Bea

As far as marks, you can either better yourself or become lower. Marks can be fair or unfair depending on
how the student answers questions from the teacher
and whether or not the teacher asks the questions a
student can answer.

> Harry A. Kagan
> (The Students Choice)

The passing mark should be "50" and not "65." Personaly I don't care but I worry about my "parents".

> Chas. H. Robbins

---

1. On the pro side marks are good to the teacher. In
   showing how much the pupil listens to her.
2. On the con side marks are bad to the pupil. If he
   doesn't do so good on a test.

> Teenager

Due to marks you can't not cheat.

                                              Constant Cheater

_____

Teachers too stingy with the marks and unfair in dishing them out. Questions are too prejudice and tests are too hard.

                                              Edward Williams, Esq.

_____

Do away with them, after all we can get along in our social life without marks.

                                              Linda Rosen

_____

Marks are important because for colleges or jobs they want your average and the average for the subject is made up of marks and the average for the term is made up of the average of the different subjects and the average for all terms is what they want.

                                              Crammer

_____

E.W. was copying from F.A. in French, also L.M. and L.R. And others!

                                              Guess Who

_____

Sometimes I do my homework and the teacher doesn't even mark it or I recite in class and it doesn't count, it's a waste of my time. Like when I studied the wrong thing.

                                              A True Pupil

Why can't they scatter exams insted of making us study severall subjects the same night, it makes no sence?

Failing

I don't think talking out or horsing around should be avaraged in with the marks. A teacher may hate you, after all he's human, Ha-ha! and he might give you a zero in conduct. One zero for talking can pull down the whole avarage! But it doesn't matter anyhow, everybody gets promoted. Sooner or later!

Lou Martin

I wrote the same identical book report for two different English teachers I had last term. One gave me 91 and the other 72 on the same identical paper. Go figure it out!

I think class discussion should be counted and not tests because you can say what you really think and not what they want you to say.

Carole Blanca

Marks encourage us to cheat though I personally don't.

Honest Abe

You either pass or fail, no two ways about it.

Zero

Best marks go to cheaters and memorizers. Marks depend on memorizing and not on real knowledge. When you cram into your head for a test you may get a high mark but forget it the next day. That's not an education. I suggest just *Good* and *Bad* at the end of the term on report cards. Or maybe nothing.

Frank Allen

The reason my marks are low is because teachers call on me the one time I'm unprepaired and never all the times I am.

Disgusted

Exams show more the paper and not the individual.

Mr. X

Teachers give tests for spite and to get even. Or just to keep the class quiet. (This is the *last* time I'm writting to answer you!)

the Hawk

Marks should be based on class work and not on tests when the nerves take over. When talking in class (English) and the teacher listens to me I feel more courage to say it.

Jose Rodriguez

I use only 10% or less of what I study. It's a *waist*.

Dropout

<u>Cheat</u> is <u>Teach</u> backwards! ! !

Doodlebug

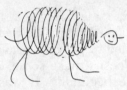

TO: ALL TEACHERS
FROM: JAMES J. McHABE, ADM. ASST.

PLEASE PLOT AND HAND IN THE MEDIAN PERCENTILE CURVE BASED ON THE MIDTERM MARKS IN EACH OF YOUR CLASSES. IF A CLASS CURVE FALLS BELOW THE PERCENTILE OF FAILURES ALLOTTED TO IT, THE EFFICACY OF THE TEACHER MUST BE QUESTIONED. TEACHERS WITH THE HIGHEST NUMBER OF PASSING STUDENTS ARE TO BE COMMENDED.

JJ McH

44 Lavatory Escort

Wed., Nov. 25

Dear Ellen,

It looks as if I might be fired from the school system—because I failed to provide a lavatory escort for Joe Ferone.

If this doesn't make sense, it's because it doesn't; but I'll start at the beginning. It was during Midterm Exams this morning. Midterms are really final exams, but they're given in November, with high pomp and protocol. Books piled in front of the room, seats in alternate rows, kids: "Can we copy?" "What's the answer to question 2?" "It's not fair! We never had this!" "How we supposed to answer this?" Confusion about money to be collected for Thanksgiving baskets; confusion about Midterm exam envelopes delivered to the wrong room; confusion about proctoring assignments; and the usual confusion about bells. Finally silence, except for the scratching of pens and shuffling of feet.

Suddenly—a problem. Ferone has to leave the room. I escort him to the door—but there is no hall proctor in sight—and he is not supposed to go unescorted. What to do? His need is urgent. We stand in the doorway for a moment, testing each other with our eyes. The situation is fraught. This may be my chance to win his trust at last. I whisper—in order not to disturb the others—my permission for him to go alone. It is understood that he is honor-bound not to use the lava-

268

tory for any but legitimate purposes; not as a reference room, not to look up any answers that may be secreted on his person, not even for a quick smoke. He goes, and I return to my observation perch at the back of the room (so that the kids can't see *whom* I am watching: a tip from Admiral Ass!). A few minutes later, the Admiral himself appears in the doorway, white with rage, Ferone at his side. Clash of swords; two enemies face to face on either side of Ferone; the showdown—but *sotto-voce*, for we have an audience.

McH: What is the meaning of this?
I: Of what?
McH: You let him out of the room *unescorted?*
I: He had to go.
McH: *Unescorted?*
I: There was no hall proctor.
McH: You should have waited for one.
I: The situation did not warrant waiting.
McH: Do you realize his exam paper may be invalidated?
I: Why?
McH: He may have been looking up answers!
I: I don't think so. He told me he wouldn't.
McH: He *told* you?
I: Yes.
McH: And you believed him?
I: I believe him.
McH: Go back to your seat, young man. Miss Barrett, this is not the time and place to explain to you the gravity of your position. You had explicit instructions; you disobeyed them. You'll hear from me later. In the meantime, you will please put his paper aside when he is finished. The outcome of his examination will have a direct bearing on you. You understand that?
I: I think so.
McH: The second girl in the third row—eyes on your paper!

Exit the Admiral.

Ferone and I look at each other. His face is impassive. Will he fail the exam to vindicate me? He is very bright; he has been an F student only because he chose to be.

Suddenly he has become a moral issue by which I stand or fall. The incident of the lavatory has brought into focus my values against McHabe's—everything I believe in as opposed to all that is petty, regimented and rote in the school system; all that degrades the dignity of my profession, and consequently, of my pupils; my desire to teach well, as opposed to bureaucracy, trivia and waste.

Perhaps I am losing my sense of humor. It's easy to do that here. But I am still new enough to the system not to take its absurdities for granted. If only the McHabes didn't keep getting in the way, I think I could move a few mountains.

Now I have to mark, over the four-day Thanksgiving holiday, 201 papers. Each is in 5 parts. Each contains 2 compositions.

I shall keep you posted on further developments of the Barrett-Ferone-McHabe Lavatory Case. In the meantime, write me what the weather is like in the outside world.

Love,
Syl

P.S. Did you know that according to the tabulation of the National Council of Teachers of English, it takes six to ten minutes to grade a single composition, and that the city's teachers carry a pupil-load of 150 to 200 pupils per term?

S.

$$\frac{20+}{60\overline{)1206}}$$
$$\underline{120}$$
$$6$$

$$\begin{array}{r} 201 \\ \times\quad 6\ \text{min.} \\ \hline 1206 \end{array}$$

20+ hrs. to grade 1 compos.

45 It Has Come to my attention

OFFICE OF THE PRINCIPAL
CALVIN COOLIDGE HIGH SCHOOL

Copy to Mr. McHabe
        Dr. Bester

Dear Miss Barrett,
  It has come to my attention that due to laxness on your part in proctoring the Midterm examinations one of our students is under suspicion of cheating. This can have a demoralizing and corrupting effect on the rest of our student body, who have always and at all times upheld our high standards of moral and ethical integrity.

             MAXWELL E. CLARKE
             PRINCIPAL

* * *

Dear Miss Barrett,
  Please bring to my office the examination paper of Joseph Ferone as soon as you have marked it. I understand that he has been a failing student in English for the last two terms.

             Samuel Bester
             Chairman, Language Arts Dept.

271

INTRASCHOOL COMMUNICATION

FROM: 304
TO: 508

Dear Bea—
 I've just graded Ferone's paper: he got 89%.

Do you suppose I'll be court-martialed?

Syl

46 From the Suggestion Box

I have known teachers to go crazy from too much teaching but not you. How come? They should put you on a pedestle.

> A Bashful Nobody

My suggestion is overthrow Mr. McHabe and you run the school togeather with Mr. Grayson. Then this would be a great place to be.

> MR. X

(In the Mid Terms the reason I flunked is because I didn't understand the questions.)

It serves them right (dishes in ruins) how we messed up the whole Cafeteria, and we'll do it again if they still treat us like jailbirds. This is the last warning I'm writting.

273

the Hawk

At first I thought to myself I'd never live through another English with a female teacher but, instead, well here I am and I owe it all to you.

Rusty

Too strick with the marks. I could use a 80.

A 55

I suggest 1. More teachers with spunk.
            A. To stick up for us.
            1. The way you stuck up for Joe F.
         2. And fight with Mac Habe
         3. Character—Excellent & not afraid.
         4. And beautiful blue eyes.

Teenager

I complaint all ready about my Midterm mark. What's the use of intergration if marks are still low?

Edward Williams, Esq.

I never knew a teacher to really care but you do. Don't ever leave us. I wish I could have you till the end of school.

Carole Blanca

Still stink.

I like to get away from war books like "Shakespeer" to the "dance" in the gym but didn't get a chance to "dance" with you. Maybe we will "next time".

Chas. H. Robbins

You took off to much for sp. and gr. and punct. and vocab. on my Exam. when you were about my age you didn't want the same thing to happen to you.

Zero

I love the frank way you speak to us and I love your methods of teaching and dressing yourself. I love your kindness and whole personality. I also love you for yourself. Tell us more about your own life like you did that time about your college. It makes you feel very human to us so we can be more like you. (I went down to size 15). I'm only misrable at home and never in English. That's why I have this new ambition to be an English Teacher. Can you tell me how you prepared your self for this career?

Your friend,
Vivian Paine

You have one of the best sense of humors I ever met. You made the lessons laughable.

Third Row

I don't like the way you dress, too loud for a teacher, you should tone it down, and a low marker.

Yr ~~Ehemy~~ Enemy

The reason I like your English is you teach English which can be used in my life to make me somebody. You have arranged your English so that it seems more interesting and it doesn't seem like English though it is. You make likable things I don't like like reading. You teach perfectly and steadily, not too fast or too slow. And you always have time to listen to our side of the book. Can I have you again?

Jose Rodriguez

I know who cheated on the midterms and got away with it, also somebody else.

Guess Who

No matter what I do my mother keeps harping.

Doodlebug

I'm not in your class, but how about a date anyhow? I am a very congenial acquaintance. I am medium tall with dark hazel eyes, sort of chubby face and a little stout around the middle. I suppose you know me already!

Passer By

Although the English Midterms were extremely interesting, they were rather hard to do in my usual well manner. I therefore wish to thank you for giving me the opportunity of raising my mark with a Extra Credit Book Report which I hope you will enjoy reading.

Harry A. Kagan
(The Students Choice)

I'm not saying there's too much homework, but I won't say there's too little. But for you I'm glad to do it even double.

Frank Allen

I was going to drop out but no more. No teacher ever gave me the break you did when you told me I could make up my briliant (Ha-ha!) marks with a book report for extra credit which I will!

Lou Martin

This is the first class I enjoyed failing because of looking at you.

Not enuogh extra credit for washing the Board!

Disgusted

Will you marry me?

PART X

Dear Miss Barrett,
 I am hereby submitting a Book Report I wrote for extra credit. I hope you will raise my mark since I need to have it raised. In the past I have always usually had excellent marks in English.

> Harry A. Kagan
> (The Students Choice)

My Reading Life

 My reading life has quite a variation and is more wider than the average student. I enjoy partaking in many types of great literature, both fiction and non-fiction books as well as others. Mr. Hemingway's works gave me a very favorable impression of Mr. Hemingway as a writer. I would recommend it to any one. One author I did not care for was Mr. Faulkner. I didn't get any enjoyment out of him. Another book I did not particularly enjoy was "War and Peace" by Mr. Tolstoy. It was much too long to read it and has too many characters with similiar names. I've also read quite a few other fiction novels that I won't mention here. I consider reading one of my most useful hobbies.

Miss Barett, You said we could put in your letter box
Extra Credit reports on books we read outside of school
and due to Midterms and horsing around I need that
E. Credit! I demand you give it to me! Ha-ha joke! But
every little bit counts!

Lou Martin

Three Important Myth

by Lou Martin

1. There was once a boy and girl but their familys were
always arguing so naturally these two children or people
would meet each other on the sly. One day a bleeding
lion came along. Horrorfied she ran away leaving her
scarf! The lion played with it for a while and then went
away. The boy came back and seeing the bleeding scarf
taught that she was killed. Remosely he took his knife
and his life! The girl saw her boy-friend was dead and
she decided to kill her self! The 2 familys seeing their
dear children dead realised how silly they were & became friends after learning a horrorful lesson. The same
conflict appears in Shakespeer.

2. Pygmalian was a myth who was a sculpture. He was
the type of man who didn't like women particulally but
this story changes this. One day he made a statue of his
wife-to-be and put in everything he wanted just so and
when it was finished he wanted to marry her but since
she wasn't alive he couldn't very well do so. What to
do? Pray, of course, which he did to the G----ss of love
who made her alive! From this we get My Fair Lady
and others.

3. Adonis was a handsome youth from Asia Miner and
Venus was the G----ss of love. She use to spend all her
time going hunting with him and fishing and other
sports. All the manly outlets of life! One day while
Adonis went hunting a wild bore killed him and all the
Gods pitied Venus so much they then allowed him to
rise from the dead to dwell as her husband part time.
During the months in which he visits we call Spring-
time.

48

What Did I miss?

INTRASCHOOL COMMUNICATION

FROM: 508
TO: 304

Dear Syl,

Welcome back! You were much missed yesterday! By Paul, who kept revising verses he was writing you. By your Joe Ferone, who wandered, listless and passless, through the corridors and out of the building before the PM check-out. By McHabe, who was summoned by the unnerved substitute to sit on your classes. By your kids. And, of course, by me.

Are you all right? Wild rumor has it that you had 1. eloped 2. collapsed beneath a pile of records 3. gone to the movies in the *daytime!* Which is it?

Bea

* * *

INTRASCHOOL COMMUNICATION

FROM: 304
TO: 508

Dear Bea—

If I have to check one, I'll take #3.

Actually, I spent the day at Willowdale Academy, being interviewed for a possible February job. From where I sit, it's very tempting.

283

Came back to find my door fixed at last; it opens and
closes now. But—two chairs are broken. Fair exchange!

Do the CC's go on the right or the left of the blue line
on the PRC?

Syl

*   *   *

INTRASCHOOL COMMUNICATION

FROM: 508
TO: 304

Dear Syl,

Fie on Willowdale! Don't you know how much you're
needed right here? My underground informs me there
was prolonged applause when your kids saw you back
in classroom.

As for Capsule Characterizations, they go on *right* of
blue line; you should have been paying attention at
October Faculty Conference. I've discovered a boy on
my register for whom I can't make out a CC or a final
mark: I never laid eyes on him! He's been spending his
English period every day, since the beginning of term,
sitting in the office, being disciplined for something or
other—no one can recall what!

Bea

*   *   *

INTRASCHOOL COMMUNICATION

FROM: 304
TO: 508

Dear Bea—

My problem is CC's of kids who *are* present. Wish I
could say something honest, like:

"Sycophant, stuffed-shirt, stinker. Has finger in every
school pie; will go far."

or "What is she doing studying French verbs? Marry
her off—and fast!"

or "Let's not lie to *him* about equality of opportunity!"

But, like the rest of us, I have to settle for:
"Leadership potential."
"Works to capacity."
"Should try harder."
One thing about Willowdale—there's no J.J. McH. there. Did you get his latest, alerting teachers to "epidemic of glue-sniffling"? And no Sadie Finch, clamping down, harder than ever, on inter-punching.
I would teach *English* there!

Syl

*   *   *

INTRASCHOOL COMMUNICATION
FROM: 508
TO: 304
Dear Syl—
The McHabes and the Finches exist in college too. There is no greener grass. Even in private high schools and so-called "better" public high schools, there are many pressures: parental pressures for Ivy League colleges, School Board pressures, social pressures. The range of dull to bright kids is about the same, and if they drive their own cars to school, they—and their parents—tend to look down on the teacher's lack of money or status.
Besides, if you leave, with whom would I exchange these intraschool communiqués to brighten my Lobby Duty period?
Besides, you're our catalyst, mascot, spokesman and in-fighter.
Besides, you laugh good, like a teacher should.
I'm not saying this to get a higher mark.
Stay!

Bea

INTRASCHOOL COMMUNICATION

FROM: 304
TO: 508

Thank you for the kind words; I need all I can get.

It may not even be *my* decision to make. After so many demerits, I expect a "U" rating from Clarke.

What did I miss yesterday?

Syl

* * *

INTRASCHOOL COMMUNICATION

FROM: 508
TO: 304

Dear Syl—

Don't worry about your end-of-term rating. "Principal's Estimate of Teacher's General Fitness"—for all its verbiage—is concerned with one thing only: "Is she loony?" And—whatever else you are—you're not loony.

You missed the Dec. Faculty Conference, as you well know, at which all vital questions were postponed for lack of time. And at which:

2 new committees were formed.

It was decided to substitute folk songs for hymns in assembly.

McHabe took a stand vs. vandalism, obscenity, lateness, smoking, and the Faculty Show.

I know, because I had to write up the Minutes.

Paul spent the hour writing you verses.

I know, because he sat next to me.

Have you forgiven him?

Bea

INTRASCHOOL COMMUNICATION

FROM: 304
TO: 508

Dear Bea–

There's nothing to forgive. He himself feels blameless.

He is—as the PRC puts it—"trying hard"; and he keeps dropping bait into my letter-box:

"A question to pursue and ponder:
Does abstinence make the heart grow fonder?"

Health Ed teacher just sent me cutting slip for Alice Blake. Apparently only today has someone bothered to take attendance in Gym. Apparently no one has as yet removed her name from Delaney Book.

I've kept in touch with her mother. Alice has been transferred to another hospital, she is in pain, she still refuses to have anyone from school visit her.

What's all the excitement about "Teacher for a day"?

Syl

o   o   o

INTRASCHOOL COMMUNICATION

FROM: 508
TO: 304

Dear Syl–

That's the day kids turn the tables on us. It always takes place just before Xmas; it's the occasion for certain responsible seniors to run the school for one day. President of G.O. becomes principal, chosen seniors prepare a lesson to teach lower classes, and it's all very sound.

But by a series of mutations and deteriorations, it is becoming more fraught and frantic each year. The humor of teachers dressed as kids cavorting on the

stage escapes me, but there is a strong faction in its
favor. They call it "the lighter side of education."
   Surely, Willowdale has nothing like it to show you!
What's wrong? You sound a bit fed up.

                                                    Bea

                        *   *   *

INTRASCHOOL COMMUNICATION

FROM: 304
TO: 508

Dear Bea—
   I am—more than a bit fed up.
   I once taught a lesson on "A man's reach should exceed his grasp/Or what's a heaven for?" I'm no longer
sure that this is so; the higher I reach, the flatter I fall
on my face.
   How do *you* manage to stand up?

                                                    Syl

                        *   *   *

INTRASCHOOL COMMUNICATION

FROM: 508
TO: 304

Dear Syl,
   Look at the cherub who is delivering this note. Look
closely. Did you ever see a lovelier smile? A prouder
bearing? She has just made the Honor Society. Last
year she was ready to quit school.
   Walk through the halls. Listen at the classroom
doors. In one—a lesson on the nature of Greek tragedy.
In another—a drill on *who* and *whom*. In another—a
hum of voices intoning French conjugations. In another—committee reports on slum clearance. In another
—silence: a math quiz.
   Whatever the waste, stupidity, ineptitude, whatever
the problems and frustrations of teachers and pupils,

something very exciting is going on. In each of the classrooms, on each of the floors, all at the same time, education is going on. In some form or other, for all its abuses, young people are exposed to education.

That's how I manage to stand up.

And that's why you're standing, too.

Let's meet at 3. If you're swamped with work, let's at least walk to the subway together.

Bea

49

Fri., Dec. 11

Dear Ellen,

I chuckled at your description of your in-laws and the shrunken turkey. I *needed* to chuckle.

The invitation to spend the Xmas holidays with you is very tempting, but I won't be able to make it. Neither am I going to visit Mother. Her letters have switched into lower gear: She now sends me clippings on marriages. No, it isn't the "extravagance of the flight," as you so delicately put it. Since I'm unable to whip up an appetite at 10:17, I've saved a fortune on lunches. It's the term papers, reports, CC's and final marks, which are due right after the holidays, "to facilitate records," although there will still be a month of school left.

Other teachers, more efficient or more experienced, seem to manage to take this time off; some (on maximum salaries?) even go on cruises!

But I'm at a loss on how to give each of my 201 students a numerical mark in a subject like English. Based on what? —Average of tests? "Class attitude"? Effort? Attendance? Native intelligence? Memory-span? Emotional problems? The kind of reading their parents had exposed them to?

About Henrietta and the Book Room Incident: She's back, galumphing more energetically than ever through the classics, devising means of bringing them to the students' level, as the phrase goes. Her latest is: *Great Poems Turned into Tabloid Headlines.* I wouldn't have believed it, had I not seen two kids in my homeroom at it:

MIDNIGHT RIDER WARNS OF FOE

SEAMAN GUILTY OF SHOOTING BIRD

WIFE TELLS ALL IN PORTUGUESE LOVE LETTERS

MAN REPORTS TALKING RAVEN

As for your question about Ferone and the Lavatory Escort episode, it passed with no repercussions. Ferone had neither failed nor cheated. As a matter of fact, his mark was 89. The day of the exam his paper was gone over, with a fine tooth comb, by Bester and me; after Thanksgiving, it was recombed by McHabe. There was no evidence of foul play. And there was no apology offered him—or me.

But the boy did finally agree to see me after school. He is coming next week. I don't know why I feel it's so important. I haven't done too well with the others.

I couldn't change Eddie Williams' conviction that the white world is against him, no matter how many proofs and protestations I offered him. He knows better. He has always known.

And I couldn't, in any way, change Harry Kagan, nor cut through the fawning politician to find the boy beneath. Perhaps there isn't any.

And I couldn't do much for Lou Martin; the need for attention that prompts his clowning is too desperate.

My victories are few; Jose Rodriguez, who learned that he counts; Vivian Paine, who learned that she is nice; and a few who learned where to put commas and periods.

I think, like me, they're all seeking a way to make contact, to communicate, to be loved.

"Hey, teach—you back?" one of my boys greeted me.

"I'm not a *teach*. I'm a *teacher*. And I have a name. How would you like it if I called you "Hey, pupe!"?

"I'd like it fine."

"Why?"

"It shows you're *with* it."

I want to be "with it," but they need some concrete proof. Like Grayson's.

Quite inadvertently (the kids had been sworn to secrecy) I discovered the mystery of Grayson.

It seems he runs a sort of one-man free kitchen, lending-bank, drug-cure center, flophouse and employment agency in the basement.

While the rest of us were busy making out graphs and Character Capsules, he gave the kids sandwiches, lent them money, found jobs for them after school, or gave them jobs to do himself. He kept them off the streets and off "the junk," and on occasion let the temporarily homeless ones sleep illegally overnight in the basement.

What Ferone and some of the other kids were getting from him was not the pedagogic gobbledygook, not concepts and precepts, not conferences and interviews, not pleas and threats, not words—not any words at all—but simple action, immediate and real: food, money, jobs.

I admit to a momentary pang of dismay: What tangibles could I offer them?

It may be easier at Willowdale.

Extraordinary—that Willowdale Academy and Calvin Coolidge High School should both be institutions of learning! The contrast is stunning. I had a leisurely tea with the Chairman of the English Department. I saw several faculty members sitting around in offices and lounges, sipping tea, reading, smoking. Through the large casement windows bare trees rubbed cozy branches. (One of my students had written wistfully of a dream-school that would have "windows with trees in them"!) Old leather chairs, book-lined walls, air of cultivated casualness, sound of well-bred laughter.

Whatever tensions, back-biting or jockeying for position exist in a place like this—and I know they do—I, as a lady and a Chaucerian scholar, was made unaware of anything but their delight at my visit. If it should prove mutually satisfactory, I would teach three classes a day, three times a week; the other two days would be for individual conferences with students. Classes are small. Although I would be stuck with Freshman Composition—the Chairman shrugged apologetically—there would be an assistant to mark the papers. I would be required to do nothing but teach. I might even have a Chaucer seminar. And certainly, they would arrange to give me as much time as possible to complete the work for my doctorate, after which, "one might rise quickly on the academic ladder."

There I sat, Sylvia Barrett of Room 304, talking in my own language, made conscious of the dignity of my profession, made to feel, like Jose Rodriguez, that I'm "real."

I know, I know. I have a tendency to romanticize; Paul keeps telling me this. But surely, anyone interested in *teaching* belongs in Willowdale rather than in Calvin Coolidge?

Bea doesn't think so. Sometimes I think she is right.

When I returned to my own classes, after a day's absence, the kids seemed genuinely pleased to see me; but I suspect they were just as pleased with the bad time they had given my substitute. It seems she had arrived shrill and jittery, because the day before she had been threatened with a knife by a boy in another school.

"We gave her a nervous breakdown," Lou told me smugly.

And Paul presented me with new verses—a parody of Gray's "Elegy"—which begins:

The school bell tolls the knell of starting day;
Ah, do not ask for whom it tolls! I see
The students stairwards push their screaming way;
I know, alas, it tolls for thee and me!

He hasn't given up courting me with iambs.

And he hasn't given up trying to publish his exotic manuscript. A new publisher is interested, and Paul is poised for flight, awaiting word. To pass the time, he's writing the annual Faculty Frolic, which is given a week before Xmas, and at which teachers and students interchange places. I'm looking forward to seeing Mary Lewis in bobby sox.

I'm looking forward to hearing from Willowdale.

I'm looking forward to resigning from the school system. Or am I?

I'm weary. Comfort me with letters of Xmas trees and hearth fires.

Love,
Syl

P.S. Did you know that attacks by pupils on teachers in the city schools average one a day?

S.

50

The Lighter Side of Education

TO: ALL TEACHERS

WITH CHRISTMAS ONLY A WEEK AWAY, THE SEASON'S GAY AND FESTIVE MOOD DESCENDS UPON OUR FACULTY AND STAFF TOMORROW WITH OUR ANNUAL FACULTY FROLIC, "THE COOLIDGE GILBERT & SULLIVAN," WHICH WILL BE THE CULMINATION OF OUR TRADITIONAL "TEACHER FOR A DAY" DAY. I HOPE AND TRUST THAT BOTH THOSE WHO PARTICIPATE AND THOSE WHO DO NOT, JOIN IN THE SPIRIT OF PROPER ENJOYMENT OF THE LIGHTER SIDE OF EDUCATION.
I WELCOME THIS OPPORTUNITY TO OFFER EACH AND ALL OF YOU MY SINCERE AND HEARTFELT WISHES FOR A MERRY YULETIDE AND A HAPPY NEW YEAR.

MAXWELL E. CLARKE
PRINCIPAL

* * *

TO: THE FACULTY OF CALVIN COOLIDGE HIGH SCHOOL
DEAR TEACHER:

IF YOU'D LIKE TO MAKE SOME EXTRA MONEY DURING THE XMAS HOLIDAYS, WE STILL HAVE A FEW OPENINGS LEFT IN OUR AGENCY IN THE FIELD OF TUTORING, SELLING, AND ADDRESSING XMAS ENVELOPES. PLEASE READ THE ENCLOSED APPLICATION FORM CAREFULLY; JOBS ARE GOING FAST!

For Linda Rosen
c/o Miss Barrett's Letterbox—Please forward!!!

Linda!!! Are you financially embarassed or your fingers turned numb or have you run out of stationery???? Why didn't you answer my RSVP???? You know I can't call you because your Mother listens in on the Ext.!!! Je me porte tres bien et j'espere que vous etes le meme. Vous comprenez ma language???? Voulez vous venir a ma noel party avec Bob? Mes parents ne serons pas dans la maison!!!! Nous voulons avoir un grand temps comme le dernier foi, parce que I got le "stuff", vous me comprenez, pour devenir haut!!!! N'est pas???? Let me know!!!

Actions speak louder than words, so I'll sign off.

Roz

* * *

CIRCULAR # 99B
TOPIC: "TEACHER FOR A DAY" DAY
PLEASE KEEP ALL CIRCULARS ON FILE, IN THEIR ORDER

DECEMBER 18, WHICH IS TOMORROW, HAS BEEN DESIGNATED "TEACHER FOR A DAY" DAY. ONLY THE HIGHEST SERIOUSNESS OF PURPOSE AND EXECUTION WILL BE TOLERATED. ALL DISCIPLINE PROBLEMS ARISING FROM THE LACK OF SERIOUSNESS OF THIS PROGRAM ARE TO BE REFERRED TO MR. McHABE.

* * *

Dear Miss Barrett,
Since I am running for re-election next term, I'm putting this in your letter box. Please enter all my Service Credits on my PRC which is important for votes. They are, to refresh your memory:
President G. O.
Captain Cafeteria Patrol
Elevator Squad

G. O. Store Superviser
Vice President Social Club
Secretary Glee Club
and *Clarion* Booster

Miss Egan said she may give me credit for laying out gauze pads and swabs in the Infirmary each morning but I don't know if she will since pressure of other work prevents me doing so.

The Students Future Choice
Harry A. Kagan

● ● ●

TO: ALL TEACHERS

THE TEACHERS' INTEREST COMMITTEE IS PLANNING A GALA LUNCHEON FOR THE LAST DAY OF SCHOOL BEFORE THE XMAS HOLIDAYS, WHEN STUDENTS WILL BE DISMISSED AT NOON. THE COST WILL BE $2.25 PER PERSON, INCLUDING GRATUITIES, WHICH IS THE MOST REASONABLE PRICE WE COULD GET.

PLEASE INDICATE YOUR WILLINGNESS TO ATTEND BY CHECKING YES OR NO. IF YOU EXPECT TO COME, PLEASE INDICATE YOUR CHOICE BY PLACING A CHECK ON THE LEFT-HAND SIDE OF MEAT OR FISH.

I WILL   ATTEND THE GALA LUNCHEON
 WILL NOT

SUPREME OF FRESH FRUIT ATTRACTIVELY DECORATED WITH STRAWBERRIES
CREAM OF MUSHROOM SOUP WITH GOLDEN CROUTONS
CHICKEN PATTY WITH WHITE SAUCE; TENDER GARDEN PEAS

FISH ALTERNATE:
FILLET OF SOLE CRISPLY BROWNED WITH PARSLEY POTATOES, SHOESTRING STRING BEANS

CHOICE OF VANILLA OR CHOCOLATE ICE CREAM
PETITS FOURS
COFFEE—TEA—MILK

INTRASCHOOL COMMUNICATION
FROM: 508
TO: 304

Dear Syl–

Your letter-box is crammed to the gills, as usual; I hope I can squeeze this note in!

I'm supposed to lure you out of 304 during the homeroom period today: I promised your cherubs I'd think of something! They want to collect money for your Xmas corsage; it's traditional, and every year every teacher pretends great surprise at receiving it. (The one with the biggest corsage wins!) So be sure to drop in to my room—on some pretext or other.

Tomorrow will be wild! It would be good to fortify ourselves with a double malted after school today, but I know you're meeting with Ferone this afternoon. Let's plan to see each other during the holidays. I'll be pretty much alone; except for a couple of nights, when I am taking some of my kids who have never seen a live play to an off-Broadway production.

I understand tomorrow's Faculty Frolic is live, too!

Bea

❋   ❋   ❋

MISS BARRETT,

  <u>Alice Blake</u> OF YOUR OFFICIAL CLASS IS OWING THE LIBRARY THE SUM OF <u>49¢</u> FOR OVERDUE BOOK OR BOOKS ENTITLED <u>The Idylls of the King</u> BY <u>Alfred Lord Tennyson</u> . UNLESS THIS SUM IS PAID AND THE BOOK OR BOOKS RETURNED WITHIN SEVEN DAYS, (HE WILL BE
                                                    (SHE
PLACED ON THE LIBRARY BLACKLIST.

——————————

Dear Miss Barrett,

Just to make sure I pass here is another Extra Credit Myth I remembered! Hero and Liandor poped into my head because I forced myself to remember that Hero is a girl! But the rest of it I don't remember so well so will talk about another Psyche. She was the sister that got left on the shelf when the others got married off but an Orcle told her parents to put her on a Mount top to wait for a husband. One day Cupid came along and became her husband but said she must never look at him! Her sisters told her to take a look and if it's a monster kill it, and if not don't! When she did he was awakened and fled away. After trying to kill herself she came to Venus to be a maiden under her. After doing some tasks she became imortal and had two children. All the other teachers are forced to pass me on, Ha-ha! because I'm outgrowing all my classes so I hope you will too with all these Extras I'm giving you!

Very truely
Lou Martin

Dear Miss Barrett,

I'm collecting money from the kids in Home Room for a Xmas present to send Alice in the hospital and would like your permision to do this. Would you care to join in? I keep thinking how she used to sit right in front of me. We want to get her one of those great big stuff animals on which we'll all autograph our names to show we didn't forget her. A pander or a kangarroo.

Sincerly,
Carole Blanca

51

Love me Back

Thurs., Dec. 17

Dear Ellen,

It is 3:30 in the morning. I can't sleep; I need to talk to you. I want to tell you what happened this afternoon, exactly what happened.

It was late when he came in; I had waited, it seems, for a long time. I remember arranging and rearranging the papers on my desk, refreshing my lipstick, switching on the lights against the winter darkness. I remember the sounds of traffic and the drilling on the street below, and the way he suddenly stood in the doorway.

He closed the door softly behind him and leaned against it, waiting. I remember thinking how nice, he had spruced himself up for our interview: the toothpick was gone; he had taken the trouble to brush his hair.

I arose. I smiled. I was glad to see him, I said. I had been wanting to see him all term. He said he knew that; well, I had my wish, here he was.

Ignoring his insolence, aware of his resentment of authority, I stepped out from behind my desk and—to bridge the distance between us—I sat down, with my Delaney Book, in a student's chair, motioning for him to sit next to me. I knew precisely what I would discuss with him: rea-

300

sons for staying in school, possibility of college, making up failing marks, attendance, attitudes. I was ready to point out the discrepancy between his capacity and achievement. I was prepared to understand his problems.

He swaggered towards me, but he did not sit down. He stood above me, leather jacket unzipped, rocking slightly on his heels, looking down at me, but not looking at my face.

I sat holding my Delaney Book like a shield against my breast, with all those cardboard names on it, last first, printed in ink. He knew what I was after, he said. He recalled my every act of kindness to him, from the first day, when I had covered for him with McHabe. And about the wallet, he said, and when they found the knife on him, and the midterms, and all that talk, talk, and asking him all the time to see me alone. Well, we were alone now.

The drilling on the street must have stopped for a moment; I remember it had begun again, more loud and insistent. I felt my heart beating against the hard, wine-red cover of the Delaney Book. He must try to understand, I said. He must believe that I wanted only— I wanted—

He wasn't listening. He was looming above me, the years between us swiftly reversed, while I sat, an unsure school girl, reciting a tentative lesson. My words never reached him; I could almost hear them drop, one by one, like so many pebbles against a closed window.

You know how you move under water, heavy and graceful? By this time I was standing. I had somehow got up. I remember how carefully I had placed the Delaney Book on the arm-desk of the chair, balancing it so that it should not spill out all those name cards. Disarmed now, empty-handed, I was standing before him. I became aware of the deserted building enclosing us, the empty room, the empty chairs, silent and abandoned as grave-stones; of scraps of paper, valueless now, scattered on the floor; of books leaning, top-heavy with words, on the splintered shelf; of papers on my desk, bulging with words. Slowly I began to step back; slowly he moved towards me, relentless as a shadow.

After a while I felt the wall at my back; there was no further place to go. I heard my words running down like a defective phonograph record, until there was silence. The drilling on the street had stopped again. He was very close. I looked at him, and with a mild shock of recognition, I saw him, as if I had known him only through photographs before, and now saw him in person. Yes, of course.

Someplace a car honked. I think he made a move towards me. Maybe not. I looked at him, and there were no words left with which to ward off feeling.

I reached out blindly. I touched his face. There were no words for the terrible tenderness. I wanted to comfort him, as if he were a child, for everything that had been done to him. I wanted to say, like Persephone in hell: My dear, my dear— It is not so dreadful here. I wanted to tell him, I wanted him to know. There were no words for this, only my hands on his face.

I don't know how long we stood, motionless, enfolded in silence. One moment his face was hard against my hands, the next, it seemed to shatter at my touch. He looked as if he were about to wrench himself away, but he didn't. Fists clenched, he watched me like a boxer poised to spring.

His eyes read me like Braille. This was the moment he had been testing me for. What was he asking me to do? Undo?

He had come for a purpose. He thought (he made himself think) it was my purpose too. It was the only way he knew to human closeness. It was also the way to diminish me, to punish.

His life outside this room was alien to me. I could not imagine or even guess it. Yet I knew him. His face told me all. The silent struggle, the clash of feeling on feeling: contempt and longing, helplessness and rage. All that he knew of good. The need to cling and to repel, to kneel and to defile.

He waited for a sign.

What could I say to show him that to survive, love was as strong as hate, and could be trusted? His world had taught him well, long before me.

Only my touch could speak. I care, it said, I do care.

His eyes grew hard. His lips moved.

"Damn you to hell"—he turned and bolted out of the room. The door opened and closed behind him, and there was the drilling on the street, loud now, and the desk and the papers and time. For some reason, I looked at my watch.

Was he crying?

If he was, he will never forgive me.

But it was I who cried. I sat down at my desk; I put my head on my arms on the desk, and I cried.

Why?

The question and answer period will come later; multiple choice, True or False, my own "probing question"; and the explanations, the interpretations, the distortions I will inevitably make.

For already, hours later, I think that what I felt for Ferone, and what I am feeling now, and what I am putting down on this paper, and what you will see when you read it—are all quite different.

"What is truth?" said jesting Pilate, and would not stay for an answer. But jesting Sylvia will stay and jest the truth away. I had used my sense of humor; I had called it proportion, perspective. But perspective is distance. And distance, for all my apparent involvement, is what I had kept between myself and my students. Like Paul's lampoons, like Lou's ha-ha's, it insulated me; it kept me safe from feeling.

I will probably, in my very next letter, or very next paragraph—see once again "the funny sides"; I may allow memory to turn flippant. But for a moment, or hour, or whatever measure of time it takes to grow, we reached each other, Ferone and I, person to person.

For love is growth. It is the ultimate commitment. It imposes obligations; it risks pain. Love is what I wanted from all, from A (Allen) to W (Wolzow) in my Delaney Book; but I had never really loved back. Oh, love me, love me back! they all cried—Alice and Vivian, all of them. And maybe now I can.

Ferone taught me. Our roles became reversed. *He* had reached *me;* I was the one who needed *him,* to make me feel.

What to do with it? I had once seen a girl's memo book on the Lost & Found shelf in the office, and on the cover— a warning in crayon: *Do Not Touch!!! Or Look!!! Personal! Private! Penalty!!!* The penalty for touching is too great. The burden of love for all the Ferones waiting for me in the classroom is not to be borne. Better by far to stand at a lectern and read my neat notes at Willowdale.

I am tired.

I had set out to tell you exactly what happened. But since I am the one writing this, how do I know what in my telling I am selecting, omitting, emphasizing; what unconscious editing I am doing? Why was I more interested in the one black sheep (I use Ferone's own cliché) than in all the white lambs in my care? Why did I (in my red suit) call him a child? Am I, by asking questions, distorting something pure? The heart has its reasons; it's the mind that's suspect.

You've read my letters from the very beginning, from the first day at school. How callow I must have been, how impatient and intolerant and naive and remote and gullible and sure of myself. And how mistaken.

It is almost morning; the alarm is set for 6:30. I have been writing and writing. "Words are all we have," I once said. Wrong again. Whatever the name for love, and there are many, it can be as silent as an unspoken word, as simple as a touch.

I must try to get some sleep. Tomorrow is our topsy-turvy day, when teachers turn into kids, kids into teachers. A fitting climax.

All my love,
                                                         Syl

P. S. Did you know that 50% of the time I've been barking up all the wrong trees?

                                                          S.

INTRASCHOOL COMMUNICATION

FROM: H. Pastorfield
TO: S. Barrett

Dear Sylvia–
    Isn't this fun?
    Have you got a Teacher for a Day kid this period?
I get a bang out of turning the classes over to the kids
and pretending I can't spell *cat!*
    Would you like to join the party in my room? Bring
your kids! We're having a "Tables Are Turned" ball!

Henrietta

*   *   *

INTRASCHOOL COMMUNICATION

FROM: 508
TO: 304

Dear Syl–
    How are you doing? You looked awful this morning!
Don't let the tumult in the halls rattle you. The wild
giggles, the dunce caps, the screams for late passes are
mostly high spirits.

306 *Up the Down Staircase*

But some of it is malice. This is the day for vengeance. I understand Loomis got a zero in Math. One of his kids had spent weeks laying the foundation: a tough question he got from someone in Graduate Math Dept. at Berkeley.

How did your interview with Ferone go yesterday? See you at Faculty Frolic this afternoon!

Bea

* * *

Dear Miss Barrett,

Joseph Ferone of your official class is absent today, but you neglected to fill out Postal card #1 (Reason for Absence).

Sadie Finch
Chief Clerk

* * *

Dear Sylvia,

Do you happen to have an aspirin?

Please send it to nurse's office—they got me to cover it while she's lying down.

Mary

* * *

FROM: James J. McHabe, Adm. Asst.
TO: all teachers

DURING TODAY'S ABNORMAL SCHEDULE TEACHERS SHOULD KEEP DISRUPTION AT A MINIMUM.
THERE WILL BE A SERIES OF THREE BELLS REPEATED FOUR TIMES TO INDICATE EARLY DISMISSAL.
FACULTY FROLIC WILL BEGIN PROMPTLY AFTER THAT.
TEACHERS MUST NOT PUNCH OUT BEFORE THEIR REGULAR TIME.

JJ McH

Sylvia!

May I borrow your phonograph? School phonograph doesn't work.

Also—stage curtain is stuck. Can you spare a couple of tall kids to be curtain-pullers?

I hope you like the show. All is madness down here. Music, lights, props, costumes—nothing works. Manheim forgot all his lines, Yum-Yum is absent, and there are hoodlums (not ours) lurking in the auditorium.

It augurs well——

Paul

* * *

FROM: James J. McHabe, Adm. Asst.
TO: all teachers

DUE TO UNUSUAL CIRCUMSTANCES THERE IS NO ONE PATROLLING THE HALLS AND ENTRANCES TO CHALLENGE UNAUTHORIZED VISITORS. TEACHERS WITH FREE TIME ARE TO REPORT TO THE OFFICE FOR PATROL ASSIGNMENTS.

JJ McH

* * *

Sylvia!

Urgent! Can you get from one of your kids a Japanese fan and some hair lacquer? If no fan is available, a ping-pong racket will do.

Hurriedly,
Paul

(Will you come backstage to help with makeup?)

* * *

TO: all teachers

Please ignore previous instructions about today's bell schedule. There will be a series of four bells repeated twice to indicate early dismissal.

Three bells repeated four times indicates fire drill and we wish to avoid confusion.

Sadie Finch
Chief Clerk

Sylvia!

Can you spare two more boys (husky) to hold up backdrop? It got unglued. Also need an obi—ask around. We'll be ready in a few minutes. Be sure to yell: "Author, author!"

Paul

(Or any wide sash)

* * *

TO: ALL TEACHERS

Please disregard bells. There has been a delay in the Faculty Show. Keep students in rooms until further notice.

Sadie Finch
Chief Clerk

* * *

TO: ALL TEACHERS

Please disregard previous notice about disregarding bells, since most students are now in auditorium.

Sadie Finch
Chief Clerk

* * *

FROM: JAMES J. McHABE, ADM. ASST.
TO: ALL TEACHERS

BECAUSE OF UNRULINESS IN CLASSROOMS, TODAY'S EARLY DISMISSAL TOOK PLACE EARLIER THAN ANTICI-PATED. TEACHERS ARE TO PROCEED TO AUDITORIUM AT ONCE.

JJ McH

PART XI

up the Down Staircase

December 22

Dear Ellen,

I'm writing this from the hospital, where I am bedded down with a fractured foot; nothing serious, but a nuisance, since I'll be laid up during the busiest time of the term: the holidays!

I was wounded in the line of duty. I might even say above and beyond. I was felled by an unhinged door with a pagoda on it.

I was not attacked or knifed; I fought no issue; proved no point. I had merely gone backstage, in the auditorium, to help Paul during the Faculty Frolic.

That whole afternoon was as macabre as a newsreel Mardi-Gras bobbing towards its grotesque denouement. Harry Kagan, as Clarke, prissy at the lectern; teachers in blue jeans and sneakers licking oversize lollipops or ostentatiously pulling bubble gum from their mouths in an exaggerated attempt at playing the good sport. Remember what's-his-name at Lyons Hall—the professor who used to perch on the windowsill in shirtsleeves and suspenders, munching a sandwich to show that he was one of us? Here was the same kind of phony camaraderie—only it got wilder and wilder. Teachers with skipping ropes, balloons, yo-yos; teachers in Japanese kimonos, pencils stuck in their lacquered hair, singing and dancing in a kind of parody of a parody: the Barringer "Mikado," to the stamping and whistling of kids jammed into the auditorium; and a separate, desperate whistle from McHabe. That was during the garbage-throwing.

I must explain that some outside kids—from a neighborhood gang, or students on suspension, or dropouts—who somehow got wind of the fact that there was a show going on, gained entry into the auditorium with contraband garbage, which they proceeded to throw around. They must have aimed it at the stage, but it landed on the audience: our kids. Naturally, ours threw it right back; they threw it back at ours; and so it went, back and forth, for a few rank moments. The auditorium, being windowless, and overflowing with the overflow of both X2 and Y2 kids, was already stifling. Eventually, the visitors were ejected, the garbage was trampled until it got lost, and the show went on.

I'm sure the songs were clever; it was impossible to hear because of the commotion. By this time I was backstage—that's when the pagoda fell on my foot. Or rather, the backdrop, which was a door, painted black with a red and gold pagoda on it. I don't know where it had originally been hinged—possibly a bank; it was heavy as metal. It hurt like hell.

The doctor says I am lucky. I could have had a crushed instep, instead of "a simple fracture of the base of the fifth metatarsal." My foot will be in a cast for a few weeks, but I'll be well in time for the new term at Willowdale.

Right now I'm in a kind of limbo: Because of clerical errors and snarled red tape, I'm not officially out of Calvin Coolidge, nor officially in Willowdale. The only thing I'm sure of is that I *am* in the hospital, lying brazenly in bed in broad daylight, while someplace bells are ringing and classes are changing and kids are waiting. Kids in schools all over the city, all over the country, pledging allegiance to the flag in assemblies, halls, classrooms, yards—hundreds of thousands of right hands on the heart, hundreds of thousands of young voices droning the singsong: ". . . one nation under

God in/divisible . . ." Someplace kids are taking a test, frowning, clutching pens, chewing pencils, thinking, thinking in a kind of silent hum. Or arguing in bus or subway about something they had discussed in class. Someplace a solitary kid sits absorbed in a book in a library.

It's absence that makes me so nostalgic. For I must remember, too, the drudgery and the waste. Frustration upon frustration, thanklessness, defeat. The 3 o'clock exhaustion; the FTG fatigue (The Sophomore Slump, the Senior Sorrows). And getting up for early session; in winter, dressing by electric light to punch in before the warning bell, to erase the obscenity from the board, to track down the windowpole, to hand in before 1, before 2, before 3 . . .

And "misunderstandings of feelings." (How often I find myself quoting a student!). And the gobbledygook, and the pedagese, and the paper miles of words.

One wordless moment with Ferone, one moment of real feeling, and I had toppled off my tightrope, parasol and all.

And Ferone—where is he and what is to become of him?

I wonder how he himself will tell it, or recall it. "I had this teacher, see, and once, on a winter afternoon . . ."

I keep remembering what he had said to me. "What makes you think you're so special? Just because you're a teacher?" What he was really saying was: You are so special. You are my teacher. Then teach me, help me. Hey, teach, I'm lost—which way do I go? I'm tired of going up the down staircase.

So am I.

What is it that I wanted? A good question. Interesting, challenging, thought-provoking, as required in the Model Lesson Plan. A pivotal question, "directed towards the appreciation of human motives"—and eliciting answers I may not like.

I wanted to make a permanent difference to at least one child. "A Teacher I'll Never Forget"? Yes.

I wanted to share my enthusiasm with them; I wanted them to respond. To love me? Yes.

I wanted to mold minds, shape souls, guide my flock through English and beyond. To be a lady-God? That's close.

I wanted to fight the unequal battle against all that stands in the way of teaching. To blaze a trail? Indeed.

Yet I am about to quit.

Am I but another dropout?

I think of new kids that will come and go, card after card in the Delaney Book, dropping without a ripple out of sight. The same kids, but with different names, making the same mistakes in the same way. I think how little anyone can do, even with love, especially with love. And I long for Willowdale. (Those windows! Those windows with trees in them!) I think I'm not so special after all.

I will have time, as I lie here alone with my fifth metatarsal, to do a lot more thinking.

They've just brought me a stack of mail from school.

Write me c/o the hospital. (I haven't told Mother or anyone at home of my accident.) Let me know if my electric rabbit reached Suzie in time for the tree, and how your eggnog recipe turned out. And a very merry Xmas!

Love,
Syl

P.S. What statistics can I give you?

Did you know that the median age for female accidents in the schools is 48.2? And that the accidents occur mostly on the stairs?

I don't seem to fit.

S.

54

Greetings on Your Illness

Greetings on your illness and best wishes for coming back soon. This sub we made her so miserable I bet she'll never show up around here again. While she's having histerics in the office we're all passing around this Round Robbin in rows alphabetically even though a lot of us are absent, to tell you your method of teaching was fair and square. If there is anything I can possibly do about it I would do it. Have a Happy New Year always.

Frank Allen

Elizabeth Elis said we should sign our real names to show that you thaught us to have the courage of our convinctions. So here goes. A man's reach should exeed his gasp is a statement true to life and I am using it daily. This proves your lessons sunk in and you didn't drum it into our heads for nothing. Hoping you will get well soon and enthuse about books once more.

Andrew Alvarez
(Use to sign Anonimus)

Some one told us a terrible rumor that you're not coming back to us. We miss you something terrible. Even
tho it's just before Xmas the whole class can't enjoy it.
Please please come back & I'll do anything for you,
even read a Julius Ceasar.

                                              Janet Amdur

A Xmas present doesn't have to be only a thing. It can
also be by telling you how you helped us this term,
which is what we decided to do. How you helped me
is in giving me a liking for school which I previously
lacked. It's awful you got hurt but they say you'll be
OK soon. If Alice was in front of me she would sign her
name too so I'll sign for her.

          A Merry Xmas from Carole Blanca
                        and
                  Alice Blake

I refuse to sign this robin.      Poisen

---

Excuse my english if I would of studied harder I could
now be riting you a nice letter like the others, if you
can read my riting you would know your class was my
happist time of life.

                        Real name Marvin Chertock

I can't believe you're not coming back. School wouldn't
be school without you. Every time you came into the

room (304) I always looked you over, no offence I hope. When I told my friends about you they all envied me. You don't make the subject too confusing, also not too hard on the eyes, which adds to my knowledge. Myself and my whole family is praying for your speedy recovery to English.

Gary Daniels
(A Bashful Nobody. Now you *know!*)

Some things can't be expressed in words. Even though I want to be a writer, I know this. But I think you know what I mean when I say only "Thank you".

Elizabeth Ellis

You and Roseanne (my imaginary twin sister) are my only friends and both beautifull to look at. Don't let anything Bad happen to you in the hospital. When I used to have my other English classes I used to have those excrushiating headaches. But since you, I don't mind if they give me English 20 times a day and I mean it.

Your Admireress
Francine Gardner

Though I made a funny face when you said you would read poetry I really disliked it. In case I don't see you in person, I hope they can save your foot, I knew some one (R.L.) who got into a foot accident and is on cruches.

I used to sign Guess Who—did you guess who?

Rachel Gordon?

I wish you a complete cure and New Years. You gave
me a deeper understanding of people like Pygmallion
and others.

Sam Harper
(Formally I signed $\mathcal{MR.}X$)

You are my most memorial teacher, you teach a subject as fast as it can enter and stay put in the brain.
And you're a person with a good sense of humor and a
touch of teacherly love.

Jerry Hyams, former Cutter

To Miss Barrett, who helped me in education as well as
my personal and business life, best wishes of the season.

Harry A. Kagan
(The Students Future Choice)

= Ronald Lipp

Now it can be told, that's who I am!
I want to join this r. robin to tell you how I feel. You
are like the gems in the ocean. I'll tell my children
about you and my days with you. My motto is "never
forget". The day is dragging out without you but you
made the period fly like wings, even a long Home Room
like this. Even the way you dressed made everything
clearer and up to date. For the rest of my life I will try
to grab higher than my reach.

Ronnie

Your not as bad as them.

> Yr Freind
> Use to be Yr Emeny S. Marino

A Happy Holiday! And Yuletide! A Happy New Year! And many more Happy Returns of English! You're the first teacher that got something into this wooden head of mine, Ha-ha! "This was the most unkindliest cut of all" (when you left us) I'm quoting from your boy-friend Shakesper (Jul. Caeser) in case you don't know! So get well right away! And come back healthful and happy to teach us some more things! Now how you helped me—I don't horse around so much, though I still do. Sometimes!

> Lou Martin

If God only makes you well I would never again be un-prepaired (Homework). I didn't mean it when I was writting those things in the Sug. Box. From the first day when I fell off my seat (remember?) I fell for you but couldn't show it.

the Hawk

(I'm really Lennie Neumark)

I still hate females but not you. This goes for me and the whole class including 16 who are absent. You can come back. But I don't know if I will.

> Rusty O'Brien

How you helped me was you didn't try to act like a
King.

Doodlebug
Jill Norris

Calvin Coolidge's New Year could be happy if only you
return to teach us again. I never met any one like you
in my whole life. I awaited every tomorrow just to see
what you were going to wear or do. You made me come
out of my shell to a size 14. My sister is size 11 but she's
got skinny legs. I will love you till the day I die.

Vivian Paine

They hogging the entire paper. I want to say is I com-
planed a lot. but I didn't know how lucky I was to have
you. until we got this jerky sub. she don't know a thing
and she's trying to teach it.

Disgusted
Miguel Rios

I would swim accross the Chanel like "Hero and Le-
ander" just to see you teaching again. And that's no
"myth", it's the truth. "Merry Xmas" and Love

Chas. H. Robbins

(I can now write without having quotion marks pile
all over me and I'm trying to not think about the "atom
bomb". I hope this makes you feel better in the hospital.)

C. H. R.

1. How You Helped Me
   A. Apreciation of Life
      1. The Road Taken
         a. (choice)
      2. Julius Ceaser
         a. (was Brutus right?)
      3. Spelling (Improved 99%)
      4. Browning (a man reaching high)
      5. Letters of the alphabet put together make up all lit.
   B. I often think of these problems
2. Merry Xmas!

> Teenager
> Alias Ricky Roche

You helped me with better knowlege also respect. You gave me a push to take out a Librarry Card and get more meanings from my readings. You have been as wonderful as my own mother to me and I loved my mother very much while she was here. I guess I love you just about the same. You are the neatest teacher in the school.

> Love and Xmas
> Jose Rodriguez

Don't think me unscrupulous but I feel towards you like a friend. You tried to make even Shakesp. understandable. Also I dress more conservitive, I wear my eyelashes only on dates now.

Maybe it's none of my bussiness but you are young and I hope you don't make teaching a profession. I would like to see you married soon so you would take care of your husband and children, teaching takes everything out of your life. If you stay home and raise a familly you will be very happy and you will see your husband quite often.

> Linda Rosen

322 *Up the Down Staircase*

A hospitle teaches you a good lesson. Only it's worst for the color people. Like today I was marked late even if it's almost Xmas. Is that fair? No mater what I do I'm always the last one, I'm next to the last one to sign this sheet.

Edward Williams, Esq.

If you read this and I hope you do you will know I'm crazy about you and if I ever did anything to show the opposite I'm sorry. It may surprize you because I kept quiet and never even wrote in the Suggestion Box but I want you to know more than anything how I think you're the most beautiful person I ever met as a teacher. I have to leave you to find a job next term but maybe I'll catch a glimmer of you sometimes as I don't live too far away, having looked up where you live.

Katherine Wolzow

55. A for Effort

Dear Ellen,

It is Xmas Eve and here I lie, with my elevated plaster foot partly obstructing the funereal flower arrangement from the Teachers' Interest Committee on the hospital bureau in front of me, and papers piled up on the bed. Papers from the Board (which still doesn't know my sex); from Willowdale; from my colleagues; from Finch; from McHabe; Accident Reports; Absence Refund slips; End of Term sheets—papers to fill out, papers to check off, papers to sign, papers to countersign, papers to notarize, papers to mail and papers to file.

I feel quite at home.

The hospital allows its semi-private patients two visitors a day. Bea has been in and out. McHabe was here for a few uneasy moments to pay a duty call. He kept looking at his watch and waiting for the dismissal bell, I think. Paul came with a clever parody of Ezra Pound in many cantos. He's begun a new novel—about a nuclear physicist marooned on a peninsula: in Kamchatka, I believe. That's in Russia. Or maybe Asia. Each of my classes delegated one student to visit me.

My homeroom sent me a round robin of appreciation and revelation: a kid who all term signed himself "The Hawk" turned out to be a tiny, scared-looking boy given to outbursts of enthusiasm; my "emeny" is now my "freind"; and I have not passed through 304 unnoticed.

My English 5 presented me with a gift on which they must have lavished much love and thought and chipped-in money. It's in such bad taste that it moved me almost to tears: a shining chrome ashtray or candy dish with glass grapes.

My English 33 SS (my super-slows, my under-achievers, my non-academics) have composed a ballad for me which they are transcribing in India ink on a special scroll and which I am to receive shortly.

Not a word from Ferone.

Thank you for your eloquent letter. I'd like to think you're right, but I have learned my limitations and my private failures. It was the idea of teaching, the idea of kids that I'd been in love with. I didn't really listen; not even when their parents, on Open School day, tried to tell me; not even when the children themselves, in their own words, said so much more than their words on paper said. Not until I had come face to face with one boy.

Bea has a way of knowing. She listens to her feelings; that's why for her it's simple. And Grayson—for him it's simple too. But I, Sylvia Barrett—what mark do I get? "A" for Effort.

"A man's reach should exceed his grasp" I once taught. This implies the inevitability of frustration. Not to lower my sights, not to compromise; to accept the "challenge," to keep fighting, to find rewards even in failure because failure is due to aiming too high; not to give up, for all the leather chairs in Willowdale.

It is too much to ask.

"Sauve qui peut," Paul once——

I hear visitors at the door——

To be continued——

Bea just left. She brought news of the latest legislation: future Faculty Shows have been outlawed. All school entrances, with the exception of the main one, will be locked "except when in use." Vigilance of patrol will be redoubled. It was suggested—but vetoed—that all visitors to school be frisked. The auditorium was to be used for assemblies only. The pagoda was scrapped.

I asked about the kids. Eddie Williams is definitely dropping out, as are several others. Jose Rodriguez is staying. So is Vivian Paine. She wants to be an English teacher, and a high school diploma is a prerequisite. Bea didn't know about Rusty or Ferone.

I don't know about Ferone either. He may be my most spectacular failure, or my one real success. If he drops out, I may never know.

"What else is happening in school?" I asked.

"Life is happening there. That's where life is," she said. It was shameless propaganda. She is still trying to dissuade me from leaving.

It's not fair. I admit my ambivalence—when I reread the round robin, when I look at the ugly chrome and glass candy dish, when I think of their faces.

I have learned how vulnerable I am.

But I must look realistically at the future. Perhaps I'm not equal to what awaits me at Calvin Coolidge. Unless I stop caring. Until, one day, I find myself punching in with indifference, punching out with relief. Until I become as bitter as Loomis, as plaintive as Mary, nursing my grievances and varicose veins.

At Willowdale, I have a chance to be "mine own woman."

If I choose to remain at Coolidge, then Clarke may justly, on his End of Term Report, call me "loony"!

In the meantime, Willowdale is waiting for clearance on my resignation from the Board and for a letter from Dr. Clarke—a mere formality. I am waiting for a "Dear Sir or Madam, Resignation accepted" letter. No regret, no gratitude, just "Resignation accepted"; that, I understand, is the usual form the Board sends.

And, of course, I am waiting for a letter from you. I shall
be here at the hospital for another week or two; after that
I'll take my metatarsal home in a "walking cast" till the end
of the term.

Remember me in your wassail, and—to quote a student
for the last time—may you have a Happy New Year always!

                                                    Love,
                                                        Syl

P.S. Did you know that teachers have been resigning from
the New York City school system at the rate of approximately
a thousand a year?

                                                        S.

Ballad

Our class was working happily,
While you were teaching us,
You gave us information which,
We learned without a fuss.

We read books and we words did spell,
The hours sped by so fast,
We always groaned to hear the bell,
At the end of our English class.

But then a traddedy occured,
An accident befell,
And you were taken from our mist,
Because you weren't well.

Come back, come back, Miss Barrett, dear,
Come back, come back, come back,
Without you days are very drear,
And this is true for a fact.

Merry Xmas and Happy New Year
from your Poets of Eng. 33 ss

BOARD OF EDUCATION OF THE
CITY OF NEW YORK

DEAR SIR OR MADAM:

IN REPLY TO YOUR REQUEST FOR RESIGNATION, PLEASE BE ADVISED THAT YOURS WAS FILLED OUT IMPROPERLY. YOU MUST OBTAIN THE PROPER FORM FROM THE OFFICE OF TENURE AND APPOINTMENTS.

* * *

January 5

Dear Miss Barrett,

We at Willowdale are looking forward to having you with us in the February semester. As you know, your appointment is contingent upon your resignation from the Board of Education and a letter from your principal. We have not as yet received either communication. Would you be kind enough to let us know the reason for the delay?

Most cordially,
Robert S. Corbin
Dept. of English and
Comparative Lit.

P. S. There is every likelihood that a Chaucer seminar will be formed, open to eight students majoring in English.

Dear Miss Barrett,

I am sending you to the hospital: Circulars #42 and #43 on Teacher's Welfare. Please fill out Accident Reports A and B and the forms Miss Finch is sending you under separate cover, and mail them back at once, with witness or witnesses to the accident.

> *James J. McHabe*
> Adm. Asst.

We miss you.
> JJ McH

*   *   *

Jan. 5

Dear Syl—

I'm glad you're up and hobbling, and that you'll be out of the hospital soon. You looked wonderful when I saw you last week—rested and relaxed. Little wonder.

School is the usual post-holiday bedlam. One forgets, when one has been out of it for a while, the pettiness, the fever and the fret; then swiftly, in a day or two, one is sucked in again! Right now we're in the midst of final reports and entries. Once more the library is closed to the kids; once more we poke and scratch in the PRC's.

It doesn't seem possible that you may not be here next term. What can we do to lure you? Give you lunch period at noon? Classes of no more than 35? All the red pencils you can use? Extra board erasers? Your broken window fixed? No patrol assignments? Honors classes? A non-floating program?

Or could you be seduced by the new building the Board has been promising us for the last seven years? According to plans carefully drawn up and dangled before us every couple of years we are supposed to be getting: a courtyard rimmed by classrooms, with "facilities for dining and study among shrubs," a complete air-conditioning system, electronic devices that sound like hoot owls to signal the end of classes, two gymnasiums and an indoor swimming pool with underwater portholes for instructors to observe and instruct swimmers!

Teaching here isn't so bad. Once you accept as one of the ineluctable laws of nature that kids will continue to say "Silas Mariner" and "Ancient Marner" and "between you and I" and "mischievious," and that the administration will continue to use phrases like "egregious conduct" and "ethnic background" you can go on from there.

And you can go much farther with adolescents than with college people—especially you, with your gift of generating excitement and provoking thinking, whether in a slow and stumbling kid or a quick, bright one. You've seen them open their eyes and walk out, blinking, into day. You've heard that sudden intake of breath, like a sigh, when suddenly it becomes clear and they see, they see! This is what it means to teach—and you are one of the few who can.

Come back!

The new term will be shaping up very much like the old; there will be the usual number of sabbatical and maternity leaves in February, and more than the usual number of new kids. Mary has been asked to volunteer for additional duties as grade adviser. Loomis, who's had an offer in industry at a much higher salary (and *without kids*), got cold feet and chose to remain in the safety of the school system. Paul has been sauntering into school in a faint vapor of alcohol. And Henrietta went and touched up her hair over the holidays: from salt and pepper to bright ginger.

I got carried away there a while back. But I feel it would be such a waste if someone like you were swept away from us.

Bea

Dear Miss Barrett,

Will you please enter final marks on the enclosed
End Term Sheets for each of your students, so the substitute can transfer them to PRC's.

Will you please send to me the CC's, Service Credits,
and number of times absent (excused and unexcused)
and late (excused and unexcused) for each of your
homeroom students.

Also, Book Blacklist of students who failed to return
their books, and any moneys you have collected for the
renewal of subscriptions to *The Clarion* and for the
G.O. Field Trip.

I hope you feel better.

Sadie Finch
Chief Clerk

* * *

BOARD OF EDUCATION OF THE
CITY OF NEW YORK

DEAR SIR OR MADAM:

AFTER 35 YEARS OF ACCREDITED SERVICE, OR AFTER
30 YEARS OF SERVICE IF AT LEAST 55 YEARS OF AGE AND
IF THE TEACHER HAS ELECTED 55–30 COVERAGE, OR IF
THE TEACHER IS NOT AT LEAST 55 YEARS OF AGE OR DID
NOT ELECT 55–30 COVERAGE, AFTER 30 YEARS OF SERV-
ICE, BUT AT A CONSIDERABLY REDUCED PENSION, A
TEACHER IS ELIGIBLE FOR RETIREMENT.

* * *

Dear Miss Barrett:

Due to an unavoidable and regrettable oversight,
your letter asking for a letter to Willowdale Academy
has been inadvertently mislaid. I shall be pleased and

happy if you plan to leave us to write a recommendation with an S rating, but I hope and trust you will return to active duty here.

Sincerely yours,
MAXWELL E. CLARKE
PRINCIPAL

* * *

Dear Sylvia,
Delighted to hear you're mending. Do you happen to have on you an extra key to the john? Can you mail it to me?

Henrietta

* * *

BOARD OF EDUCATION OF THE CITY OF NEW YORK

DEAR SIR OR MADAM:

APPARENTLY YOU WERE SENT THE WRONG FORM. THE FORM YOU WERE SENT IS A RETIREMENT FORM. YOU NEED A RESIGNATION FORM.

BUREAU OF APPOINTMENTS AND RECORDS

* * *

Dear Sylvia,
The Teachers' Interest Com. (they've stuck me with that too!) want to know if and when you are leaving, so that we can start collecting money for your going away gift and farewell tea.
I've been meaning to visit you, but the work has been piling up so high I have to take it home every day to get it in on time. I wish I could just lie down someplace like you!

Mary

BOARD OF EDUCATION OF THE
CITY OF NEW YORK

DEAR SIR OR MADAM:

IN ANSWER TO YOUR REQUEST FOR A RETIREMENT FORM, YOU WERE SENT THE OLD RETIREMENT FORM INSTEAD OF THE NEW RETIREMENT FORM.

BUREAU OF APPOINTMENTS AND RECORDS

*   *   *

Dear Miss Barrett,

Due before 3: All items on the enclosed Circular #134 are to be checked off. See also Addenda to the Circular.

I'm sorry you've been getting the wrong forms from the Board. You must apply for the correct form to the Division of Appointments and Records.

Sadie Finch
Chief Clerk

*   *   *

Dear Miss Barrett,

I recall a lesson on "The Road Not Taken," and a fruitful discussion on choices. I hope you've made the right one; though whichever it is, as you yourself pointed out, it is bound to be charged with regret.

With best wishes for a speedy recovery—

Samuel Bester

*   *   *

Dear Miss Barrett,

No matter how I add up my marks my average is still 61%! Well, well! Here's hoping that one more Extra Credit will pick me up to 65%! I have no more books I read but will try to read some more if I pass!

Odyssus

Odyssus left Troy after killing a couple of million people and with his men were going home. But these giants at an island they stoped at smashed Odyssus men to pieces! After that they went to the Cyclopes who ate them gradually, but Odyssus stuck something in his eye blinding the Cyclope and which resulted in the Cyclope not being able to see. After that they went to Circe who changed the men into pigs but Odyssus changed them back! Finally they went to the island of the sun and ate up all the sun's cattle. But Zeus killed all the men except Odyssus since he was the hero. By now all the men are dead! Odyssus lands in Ogygia and stays there for 7 years. Finally he comes home.

Even if I don't pass I hope you come back! Because you know you can't get along without us, Ha-ha!
(I laugh a lot but mostly I don't mean it)

Lou Martin

PART XII

58 Hi, Pupe!

Is this 304?
Hey, she's back!
You out of the hospital?
Hurray, we got Barrett!
How's your foot?
Let's give her a round of clap!
Thank you for the applause, but that's enough. That's enough, thank you. I'm glad to see you again too. And now, please fill out these Delaney cards while I call the roll——
What's the date?
February first, you moron!
There's not enough seats!
Hey, we got a lot of new kids here!
I'm not late—the bell is early.
You gonna be our English too?
Is Lou Martin here? Oh, there you are.
Who, *me?* I didn't do it! Honest—cross my——
Stop clowning, Lou. I just want you to know you were right. You were absolutely right.
You got a cold?
Who's got a pen to loan me?
You want my Kleenex?
Quit pushing!
I don't need a Delaney, I'm dropping out.
See me after school, and we'll talk about it.

Lc

Can I have a pass? I've got to leave the room—I've got a
doctor's note to prove it!

Hey, the window's broke!

Pipe down, you guys, you know she means business!

Acevedo, Fiore?

Here.

Adamson, Ruth?

Here.

*Please come to order. I can't hear you when you—— Put
that chair down! Amdur, Janet?*

Here.

Good morning, Rusty. Why are you late?

I'm not late—I had my English changed. I wanted *you.*

*I'm glad. Well—find a place to stand. Axelrod, Leon?—— No,
don't bother me with these circulars until I'm through with
attendance. Axelrod, Leon? Is he absent?*

Him? He's always absent!

You're lucky he's not here!

Boy, will he give you trouble!

Hey, I'm too crowded!

My desk is full of holes!

Is this the right room?

Hi, teach!

Hi, pupe! . . . Belgado, Ramos?